In the midst of a summer storm, sev
swerves to miss a strange creature in
leaves her mother in a coma with doct
Desperate for answers, Jocelyn returns to the scene of the accident to discover that the creature was one of the good folk—a faerie. Not only that, but the queen of Faerie herself is willing to listen to Jocelyn's story and offer her help.

For a price, of course.

The two strike a deal: Jocelyn will paint the queen seven portraits and, in exchange, the queen will heal Jocelyn's mother. Unfortunately, nothing in the faerie realm is ever that simple. The closer Jocelyn comes to finishing the paintings, the harder malicious magical forces try to ensnare her. If she isn't careful or can't complete the portraits by October 31st, the day of the Hallowed Offering, her mother's life won't be the only one in jeopardy.

PORTRAITS OF A FAERIE QUEEN

The Faerie Court Chronicles, Book 1

Tay LaRoi

Published by
NineStar Press
PO Box 91792
Albuquerque, New Mexico, 87199
www.ninestarpress.com

Print ISBN #978-1-947139-39-8
Cover by Natasha Snow
Edited by Jason Bradley

Words of Thanks

Roz, thank you for sitting through month after month of rewrites and hilarious misspellings. This book might not have made it if not for you.

Kelsey, thank you for being the first person to ship Jocelyn and Rina. It's comforting to know I can write a ship-worthy couple.

Catherine, thank you for being the first person to ever read this book at all. Your encouragement kept me going, even though I know that first draft was terrible.

Devin, thank you for your words of insight and wisdom, even though they weren't always what I wanted to hear. Jocelyn, Rina, Anna are all stronger characters thanks to you.

Mom, Dad, Savanah, and the rest of my brilliant family, thank you for always having my back and inspiring me to set out on this journey. I love you all.

One

I DON'T BREATHE.

The slightest nudge could ruin the brush stroke, destroying the entire effect I want. According to the Faerie Queen, I have yet to properly capture what she calls her "unique blend of splendor, grace, and power." She rejected the first two attempts in mere seconds. She's a picky one, Her Majesty.

On the canvas, she looks over the wild fields outside as if she has just conquered them. Wreaths of roses surround her in honor of the fallen. An auburn waterfall of braids frames her heart-shaped face, tumbling over her bare shoulders and brushing against her elegant gown. It's a funeral shroud that silhouettes her curvaceous body. She could be wearing it in memory of any number of the dismembered skeletons beneath her feet.

Or is it to honor her next victim? It's a toss-up.

All those details were a cakewalk this time around, compared to the depths of her green eyes. Those eyes are always the hardest part. It's nearly impossible to mimic the way they trap you. The way they sparkle as you pour out your heart and plead for a miracle. The way they coldly calculate whether you're worthy.

I lift the brush from the canvas, leaving all of her mystery and seduction embodied in oil paint. My body and soul alike give a relieved sigh.

Six paintings down. One to go.

One more painting and Mom will wake up.

Thanks to my housemate, I don't get to savor the moment.

Faeries like him have this power about them. They heighten your senses, bringing the world to life and sharpening everything in it. He thinks I spend too much time in my head and the only suitable remedy is spontaneous guerilla attacks, apparently.

I take a breath, then tumble out of my chair and fling a clean paintbrush at him, letting loose a war cry like the world has never known.

The kitchen broom comes down and raps against the back of my chair. The brush sails past my housemate's face and he watches it land in the hallway.

"Better, Jocelyn," he concludes, "but now you're defenseless. And what exactly was that god-awful noise?"

"My war cry," I answer, propping myself up on my elbows. "It was supposed to either startle or confuse you. Judging by your expression, it worked."

He smirks, drops the broom, and offers me his hand. "Oh, I'm confused, all right. Confused as to why you thought it would startle me."

I take his hand, stand up, and point a paint-covered brush at him. "Keep it up, and I'll give you whiskers while you sleep."

"Do so and I'll steal your firstborn child."

I study him and wonder if he's serious. He can't be. Can he? He can't.

The day we first met, the day I made the deal with the Faerie Queen, he asked me to call him Dominic, but I doubt that's his real name. Faeries aren't keen on giving them out, especially to the lowly humans they're supposed to babysit. Lucky for me, he doesn't take his job seriously. Given his disheveled clothes and messy pine-green hair, he's literally been sleeping on the job.

"You feeling okay?" I ask, retrieving the clean paintbrush.

"Right as rain." He yawns, itching a pointed ear. "Just needed a nap before I meet a friend." His yawn closes to a grin when his obsidian gaze falls on the painting. "You finished it?"

"Sure did," I reply as I begin to wash the paint-covered brushes. "Come have a look."

Dominic sets his hands on his hips and studies the canvas. "To be fair, ruining this would have been a pity. This is stunning, Jocelyn."

"It better be." I sigh. "That's my third attempt."

"I'm sure Her Majesty will love it." Patting me on the shoulder, Dominic adds, "You deserve a break. Could you take something to Iver for me?"

"Running errands counts as a break?" I tease.

Dominic digs in his pocket and pulls out a small wrapped package. "Well, you don't know how to relax, and it's pitiful for a seventeen-year-old to stay home on a Friday night. Maybe you'll find inspiration for your last painting."

I take the parcel. "How is a nightclub going to inspire me to paint the Queen of Faerie?"

Dominic shrugs. "You tell me. You're the artist." He points to my shirt. "Change first, please. You know how we folk are about appearances."

"Paint spatter and turpentine aren't all the rage in the Faerie Realm?"

"Not at the moment, no," Dominic replies crisply.

I quickly change into clean jeans and a black T-shirt, barely noticing the large scar on my chest shaped like deadly nightshade; its badass aura wore off a while ago. It's the only real noticeable mark left on my body. The scars from last summer's car accident, the beginning of all this faerie craziness, have mostly faded.

After my mother and I swerved to miss a small figure in the road early last spring, everyone told me it was a fawn, or maybe a lost bear cub. Neither of those walk upright on twiglike legs with a hunched back, so I went looking for answers shortly after being released from the hospital. Imagine my surprise when I stumbled onto a whole hidden world of strange creatures, including the Queen of Faerie herself. And, lucky me, she was in a bargain-making mood. *Un*lucky me, she likes to physically mark those she makes a deal with. Apparently a simple signature isn't binding enough.

A metal cross hangs around my neck. My sister, Annalise, gave it to me before I moved to Grand Harbor, supposedly to enroll in an intensive art program for high school seniors. In reality I'm here under the queen's orders since it's the closest human town to the Faerie Court. I'm only an hour away from them, but they feel a world away sometimes. It's better than Her Majesty's original idea of making me live with her at court, I guess. Dominic stepped up and offered to look after me, thank God. I don't like to think about the kind of life I'd be living now if he hadn't. All I know is that it would be the farthest thing from a fairy tale.

I look in the bathroom mirror long enough to rake a comb through my hair. Light-blue eyes that match my dad's stare back. I've got his thin Anglo features too, but with a softer jaw, longer lashes, and a slender figure. Mom always said he was good looking and I guess I am too, except in a girlish sort of way. Emphasis on the "*ish*." My shaggy pixie cut, lack of makeup and simple wardrobe prevent me from being labeled anything close to "girly." That's okay, though. I've also got my dad's killer sense of humor to help me get the ladies.

I mean, it hasn't helped me *lately*, but it will one day. Mark my words.

Downstairs, Dominic skims his vast collection of herbs and spices. There are so many jars, bags, and boxes that I hardly remember what the counter looks like. "Care for some tea?" he asks.

"No, thanks," I reply, hunting for my tiny leather satchel and keys. They're on the table. The only photos in the house catch my eye as I slip them into my pocket.

Nine-year-old me took the first, so it's crooked. I took it in our backyard. Annalise stands behind my mother in a bright yellow dress and weaves flowers into Mom's hair. A temporary unicorn tattoo glitters on her chubby cheek. My mom kneels in a matching dress with her crow's feet revealing how often she used to laugh. I hope she still laughs like that once she wakes up from the coma.

The other photo is of my dad. He sits at a picnic table wearing flannel and denim, warming his hands by a campfire as he grins at the camera. Our hair even seems to fall in our faces the same way.

He died of leukemia shortly after I turned thirteen. Annalise was ten.

He would never let us know how much the disease ate at him. Even toward the end, when he couldn't even sit up, he'd crack jokes and tell stories. He only got serious when we were leaving the hospital. He would always say, "You're in charge till I get back, Jocelyn. Take good care of your mom and sister for me."

Safe to say I wasn't the best woman for the job.

Dominic breaks through my thoughts. "Are you sure? I need a taste tester."

"Save me some. I'll drink it when I get back."

Dominic frowns but doesn't argue. "If you insist."

I grab my jacket and head out the door.

The crisp evening air blows through the woods surrounding the old farmhouse where we live, carrying the smell of fall leaves. Even on gloomy days, the surrounding trees glow with bright reds, shining yellows, and warm oranges. I imagine it's because we're so close to the Faerie Court.

That's probably why the shadows look so sinister after dark too.

My old green Volkswagen coughs to life and sputters down the dusty driveway. One thing I didn't inherit from my father was his knack for cars. At this point, I'm pretty sure it runs more on prayers than gas.

The worn brown "Welcome to Grand Harbor" sign flies by as the town springs up from the northern Michigan forest. Tall old houses with wraparound porches line the street. Smaller brick homes and tiny shops sit in the mix. All of them hold their own against the newer seasonal cabins and retreats.

Two of the main reasons people come to Grand Harbor pan out on either side of Main Street: Lake Michigan on my left and James-Child College on my right. It's a small private college with a tiny student population and little athletic merit but nationally renowned academics. At least, that's what I've heard. I never had the grades to even sneeze near the place.

The town passes by in a flash, and I cross the railroad tracks into the old run-down industrial area. Most of the buildings are tombs of abandoned outdated manufacturing practices and home to a plethora of supposed hauntings and campfire stories. It's probably the work of faerie troublemakers—imps and pixies and such—but I'm not stupid enough to go investigating.

Besides, I already know exactly where to find said troublemakers.

The Time Between is a refurbished factory-turned-nightclub packed with local fae who live in or near the Human Realm. Many come wanting to escape the watchful eye of the Faerie Court. Others find humans fascinating. Some see us as easy pickings.

They all stop by the club to purchase spells and charms to ward off the effects of iron, which saturates the human world. For faeries, iron is like an allergy with a license to kill.

The burn on my chest grants me protection and entrance. No faerie in their right mind would touch someone wearing the queen's mark, human or not. The bouncer gives me a nod, and I sink into the sea of music, magic, deception, and alcohol.

Iver, the elven bartender, spots me, pours me a cola, and waits.

I yell over the pounding music, "Hey, where's the rum?"

Iver lets out a booming laugh far bigger and deeper than one would expect from his slender frame. "I think not, young one," he chortles in his Scandinavian accent. "Human Realm, human rules."

"Since when do faeries care about human rules?" I ask, taking a sip. Drinks with blood, poisonous plants, and insects are on the menu, but serving a minor alcohol is not allowed? How is that fair?

"Since you're an important human," he answers, tightening his long pale-blond ponytail. "How are the paintings coming along?"

I sit up a little straighter with pride. "I finished number six. Just gotta paint one more, and I'm done. In the meantime—" I pull the package from my pocket. "—Dominic has me running errands."

Iver's expression hardens as he takes the delivery. He looks it over and puts it into his apron. "Thank you, Jocelyn. The drink's on the house."

He goes back to serving patrons with a new smile on his face, leaving me to survey the crowd for a bit.

The flashing lights from the dance floor and the shadows around the bar make it hard to tell who's what in here. A lot of them are probably wearing glamour, a disguise woven of magic. Most of the faeries appear humanoid with a hodgepodge of deviations: translucent wings, the occasional pair of goat legs, deer noses, stonelike skin, long floppy ears, and eyes that resemble the cosmos. I wish they'd stay still enough for me to sketch them.

Someone bumps into me and plops down on the next stool. He takes off his bright crimson beanie and runs a hand over his spiky black hair. The smell of blood on him is impossible to ignore.

The smell and the beanie tell me that he's a redcap. Dominic once told me they have to dye their hats with blood on a regular basis to stay alive. The universe must have been in a pretty bad mood when it made these guys.

"Give me the strongest thing you've got," he barks at Iver. "No ice."

"Bad day?" I ask.

"Terrible," the redcap grumbles. "Source fell through. Had to get my own damned fix. One of the queen's knights spotted me and asked all sorts of unpleasant questions. Had to think fast."

Iver sets a glass of clear liquor in front of him and the redcap takes a sip.

"And I thought life was rough under Queen Titania—she was an angel next to her sister. At least she left us solitary folk in peace."

From my understanding, solitary fae are the vagabonds of their realm. They normally live outside the queen's lands and do as they please but behave themselves in her territory for their own sake. That's how it's *supposed* to work, anyway.

Grand Harbor is close enough to the queen's borders that one would think she'd do more to stop her subjects preying on humans, but no. Such stories are commonplace. How they stay clear of human suspicion is even more baffling. Magic and all that jazz, I suppose.

The redcap twirls his beanie in one hand, looking at it with disdain. "I was nearly out of juice, too." With a sigh, he puts it down and nurses his liquor. "And I had to settle for A positive again. I'm damn near sick of A positive."

Well, there goes my quitter's streak.

Shortly after moving to Grand Harbor, I started smoking. It's not exactly legal, given my age, but after the first month of this madness, Dominic's teas stopped being sufficient stress relief. Lucky for me, Dominic is the worst babysitter ever. I collect plants from the woods around the farmhouse for him and he buys me cigarettes. I'm trying to quit, but this conversation is kicking my craving into overdrive. The idea that someone is out there, possibly bleeding to death, while this asshat is complaining about what kind of blood he had is stressing me out. I can't do anything for him, and that gets under my skin. That's probably exactly what this jerk wants. "You humans aren't easy to nab these days," the redcap continues. "You're all so suspicious. Greedy, too. Want to keep all your blood to yourself."

"Gee, can't imagine why," I mutter, fishing in my jacket for my pack and lighter. Guess I "forgot" to check it when Dominic and I purged the house.

The redcap gulps down the rest of his drink and motions to Iver for a refill. "It's not like I killed the guy. A few transfusions and he'll be fine." A sharp-toothed smirk creeps onto his face. "If they find him in time."

He should know better than to mess with my head. I've been around his kind too long to take such obvious bait. I light my cigarette and take a long drag instead to calm my nerves.

The redcap finishes his second drink and says, "You're the painter girl, right? You go to the court a lot? Any juicy gossip you'd like to share?"

"I actually haven't been there in a while." I take another drag to replace the redcap's toxicity with something less poisonous. "You?"

"Nah. They don't like my kind poking around. I hear tell that the queen's changeling daughter is getting popular, though. Her Majesty must be slacking if her thrown-away kid has more fans than her." The redcap orders yet another drink, even though his speech has started to slur.

Fun fact: faeries are lightweights.

"No idea why she keeps her," he continues. "Most monarchs would have slaughtered a changeling that came crawling back. The queen's losing her marbles."

I just want to finish my rum-less cola in peace. Is that too much to ask?

Since there are no more empty seats, I chug it and get ready to leave. My gaze falls on the exit as I search for Iver to say goodbye.

Five human girls walk in and catch my eye.

Five very lost, very oblivious, and very vulnerable human girls.

Two

THE REDCAP SNEERS in the girls' direction. "This night just got interesting." He snickers.

"Don't bother. They're out of your league," I scoff.

The redcap whirls with a glare. His pupils, irises, and whites turn into a soulless black ink, and his face morphs into hollow angles.

"Watch yourself, girly," he snarls. "Wouldn't want to leave those paintings unfinished, would we?"

I blow cigarette smoke in his face. He coughs and growls but just keeps glaring since I've called his bluff. Thanks to the queen's mark, he can't touch me.

The girls weave through the crowd and head toward the dance floor. They're dressed in flashy outfits befitting a nightclub and look a bit older than me. They must be students from James-Child.

Shoot, if getting into James-Child means I get to study with girls that hot, I might have to pull my grades up and apply once I get back to school.

I bring my attention back to the bar. "I'm saving you the disappointment. They look like trouble."

The redcap scoffs, tipping back to catch the last drop of alcohol in his glass. Several others at the bar laugh as he topples off the stool. Getting to his feet, he says, "No, they look feisty. I love feisty women. They're more fun to break."

This guy is officially begging to get his ass kicked. If the music wasn't blaring, he could probably hear the blood rushing in my ears. He takes a few stumbling steps toward the girls, and I snatch him by the collar of his shirt. A few patrons back away as he turns on me with murder in his eyes.

When Dad was in the hospital, I promised to stop getting into fights. I think he'd let this one pass. He's the one who taught me how to throw a punch after the school bully started pulling my ponytail at recess, after all. "Let me rephrase that," I say. "Mess with them and *I'll* be trouble."

"You wish," he cackles, gaze locked with mine.

My body starts to tingle and the world goes quiet.

"You're on your way out, remember?" His voice echoes in my head.

The redcap weaves through the crowd toward the girls, a triumphant grin on his face. It looks like he's moving in slow motion. The whole club is.

The tension leaves my body, and I move toward the exit.

He's right. There's no reason to fight. They're just human girls. Who cares what happens to them? I was leaving anyway. It's not my business. I shouldn't get involved—

An intoxicated patron bumps into me, making the world abruptly speed up. I shake my head and slap myself in the face. That prick just bewitched me. That makes this my business. Thank God he was too drunk for the magic to stick.

I hunt for the redcap in the crowd. He didn't get far. I spot him as he grabs one of the girls and spins her around. The music's too loud for me to hear their exchange, but judging by her flabbergasted expression, she's not happy about the interruption.

They get into a shouting match, and her friends step in. One of them shoves him. He tries to flip up her skirt.

Red tints my vision and I clench my hands into fists. When I get my hands on—

The shortest girl in the group nails him in the jaw with a mean right hook and the redcap tumbles like a chopped tree.

Can't say I saw that coming.

Faeries scramble out of the way as the redcap clambers to his feet. Teeth bared, he launches himself at the girl who socked him. I jump between them, hoping the queen's protection will stop him. It doesn't. He's too furious and too drunk to care. His pointed nails swipe under my left eye. The attack throws me off balance, but speed is still on my side, thanks to the redcap's blood-alcohol level.

I land a hit to his gut. My elbow collides with his right eye. He throws a punch that splits my bottom lip and I stumble back.

The girl with the right hook steadies me. "Are you okay?"

I want to answer, but her eyes catch me off guard. They're pools of soft ebony framed by long lashes and dark, rich sepia skin. What I wouldn't give to grab my sketchbook and draw them before this girl disappears forever.

The redcap pulls me back into the fight, so no chance of that.

He winds up a punch. I throw my weight against him, and we both go down.

A set of arms lock around me and lift me off the ground. It's Iver.

A huge lumbering man—probably a troll in glamour—yanks the redcap to his feet and props him against a table.

The redcap doesn't seem to notice his helper. He cackles as blood drips from his nose. "Damn, kid," he sneers. "If you really wanted one, you could have asked. Take the black girl. They're too obnoxious for my taste."

Right-hook girl pops her knuckles in response and steps forward.

Another patron intercepts her.

"Hey!" she snaps. "Don't—"

"That's enough!" Iver barks. He turns to the redcap. "Fuloch, that's your third strike. If I ever see your ugly face around here again, you'll *wish* you got beat up by a couple of teenagers."

"These *teenagers* had it under control, thanks," I grumble.

Iver squeezes me tighter to shut me up.

The redcap, Fuloch, goes crimson in the face and snarls, "They started it."

"I'll handle them. Get out of my club."

The troll drags Fuloch toward the exit, literally kicking, screaming, and swearing vengeance on us the whole way. Especially me. "You'll regret this, kid. Just you wait. Don't think you're getting off easy because you're a girl."

Iver ignores him and turns to the college students. He puts on his best human-esque air and bows. Their tight little huddle relaxes.

"I'm so sorry, ladies," he says with a charming grin.

At least, I assume it's charming, given that they all go doe-eyed. Except for Right-Hook. She still looks ready to fight. Her gorgeous eyes are sharp enough to cut steel.

Iver keeps laying on the charm. "I try to be an understanding host, but there is just no hope for some people. Might I offer you some courtesy drinks?" He eyes the black marker Xs on their hands. "Nonalcoholic, of course."

The girls blush and giggle. Even Right-Hook seems to be softening up. I get the feeling that their ease has magical properties to it, but I'm not about to ask. After a few giddy whispers, they agree and follow Iver back toward the bar. He drags me along and forces me to sit.

The girls thank me, so I stand taller and reply with "don't mention it," and "no problem," hopefully sounding smooth.

Right-Hook nudges me and takes the seat next to mine. "Thanks," she says. "That guy was a grade-A douche. Can't believe he only got kicked out."

She's talking to me. This gorgeous woman isn't just thanking me, but *talking* to me.

My brain short-circuits. "Y-Yeah. What a creep." C'mon, Jocelyn. You can do better than that. Is she probably straight? Yeah. Will you never see her again? It's likely. Step your game up anyway.

Once he serves the girls, Iver plops a dusty bottle of alcohol and a wad of napkins in front of me. "Clean those cuts," he orders.

I uncork the bottle and take a whiff. The smell could peel paint. "Shouldn't I do this in the bathroom?"

"And start brawling on the way? I think not." Iver huffs. "You're staying where I can see you." He points to his own eyes, then to mine, before going to help other patrons.

The girl next to me gives me a sympathetic smile. "Sorry. I think we got you in trouble."

I wet a napkin with the solution and flinch as it burns my split lip. "Don't sweat it." It would be nice to see just how bad it looks. "Would you happen to have a mirror I can use?"

The girl swivels on her stool to face me. "I'll do you one better." She gently takes the napkin in one hand and my chin in the other. The warm touch of her hand makes my stomach flip and my mouth go dry.

Please let her like girls; please let her like girls.

The sting of alcohol restarts my brain as she dabs the napkin against a cut under my eye. I wince, definitely looking far from cool.

She winces too. "I really am sorry."

"Look on the bright side," I say. "You got to look like a superhero tonight."

With a smirk, she applies more disinfectant. "Thanks. Glad those self-defense classes paid off."

As she dabs at another cut, I take the chance to really look at her.

This time I notice sparks in those dark eyes that probably turn to fireworks when she smiles. Big beautiful black curls frame her oval face and hover above her dark slender shoulders. When she shakes a loose ringlet out of her face, I'm flooded with the smell of ginger and citrus. Her thin eyebrows pull together and her full cherry-red lips scowl.

"I hate people like that," she grumbles. "Thinking they can just touch whoever they please. Makes me sick."

We should change the subject. Maybe it's time to work some magic of my own.

"It's okay," I say. "You made sure he had a rough *night.*"

She leans back and gives me a puzzled look.

I motion around the club. "You know, because we're in a *night*club?"

Her lips pucker and her broad nose crinkles as she fails to keep a straight face. Her laughter sounds like bells and those sparks in her eyes come alive.

Jeez, tone it down a bit, Jocelyn. You just met this girl.

"That joke was atrocious," she chuckles, putting down the napkin.

It hurts to smile, but it's worth it. "Can't be that bad if you laughed."

She scoffs. "Yeah, it can. That's *why* I laughed." She studies me for a nerve-racking moment, then offers her hand. "I'm Asterina Fischler. Call me Rina."

"Jocelyn Lennox." I take her hand. It's soft, but strong.

"Pleasure to meet you, Jocelyn."

"The pleasure's all mine." Now for some questions. "How'd a group of girls like you wander in here? It's kinda off the beaten path."

Rina rolls her eyes and dabs at a scratch on my forehead. "It was my roommate, Megan's idea." She motions to the blonde girl Fuloch initially grabbed. "Heard about it through the grapevine and wanted to check out. I told her they wouldn't let me in since I'm seventeen—"

Hello. A college girl my age?

"—but when she saw that I was studying, she dragged me along anyway."

A girl that studies on a Friday night? Never mind. I doubt I have a chance. This girl's in the NFL and I'm in pee-wee football.

She tosses the bloody napkin in a nearby trash can. "I think you're good."

"You're all at James-Child, right?" I ask.

Rina nods.

"Seventeen's a bit young, isn't it?"

"I graduated early." She rolls her eyes and makes air quotes. "Well, 'graduated' as much as I could. I was homeschooled."

"What are you studying?"

"Astronomy with a computer science minor."

Forget the sports analogy. We're not even on the same planet.

And yes, that space comparison was deliberate.

Rina's smile falters as she lifts her drink to her lips. "I know. I'm a giant nerd."

I shrug. "It's pretty amazing if you ask me." Not to mention hot. It sets me up for a lot of rejection, but I've got a thing for smart girls.

She raises an eyebrow. "Really?"

"You don't believe me?"

Megan drapes herself over Rina's shoulders before she can answer. "Ri-ri," she whines in a drunken slur. "C'mon, let's go dance." Sounds like Megan's party started long before they arrived.

Rina squirms out from under her. "Meg, give me a second—"

Latching onto Rina's arm, Megan reaches out and tries to tousle my hair. "You should bring our new friend too," she says.

"Thanks, but I don't dance," I reply, dodging her.

"Oh, that's no fun." Megan sighs, tugging on Rina. "Let's go."

"Megan, wait—"

"Go on," I say. "You came to have a good time."

Rina studies me skeptically. "You sure?"

"Of course," I assure her. "Go take advantage of the fact that they let you in."

She reluctantly lets her friends drag her toward the dance floor.

Iver walks by, and I grab him by the sleeve. "What did you put in my drink?" I demand.

Iver watches Rina across the room, then smirks down at me. "Nothing. It's called 'romantic attraction.' You'd recognize it if you left your easel more often."

Damn. I was hoping I could blame him.

"Aren't you going to do something about them?"

Iver ticks up one pencil-thin eyebrow. "Why would I?"

"Um, because they're humans running around a faerie nightclub? Fuloch was the tip of the crazy iceberg."

Iver sighs. "I'm busy, Jocelyn. If you're so worried, you get rid of them. Though if they're resilient enough to stay after that, I'm sure they'll be fine."

I'm not convinced. And I can't shake the feeling that tomorrow's headline might involve dead or traumatized college students. I could tell them to leave, but if Rina's tough enough to sock a redcap, I doubt it'll be that easy. A glimmer of gold near the door catches my eye and I let out a sigh of relief. Finally, someone who will listen. At least, I hope she will.

A local nymph, Calista, strides into the nightclub. What little clothing she wears sways with her movements and sparkles in the shifting light. Intricate dark braids bounce while shimmering jewelry jingles in time with her steps. Iver catches me watching her and gives me a warning look that I blatantly ignore. One more deal with a faerie won't kill me.

Hopefully.

I catch her by the arm as she walks by. "Calista, I need your help."

Her frame is so slight and slim that the sudden weight threatens to knock her over. She turns to me, first in bewilderment, then with a mischievous grin that I know means trouble.

"It's been a while, Jocelyn," she coos. "I've missed you."

The smell of cloves makes my head spin as she tosses her hair. That's probably exactly what she wants.

"I need a favor," I say, not sounding nearly as seductive or smooth as her.

She giggles and folds her arms. "What kind of favor?"

"Five human girls are in the club." They're too deep in the throng of dancers for me to point out. "Can you get them to leave?"

Calista bites her bottom lip and clicks her nails together.

"*Without* making a scene," I add.

Calista hooks one finger into my belt loop, turns my stool around, and slips between my legs. She leans up against me, slipping her other hand beneath my shirt and pushing me against the bar. Her touch is cold but pleasant, like ice on a summer day.

"And what do I get in return?" she whispers in my ear.

Her breath ignites every nerve in my body.

Here's another fun fact: faeries are pretty flexible when it comes to hooking up.

That's great for them and all, but given some of the bad things I've heard happen to men when they mess around with nymphs, I'd rather not try my luck, even as a girl. Even if I liked hooking up, how am I supposed to enjoy it if I'm worried about ending up addicted to her, losing my mind, or enduring whatever kind of magical mind games Calista might want to play? That doesn't sound like my idea of a good time.

My body screams in protest as I push Calista away and smooth down my shirt. It's even hard to release her shoulder. She tsks in annoyance.

"Think a little harder, Calista," I say. "I can't finish the queen's paintings if I'm catatonic."

She folds her arms again and pouts like a child denied a toy. "The queen never shares," she huffs. Reaching behind her neck, she adds, "Fine. I have something else you can help me with."

She offers me the plainest of her many necklaces, a glass butterfly dangling from a simple leather cord.

"I need you to hang on to this for me. Just for a little while."

"That's it?" I ask, watching the butterfly swing to and fro. It can't be that simple. Nothing ever is around here.

Calista scoffs and tosses the necklace over the bar. "Iver, catch!"

The elf snatches it from the air without looking up. He rolls it over in one hand while still mixing a drink with the other. "It's safe, Jocelyn," he calls. He tosses it back, this time to me, and sure enough, I don't feel any different. The world looks the same. My emotions don't shift. "Why do you want me to hold on to it?"

"It belonged to a friend who died," Calista answers, "Now a kelpie wants it, but I want it more. Just hold on to it until he's convinced it's lost. Shouldn't take long."

I look for any sign that she's playing me. She holds my gaze and her face stays stern.

"Do you want those human girls gone or not?" she demands.

I mull it over. The last thing I need is a faerie enemy, but if she's going to convince him that the necklace is lost, not that someone else has it, I should be fine. A small spark pricks my palm as I shake her hand. Calista rolls back her sleeves and heads for the dance floor.

"Want me to describe them?" I ask.

"No. Humans stand out well enough," she replies, sashaying into the crowd.

I turn back to find Iver glowering at me.

"Hey, you told me to deal with it. I'm dealing with it."

"You had better hope the kelpie in question isn't Essen," he warns. "He can be nasty."

"So can Her Majesty," I remind him. "It'll be fine."

Iver sighs. "It's your funeral," he says and goes back to work.

"Thanks for the vote of confidence," I mumble, turning to face the crowd.

Five minutes pass. Rina's friends stumble toward the exit, bumping into patrons with the signature slack-jawed expressions of people who have been bewitched. I had hoped for something a little tamer, but can't say I'm surprised either.

A fifth woman follows. She's Asian, petite, and covered in tattoos.

Rina's nowhere in sight.

Three

Cursing under my breath, I head to the dance floor in search of Calista. I find her grinding on a gangly pixie boy who seems to be enjoying it of his own free will, the poor sap. She spots me and beckons me closer.

I stop just out of her reach and shout over the music, "You missed one."

Calista groans. "You said get rid of five human girls, so I got rid of five human girls. That's all that was on the dance floor, I swear."

So where did Rina go? I look around for her, hoping she noticed her friends leaving and followed them, but that would mean I'm lucky. Sure enough, she emerges from the hall leading to the bathrooms, apparently oblivious of what's just happened.

Calista giggles at the sight of her. "That explains it. Want me to get her?"

"Will it cost me another favor?"

"Naturally."

"Never mind, then," I reply, making my way off the floor.

Rina smiles when I reach her. "Do you dance after all?" she teases.

"Your friends left," I explain, taking her hand and leading her toward the exit.

Rina yanks out my grip. "Wait. What do you mean?" She glares at me and takes a step back. "What are you doing?"

I take a deep breath, trying to stay calm. "I'm trying to make sure you get home."

Rina pushes past me and surveys the crowd. Her expression shifts to worry, and she makes a beeline for the door.

She's leaving of her own accord. Good. I'm probably less likely to get sucker punched that way, but I don't really want her to go. Human contact, especially of the cute girl variety, has become a rarity as of late, what with the Queen of Faerie practically owning my soul and all.

"I got this under control," she snaps, letting the door shut on me.

I catch it and ask, "What if that guy from before is hanging around?"

"I think we established that I can handle him," she scoffs. "Besides, it's not like they'd—what the hell?" We come to a halt in front of an empty parking space that was no doubt occupied by Rina's friend's car not too long ago.

I sincerely hope Calista's laughing it up inside. Really, I do. There's nothing more hilarious than leaving someone stranded in a seedy part of town.

"They *ditched* me?" Rina exclaims, hands thrown in the air. "This was their stupid idea, and they *ditched* me?" She whips out her phone and punches in buttons. I can faintly hear the other end ringing. Thanks to the bewitchment, that's probably the only answer she's going to get.

Patrons of the club come and go, watching us with sneers and whispers. Maybe it's the amber shade of the streetlights or the towering run-down buildings, but they look more menacing out here.

"I can take you home," I offer. "James-Child is on the way."

Rina dials a new number. As it rings, she looks me over skeptically. "Thanks, but no."

Given the part of town we're in, I don't really blame her. Besides, getting into cars with strangers late at night sounds like "How to Die 101," but I can't leave her here. I plop down on the curb as she has a heated conversation on the phone.

She snaps it shut and looks down at me. "What are you doing?"

"Waiting with you. It's not safe out here."

Her eyes narrow, drilling into mine as she probably wonders what sort of weirdo she accidentally started to be friends with. Given the punch she threw earlier, she shouldn't worry. She must reach the same conclusion, because she sits a few feet away from me.

Pulling her coat tightly around her, she grumbles, "Bar fights and getting stranded. I should have stayed home and studied after all."

"It's Friday night," I remind her. "What could possibly be that interesting?"

Rina pulls her knees to her chest and grumbles behind them, "I have a test Monday on constellations."

That gives me an idea. Making sure the sidewalk is free of glass, I lean back and look up at the sky. An abundance of stars blink above us thanks to the darkness of the surrounding buildings. "Looks like you've got a big review sheet right here," I say. Rina's eyebrows pull together as she stares at me.

I point up at the sky to draw her attention. "Quiz time. What's out tonight?"

She looks up and studies the sky. "Let's see…" Leaning a bit closer, she points toward our upper left and traces a shape. "That's Leo."

My heart skips a beat as the smell of ginger hits me again. I'd rather look at her, but I lift my gaze to where she's pointing. There's not a lion in sight.

"Looks more like a puffer fish," I say.

Rina chuckles. "How does it look like a puffer fish?"

I point around the shape. "All those little stars are the spikes. See?"

She squints, then shakes her head. "If you say so." Pointing to squiggly line of stars, she says, "That's Hydra over there."

"Hydra looks like a heavy drinker."

Rina scoffs. "How exactly did you reach that conclusion?"

I point to a group of stars near the top of the constellation. "Doesn't that look like a giant beer bottle?" I point to another. "And there's a martini glass."

Rina shakes her head. "The Greeks are rolling in their graves."

"Bummer. They're missing out on all these cool new constellations. Like the giant roller coaster that sends the passengers flying over Leo's head. See it?"

Rina leans in even closer and squints in an effort to see where I'm pulling this nonsense from. "Bummer indeed," she says. "Looks like a fun roller coaster."

She smiles at me, and I stop breathing. I can't think straight enough to come up with another constellation. A curl falls in her face, and I resist the urge to tuck it behind her ear.

A nearby voice booms with laughter, startling both of us.

Rina sits back and lowers her eyes. "If you don't dance, why go to a club?"

"I'm friends with the bartender," I answer. "And most nights you meet some interesting characters. Not everyone who hangs out here is a creep. I promise."

Rina laughs. "I'll take your word for it." She shivers and huddles farther into her coat. It's pretty cold for mid-October. "I still don't get it," she mutters, "Why would they take off *and* not pick up the phone?"

I shrug. "Maybe they were bewitched or something."

Rina elbows me with a smirk, clearly convinced that I'm just messing with her.

A pair of headlights come around the corner. They belong to a small black Jetta that pulls up next to us. A redheaded girl waves at Rina from inside. Whoever she is, she drives too fast. I was just getting warmed up.

The window rolls down, and the girl grins. "You sure you need a ride, Rina? You look fine to me."

Rina scrambles to her feet and grabs her purse. "Jocelyn, this is Brook. Brook, Jocelyn," she says. "Thanks for waiting with me."

"No problem," I reply, getting to my feet. "Don't go starting fights on your way home."

Rina walks around the car to get in. "Ha. I won't if you won't."

"No promises."

With the door open, Rina's gaze lingers on me like she wants to say something more.

Brook doesn't give her the chance. She leans out the window and winks at me. "You're definitely Rina's type, if you get my drift, *and* she's single. Just FYI."

"Brook!" Rina exclaims. Avoiding my eyes, she adds, "Thanks again, Jocelyn," and slides into the car. They drive around the corner and into the night.

Once they're out of sight, my brain properly processes Brook's words, and I kick myself. Damn it! I should have asked for her number after all. Grand Harbor isn't that big of a town...

My phone rings, sparing me too much wishful thinking. Dominic's number flashes on the screen.

"Last time I checked," he chastises on the other end, "the Time Between was on the other side of town, not the other side of the planet."

"Things got complicated," I explain. "There was this really cute girl—"

"Tell me later," Dominic says. "The queen wants to see the painting."

Wonderful. I hope she didn't hear about my little spat with Fuloch.

I make my way back to my car and head for home. Halfway there my phone rings again. I prepare to assure Dominic that I'm on my way, but the Caller ID reads Annalise.

"Hey, baby sister," I answer.

"Hey, big sister. Question: can you come home for Halloween? Mrs. Jones is throwing a block party and wants a head count. I was supposed to call you after school, but I forgot."

"I should be able to swing by," I answer after a moment of thought. If the queen accepts this painting, I'll only have one more. I probably can't finish by Halloween, but it might be a nice break.

Anna squeals with joy. "Think we're too old for joint Halloween costumes?"

"Absolutely," I reply. "Besides, aren't you supposed to be asserting your independence? You know, being a teenager and whatnot?"

"Meh. We Lennoxes have to stick together. Mom would love to wake up and see us as Wendy and Peter Pan like when we were kids. You'd still be Peter Pan, just so you know."

I try to keep my stomach from sinking too far. For her, the notion that Mom will wake up is just wishful thinking. I'd love nothing more than to tell her the truth, but I can't bring myself to say the words. As crazy as everything is, she just might believe it's all true, and that puts her in danger. I refuse to do that.

"Wanna bring Uncle David?" Anna asks.

Ah, yes. Uncle David, the supposed relative I live with while I'm in that supposed art program. Dominic played the part of our estranged relative and convinced our current guardian and Mom's older brother, Uncle Rick, to let me move across the state to enroll. We convinced my sister too, for good measure. And by "convinced," I obviously mean "bewitched" since none of us have actually met the real Uncle David. He and Dad apparently never got along.

"I'll be sure to ask him," I answer.

"All right. Other than that, how are you?"

"I'm fine. You?" The less we talk about me, the better.

"Same as always, I guess."

I hate that answer. It doesn't actually tell me anything. Sure, I constantly lie through my teeth, but I'm the oldest. I get a pass.

"Shit! Rick heard me. I was supposed to be asleep at eleven. Love you. Bye."

"Stop swearing. Love you too."

I pull into the driveway and push away the usual guilt that comes with talking to my sister. Soon everything will be fine. Mom will wake up, I'll move back home, and our family will be fixed. Anna and Uncle Rick never have to know the truth about anything. It's just a little longer.

I walk in the kitchen to find my painting wrapped in a sheet on the table. Before I can have a heart attack at the sight of fabric touching fresh oil paint, Dominic reminds me to breathe.

"I dried it with magic," he assures me. "I wouldn't have touched it at all if Her Majesty hadn't been so insistent on seeing you."

I rip off the sheet and see that there's not a brush stroke out of place, thank God. I probably would have killed Dominic if he messed up the painting, which would have sucked. He's grown on me these past months.

"She usually lets me come to her," I say, wrapping it back up. "What gives?"

"She mentioned Iver's nightclub."

"I was afraid of that."

"What did you do?"

"I'll explain later. Just let me get rid of this thing first." With the painting tucked under my arm, I head into the night.

I've never told anyone, but my fear of the dark lasted long into high school. Since striking the deal with the queen, however, the monsters that hide here can't hurt me. It's a comforting thought as I walk through the trees.

In a small clearing sits a large hill ringed with white mushrooms. Its grass is still lush while the surrounding area lays covered in dull brown. As I climb over it, the energy of the world shifts. The air feels thinner, the colors sharper, and the earth more alive. It feels like a fresh spring morning rather than a bitter autumn night.

If that doesn't tell me I've entered Faerie, the houses protruding from trees and rocks certainly do. Lights glow in windows like fireflies and bonfires. Colorful smoke and earthy herbal scents waft down from chimneys built from hollowed branches. Hushed conversations ride the wind, and I can pick up English and a few modern European languages, but I suspect others are older than these woods. The unease in all the voices crosses any barrier made my language. Nervous figures peek outside at the sound of my footsteps. Some are only as big as a human hand and others stand twice as tall as any adult.

Members of the queen's guard patrol the paths. They scowl at me from the slits in their black helmets. Once they spot the painting, they ignore me and look for other people to harass. I'd scowl back, but I'd hate to cause a scene, mainly because that scene would end with me getting my ass kicked.

The queen's labyrinth of a keep rises out of the night. Its trunk and roots are so massive and sprawling that they remind me of a mountain range. I don't raise my eyes to the branches anymore. The sight makes me dizzy, and I know the sky is hidden, even as the autumn leaves fall. Two knights stand at the entrance, a root arching tall enough to walk under, and let me pass without a word.

Once inside, the bark turns into a system of corridors and chambers too vast for anyone to explore all at once. If they didn't drive you mad, the thick aura of magic would. It hangs in the air like a muggy scentless perfume. Luckily, the path to the Grand Hall is a short one.

Red, gold, and brown banners wave limply in various states of decay. They span from new and silky to moth-eaten and crusted with dirt. The tablecloths and silverware are in a similar state, as are the decorative paintings and tapestries. The scenery has nothing on the patrons.

They wear similar autumn colors as they dance and peruse the tables. Many of them sport ripped gowns and trousers spotted with dried blood and dirt. Leaves and acorns adorn elaborate and simple hairstyles alike, which complement corsages made of dead flowers. Those wearing clean clothing stand out with their otherworldly physical characteristics: skin like bark and twiglike fingers, enormous onyx eyes and sharp jagged teeth, hair like weeping willow branches and bodies with more thorns than a rose bush.

I know better than to stare into the crowds, but I can't help it. Both the beautiful and horrifying enchant me with the way they move. The way they dance and weave together.

The way they torture each other.

The only folk who look like they could be from fairy tales are living a nightmare. One small mangled arm hangs out of a gremlin's bloody grin. To my right, a doe-like woman kneels as a footrest for a harsh-looking pair of gentlemen. A young man gingerly weaves past me, his back hunched with defeat, to set more food on the table. Two dark bloody holes protrude from his shoulder blades where a pair of glistening wings once fluttered.

If I stay here too long, I'll be sick. I need to deliver this painting and get out.

I lift my gaze to the most beautiful and terrifying being in the court. My refuge from all this ugliness and my worst nightmare.

The Queen of Faerie.

Four

I DON'T THINK anyone will ever capture the awe that the Faerie Queen inspires. Maybe if I painted here at court like she initially suggested, I'd get pretty close, but I'm set on living. Even when she's not looking right at you, the spell she weaves, compelling you to be whatever she wants, can threaten to swallow you whole.

As she surveys her subjects with passive amusement, she swirls a glass of ruby-red wine in one hand. She twirls a copper curl with the other. The crown she wears is a similar color, ornamented with vines dotted with thorns, dead leaves, and lifeless buds. Her golden dress shimmers as she crosses one long leg over the other, revealing a slit that runs all the way to her hip. She sits up straight once she spots me, making the amber stitched into the dress sparkle, and pats the arm of her throne with subtle well-controlled glee.

Lyle, her champion, regards me with disdain from beside the throne. With his pale eyes narrowed, he stands a little taller with his chest puffed out and his muscular arms folded. If he's trying to intimidate me, he's wasting his time.

He accomplished that months ago.

I try to keep my breath steady as I perch on the arm of the throne, ready to run at the first sign of trouble. That should be in about ten seconds.

The pendant around the queen's neck catches my eye. It's made of two trees, one opal and the other onyx, joined at the base of their trunks. Their outermost branches intertwine to create a circle. It emits a faint glow that, if I look close enough, pulsates like a heartbeat.

The queen runs her slender fingers, dripping in jewels, up my back. I go rigid and try not to shiver. It's nearly impossible to convince myself I don't want her touching me.

Her Majesty must know it too, because she giggles. "It's been too long, Jocelyn," she coos in a voice like poisoned syrup.

"Only about three weeks," I reply coolly, unwrapping the portrait. "I think you'll really like the changes I made."

The queen gives a small gasp of joy, gets to her feet, and takes the painting from my hands. "Oh, I do. It's marvelous." Turning the canvas to Lyle, she asks, "What do you think?"

Lyle scowls and surveys the crowd instead of giving an answer. Everyone's a critic.

The queen pouts at him and hands the painting back to me. As she sits down, she says, "Forgive him. He's been a bit put out lately." She lazily strokes my arm with one hand and sips her wine with the other.

My body locks up again.

Her gentle features pull together into a frown. "You're always so tense, Jocelyn. You should stay for a while." She offers me her glass. "The Faerie Court has a way of calming one's nerves."

"No, thank you, Your Majesty," I say. "I have to get home and faerie wine is rather...potent, from what I hear."

Translation: Nice try, but Dominic told me how addictive faerie wine can be for humans.

The queen drops her hand to my thigh, binding my muscles like metal cords. "Such a responsible girl." She gestures to the dancers with her glass. "We could use a bit of that here."

As much as I hate this woman, I have to admire her persistence. From the second I could stand after the nightshade scar appeared on my chest, she's been trying to ensnare me. If Dominic hadn't volunteered to watch me in the Human Realm while I painted, I probably would be trapped here.

"I need peace to work," I reply, keeping my eyes on the crowd and off the queen. "You would be too much of a distraction."

Her Majesty raises an eyebrow and turns her attention to the portrait. "While this is quite stunning, Jocelyn, you could use a distraction. You never seem to rest. Besides"—she leans against the opposite arm of the throne, causing the left shoulder of her dress to slide down—"don't you want to paint from life?"

Lyle glares murder over his queen's head, daring me to take the invitation.

I pull at my shirt collar and swallow hard. "With all due respect, the fewer distractions, the better. The sooner I finish the last painting, the sooner I'm out of your hair."

The queen's smile droops. "If you're so eager to finish, you should be at home painting instead of attacking my subjects."

My blood runs cold. She knows about Fuloch.

The queen sits up straight and lowers her voice. "I heard about your little spat down at that horrid club over a few human girls."

Trying to keep my voice steady, I say, "Your Majesty, I gave him fair warning—"

The queen jabs me with the pointed red nail of her index finger. "I don't care what you gave him. I will not have you attacking my subjects over affairs that don't concern you. You are not to abuse my protection, and you will not assault one of my kind again, do you understand?"

"If you kept your kind in line, I wouldn't have had to assault him."

The music stops. The patrons freeze. They all know I'm dead.

Lyle draws his sword and I jump to my feet. The painting clatters to the floor, and I look for the quickest escape route, which will just delay the inevitable.

The queen rises to her feet and holds a hand out to stop Lyle. I don't know whether to be relieved or terrified. Judging by the way her eyes darken, it's the latter.

"She insulted you, Majesty," Lyle growls.

"I will handle it." Her voice sounds like cracking ice.

"But, Majesty, it's nearly time for—"

The queen turns to him and shouts, "I will handle it!" Fury smolders in her eyes as she looks back at me. "Come with me, Jocelyn."

"Your Majesty, I—"

"Get over here," she shrieks, "or I will make you wish the last three generations of your family were never born!"

I believe her, so I follow and keep my eyes down.

She glances at Lyle. "Keep an eye on things for me."

We disappear behind the curtains that hang behind the throne and walk down a short hall that opens to a series of wider corridors like the ones I followed to the Grand Hall. The queen is so still and cold that I feel like I'm walking on frost. The few servants that scurry about stay clear of us.

She stops before an enormous door encrusted with jewels. They form the same pattern as her pendent, but the door seems alive somehow. The gems catch the light and sparkle like sunlight on waves. The branches of the trees swirl and bend in a nonexistent breeze. The opal tree shifts in color from faint blues to pinks while the onyx one alternates between deep cobalt and deeper browns and crimsons.

Animals and faeries look out at us from the ever-shifting branches, calculating our place in this world and our relationship to it. A buck locks eyes with me. It's only for a bone-chilling second, but it tells me something both horrifying and reassuring: I'm looking at magic itself.

The queen unlocks the door and shuts it behind me. An extravagant four-post bed sits hidden in maroon curtains and beside it stands two black lacquered nightstands. All of the furniture is black, actually, except for the gold detail around the full-length mirror we're facing.

The queen traces the decoration along the top of the mirror and it begins to glow. The mirror swings open to reveal a stone staircase leading into the depths of the earth. A torch juts out from the tunnel wall. The queen takes it and descends the stairs. I take a deep breath, gather what's left of my nerve, and follow her.

At the bottom of the stairs, a series of damp rotting halls fan out before us. Her Majesty holds the torch up to each of them. When she reaches the one farthest to the left, the flames turn purple. That's the path we take.

I don't dare ask how much longer we have. I just trail behind as the queen continues picking tunnels and pray that, if she's leading me to my death, she'll drag my body back and leave it in the human world.

Who am I kidding? She'll have her cooks use me in tomorrow's supper.

Eventually we can't go any farther. A sharp, jagged pile of junk blocks our path.

The firelight casts ghostly shadows on marble statues reduced to rubble. Emerald-green tapestries and banners function as their damp, moldy shrouds. Slashed, mud-caked portraits jut out as their tombstones.

I dare to ask, "What is all this?"

The queen walks a little closer. "This is all that's left of the former queen of the Seelie Court," she answers. "The *last* queen of the Seelie Court before I unified our realm. It serves as a reminder of what will happen if I fail."

Her gaze drifts off into the inky distance. "If that happens, all of Faerie will fall."

I take a few cautious steps back. "That sounds like a lot of pressure. I apologize for my rash words."

"Oh, Jocelyn..." She sighs, turning to face me. "An apology isn't enough." She matches the steps I take with a few of her own. "If I allow you to speak to me that way, what's to stop the solitary folk? After that, it's the members of my court, then my knights, and then all I've worked so hard for crashes down around me. With no queen to lead, no channel for magic to enter our world, we'll become the myths humans think we are."

"I didn't realize the politics of your world was so complex," I say, backing up to the last stair. "I'll keep that in mind in the future."

"No need," the queen insisted, reaching behind her back.

She swings like lightning.

Her long, curved dagger rips through my shirt. Pain slices across my chest. I trip and my head collides with the edge of a stair. White bursts flash across my vision and the world spins. It stops just as Her Majesty throws herself on top of me. I catch both her wrists before that dagger can do more damage.

The queen throws her head back and lets out a high, shrill, terrifying laugh. Leaning over me, she giggles. "When I'm done with you, you won't have a mind to keep anything in."

She hardly weighs anything, but it's not her physical strength I need to worry about. She has a far more dangerous weapon on her side. With her curls forming a curtain around our faces, it feels like she's the only thing that exists.

"Why couldn't you just keep quiet, Jocelyn?"

Her breath raises goose bumps on my skin.

My grip on her empty hand loosens on its own. She brushes the hair from my eyes and traces my jaw. Every bit of skin she touches aches for her to linger. She slides her hand down to the cut in my shirt and slips her hand through the torn fabric. The touch of her skin bites, then, suddenly, I'm in the most comfortable bed in the world.

Underneath the most beautiful woman in the world.

The queen's lips brush against mine, soft and cool. "I like your spirit, Jocelyn," she whispers. "It's been awhile since a human resisted me like this, especially a woman." She moves her mouth to my ear. "It would be more fun to break you slowly, but you're starting to cause me trouble."

"B-but the p-painting." It's impossible to think straight.

The queen kisses my neck, her lips like a match setting me on fire. I bite my bottom lip as hard as I can, but the pain isn't enough to clear my head.

"Forget it." Her Majesty titters as she reaches my collarbone. "Let me have you and you'll never have to paint again."

That sounds nice.

Wait. No.

Wake up, idiot!

She still has the dagger. If I'm not careful, it's going to end up in my chest.

The queen hikes her hips up farther. I hold my breath in anticipation of what she'll do next. I know what I want her to do next and I hate her for it. I hate myself for it. Waiting hurts.

My free hand slides up her thigh, under her skirt, of its own accord. I don't mind, but I know I should. Like Calista, the queen feels cold. Cold enough to put out this fire, but she'll only make it worse.

Worse is the last thing it would feel like, though.

Maybe...

"Will you save my mother?"

The queen stops.

The tunnel comes into focus. It's easier to breathe. I'm still *very* aware that the Queen of Faerie is on top of me, but it doesn't feel like she's about to devour me.

I seize the moment of clarity. "If I stay here, will you still heal my mother?"

Her Majesty sits up straight and stares down at me like I'm a stranger. "You're still trying to bargain with me?"

"Well, yeah," I reply. "I have to protect my family."

The queen's face contorts in disgust. "Your family," she spits. "Leave it to a human to think blood counts for anything." Her gaze darts up the staircase and her face goes pale.

With a horrified scream, she throws herself off of me and scrambles away from the stairs. "Get away!" she pleads. "Hide in my skin if you must, but I'm begging you. Get away!"

Five

OF ALL THE people to come to my aid, it had to be Lyle. There's a stranger with him too. She looks strikingly like the queen except she appears confused rather than mortified.

"Your Majesty, it's me, Shaylee," she exclaims, rushing to her queen. Lyle follows, setting his torch in a ring on the wall.

The queen scrambles back farther, bumping into the mountain of rubble. The woman kneels and gives the queen a comforting smile while Lyle takes her hands.

"It's us, Your Majesty," he coos, stroking her cheek. If they weren't both psychos, it might be a touching scene.

The queen's breath slows and she stops trembling. As the color returns to her face, recognition slowly creeps into her eyes.

So does fury.

She pulls away from Lyle and strikes Shaylee across the face, causing her head to snap to the side. I wince as all those jewels hit flesh. That's gotta hurt.

"Idiot girl," the queen snarls, then gets to her feet and snatches up her torch from the ground. "Don't sneak up on me like that."

"My apologies," Shaylee murmurs. "We came to inform you that the emissaries from the Unseelie Lands have arrived." Our gazes meet as she stands. Her cheek glows red from the impact.

The queen's eyes narrow to murderous slits in my direction, practically burning a hole in my soul. "Tell them I'm busy."

Lyle grabs her attention. "They caught an old court loyalist."

The queen pauses, tapping her foot and drumming her nails on her arm. All the while, she stares at me. I don't feel any magic, just annoyance and disdain. The queen strides toward the stairs, and I scramble out of her way.

Her Majesty picks up her dagger and slips it back into the sheath against her back. Glaring at me she hisses, "Put the painting with the others and get out. If you harass any more faerie folk, your mother will be the least of your worries. That unfortunate loyalist has put me in a generous mood."

The fear of failure, both for myself and Mom, squeezes my heart so tight it might implode. "Yes, Majesty," I mutter.

Lyle scurries after her. "Before the meeting, Majesty, it might be best to have another dose—"

"Prepare it while I meet with the emissaries," the queen snaps. "It shouldn't take long." She and Lyle march up the stairs, leaving Shaylee and me among the skeletons of the past.

I lean against the wall and try to slow my pounding pulse. All the adrenaline and magic wears off at the same time and leaves me shaky and nauseous. I owe that loyalist big-time, if he survives the queen.

"You gonna make it?" Shaylee asks, taking Lyle's torch from the wall.

"Hopefully." I sigh. "You?"

She shrugs. "Ain't the first time she's hit me, or the hardest. I'm more worried about you. You got the worst of it."

"That's not what it felt like," I reply, rubbing the queen's phantom touch off my skin.

"That's the point." Shaylee chuckles. "Magic and whatnot." She cocks her head to the side. "I don't think we've met." She offers her hand. "I'm Shaylee, princess of the Faerie Court."

I shake her hand. The strength of the muscles underneath surprises me. And I've never heard of a faerie with calluses before.

"I'm Jocelyn," I say. "Idiot human who made a deal with your mother."

That makes Shaylee laugh again. "Thought so. Saw your painting in the Grand Hall. Nice work, girlfriend. Let's go put it up so you can go home."

"Please and thank you."

As we climb the stairs, I look for a way to phrase the question weighing on my mind. I'm not even sure I want it answered. Against my better judgment, I decide to ask anyway.

"Princess—"

"Just Shaylee is cool."

"Okay. Shaylee, what would have happened if your mother had...won?"

She goes quiet for a moment, clicking her tongue. "Time and space would never matter again. The queen would have been your whole universe. You'd need her more than food or water. More than air. Centuries might pass before you realized what happened, but by then..."

My stomach churns. "I was afraid of something like that."

"But you won!" Shaylee slaps me on the back.

"I didn't win. You showed up and scared the bejesus out of her."

Her Majesty had stopped when I mentioned Mom, though. It was probably a fluke. That woman can't be capable of anything resembling sympathy.

"Well, shucks. You're welcome then," Shaylee says.

The twang in Shaylee's voice sounds incredibly out of place.

"Shaylee, why do you sound so...human? And...Southern?"

A grin spreads across her face. "So glad you noticed. I was raised with humans, actually. I'm what you call a changeling. Somebody snatched a human baby and left me behind. Hung around for quite some time until people started noticing that I make weird things happen."

The queen abandoned her daughter? How wicked can she get?

Shaylee must read the question on my face, because she continues the story. "Crazy as it sounds, that's the least of the queen's crimes. Dumping sickly and dying faeries is pretty standard practice. Half-human ones like me, too. Once she saw I was healthy, though, she was more than happy to take me back."

"You have a weird definition of *happy*," I mumble.

Shaylee shrugs. "Can't argue there."

A light shines ahead, and we emerge nowhere near the queen's chamber. Judging by the servants and the smell of food, we're somewhere near the kitchens.

We pick up the painting from the Grand Hall and go to put it with the others. Shaylee chats the whole way. She seems happy to have someone to talk to, and it's nice to have a guide. At least there's one faerie around here who doesn't want me dead or driven mad.

The queen's Hall of Vanity, as I've come to call it, is always tricky to find, but with Shaylee's help, I reach it in record time. Statues of Her Majesty glower down at us. Embroidered queens on blanketlike tapestries look anything but warm and inviting with their icy, calculating expressions. Portraits by other artists cover the wall so densely that I wonder if I'll find room for one more.

Together we search for an empty patch of wall big enough for the latest painting. Shaylee finds one toward the back and hollers for me to join her. Standing on my toes, I manage to reach the tiny hook-shaped branch with the frame. I stand back to admire it, but only for a moment.

"All right, let's get out of here," I say.

"Good plan. I'll see you out, but let's hurry. Her Majesty will probably want to smack me around again if I don't get back soon."

A series of bruises are already becoming welts across Shaylee's cheek.

"I can get out myself," I insist. "It's all right."

"We're not too far from the exit. Besides, I have a few more questions."

Shaylee leads me back toward the entrance, drilling me about global events that date back to the end of the Vietnam War. Something tells me she's been away from humanity a little longer than she realizes.

A knight approaches us near the entrance, holding a dazed, half-starved, scruffy human man by the arm. The knight stops and bows before Shaylee. The man stares into space.

"Your Highness," the knight greets.

Shaylee goes into princess mode. She stands taller in her dress made of pumpkin and corn husks, folding her hands in front of her. All traces of her accent disappear. "What do we have here?"

She sounds eerily like her mother, so I inch away, seeing as I only signed up to deal with one crazy monarch.

"Found him wandering the halls," the knight explains. "I imagine an imp unlocked his door as a prank."

The man's hollow eyes widen at the sight of Shaylee. He falls on his knees and crawls toward her. "Where is my lady?" he whimpers. "I beg you, take me to her. I haven't seen her in days. How am I supposed to play my flute without—"

"Enough," the knight growls, yanking the man back to his feet.

"Take him back to his room and get him something to eat," Shaylee orders. Wrinkling her nose, she adds, "And, for goodness sake, make sure he gets a bath."

The knight bows and drags the man away. Shaylee walks on with me close behind. The man's pleas and cries follow us like a ghost, sending a shiver down my spine. I want to get out of here *yesterday*.

"How sad," Shaylee mutters. "Maybe the queen will show him mercy and make him the Hallowed Offering."

I process her words and stop in my tracks. "The Hallowed what?"

Shaylee bites her lip and blinks a few times before pushing me along. "Don't worry about it. You've got enough on your plate."

"But that man—"

"It's faerie business. You wouldn't understand. All you need to know is that once a human gets hooked on this place, there's no going back. The only release is what lies beyond the grave. Sometimes, that's better than staying in Faerie."

The thought makes me nauseous. I knew I'd end up trapped here if I ate faerie food, and staying here would mess me up, but to see it in action sends my pulse racing in panic.

How close had I come to turning into that?

We round the corner and see the exit, but home has never felt farther away. With a rushed friendly wave, Shaylee shoos me out the door.

"I'd love to chat more, but duty calls."

So does the safety of the farmhouse. My muscles don't unwind until I leave Faerie completely. The dulled colors and thicker air put me at ease, and once I stand in the warm light of the farmhouse windows, the nightmare begins to melt away.

I zip my jacket up to hide the rip and the blood on my shirt. Dominic doesn't need to know about what happened.

The sound of a pan flute coming from his room pushes the court farther away. The music stops when the screen door slams. He emerges seconds later, and as always, he locks the door behind him. As if I'd be stupid enough to go snooping around a faerie's room. He'd *definitely* steal my firstborn if I did.

"How was it?" Dominic asks.

"The usual." I sigh, dropping into a chair. "Her Majesty praised my work, then tried to seduce me into staying. Nothing new."

Dominic frowns as he crosses the kitchen and fills the kettle with water. "Your casual tone troubles me, Jocelyn."

Behind him, the stove clock reads two A.M. That's all? It feels like I've been gone for days. No wonder Shaylee doesn't know what decade it is.

"I met the princess."

Dominic perks up. "How is she?"

"Very...human."

"She must have warmed up to you quickly."

"Well, she did save my skin. Breaks down the barriers of formality, I think."

The troubled expression comes back. "That makes me think your visit wasn't as 'usual' as you say." Dominic snaps his fingers and the kettle whistles. He brings down two mugs and pulls out two tea bags from a drawer. Filled mugs in hand, he sits across from me, then hands me my tea. "Anything I should know about?"

I shake my head and take a sip. I can't tell Dominic what happened. He might actually start doing his job and keeping an eye on me, which I don't need. Besides, I only have one more painting. Once I get it done, I won't have to deal with the Faerie Queen ever again. The fact that Shaylee can stand her is magic all on its own. And how long has that poor old man been there?

"Dominic, what's a Hallowed Offering?"

He chokes on his tea, sputtering it down the front of his shirt. Whatever it is, it's a big deal if I can catch him off guard. I never catch him off guard.

Jocelyn: 1.

Dominic: 500-ish.

As he mops up the tea, he rasps, "Who told you about that?"

"Shaylee," I answer. "We passed an old man on our way out. Shaylee said he should be the Hallowed Offering."

Dominic gets up and throws the napkin in the trash. "Lovely," he grumbles. Instead of coming back to the table, he begins organizing tea ingredients on the kitchen counter. "Thanks ever so much, Your Highness."

"Well, what is it?"

"It is a pact, Jocelyn," he finally answers. "A pact born of blood that ensures the Faerie Realm keeps its magic. We would all waste away to nothing without it."

I hold my mug tighter, but it fails it keep off the chill of Dominic's words. "Does someone have to die, though?"

Dominic pauses, then gives up on the ingredients. "Long ago, when Queen Titania ruled and the emerald banners waved, no one did. The two courts, Seelie and Unseelie, gave animal offerings, but when the current queen seized control and united the two, the Offering took a darker turn. Someone must die now."

"Why?"

"No one's sure. Most think it's a punishment from the Other World, the ancient powers that gave us magic. The queen went against the natural order by unifying the courts, so she must pay a greater price. For the past hundred years, she has done so willingly.

"At first, no one in the Unseelie Court cared. They control the entire realm and subjugate the Seelie faeries. But now, as the queen becomes less and less stable, more and more of them are finally waking up and seeing that something is very wrong."

"Can things change before the next Offering?"

"Seeing as it's on October thirty-first, I doubt it." Dominic faces me, leaning against the counter. "We have too many squabbles and personal agendas to get anything done. We faeries are vapid, selfish creatures."

"You're not vapid or selfish," I argue.

Dominic chuckles. "Thank you, but you don't know me well enough to reach that conclusion." He takes his empty mug from the table and begins rinsing it in the sink. "Take yourself to bed. It's late."

I scowl behind his back, mostly because he's right. I don't know much about Dominic, besides his enthusiasm for tea. He can tell me about all this cultish blood sacrifice craziness, but not a word about himself. He's not vapid or selfish, but he's certainly secretive.

I run the shower as cold as possible to get the queen's touch off my skin. The thought of turning out like that old man makes it hard to fall asleep. It shouldn't, though. There's only one painting left and then I'm free. Once I'm home and Mom's awake, I'll never have to step foot in Faerie again.

But I can't help but wonder, how much of Faerie will follow me home?

Six

I'M GRATEFUL THAT I have to work on Monday. After all the fruitless sketches, false starts, and countless stress-induced cigarettes, it'll be nice to stare at something other than a blank canvas for a while.

Thanks to the reliable lack of traffic, I make it to the Novel Spell at 7:35. Like the Time Between, it used to be a factory. Now it's a three-story used bookstore. It's one of the biggest in the state and the best in the world, in my opinion, but I'm a tad biased.

The musty smell of old books and dust greets any who enter, along with the sprites that call the store home. They flit around as small darts of earthly color, squeaking, chirping, and pulling my hair and clothes in their constant need for attention.

"Morning," I say, holding up my hand. They snuggle against my palm and fly off as quickly as they came. Some dart off to play hide-and-seek in the bookshelves. Others return to their nests hidden above. Most go looking for trouble.

"You're late, Jocelyn," my boss croaks as he emerges from the basement.

He waddles toward me, scowling with dark beady eyes that routinely get lost in the ancient wrinkles of his face. His long, ragged ears bounce in time with his heavy steps. The smell of freshly turned dirt follows him and a bit shakes itself loose as he raps his cane against my shin.

Wincing, I apologize. "My bad, Mr. Hob, but I brought you something."

His eyes widen as I pull a pair of toaster pastries out of my bag. He snatches them out my hand and mumbles, "You're forgiven," around a mouthful of crust and strawberry jam. "Consider yourself lucky. I was considering turning you to stone."

Yeah, right. He always says that.

As far as faeries go, I've known Mr. Hob the longest. While investigating the woods for that strange creature we almost hit, I slid into a creek bed and bumped into Mr. Hob, who was out for a stroll.

"Away with you," he snapped, "or I'll turn you to stone!"

The lunch I brought dissuaded him and convinced him to take me to the Faerie Court in search of answers. I never found the faerie I nearly hit, but I did find the Faerie Queen. The rest is history.

"Get the store ready to open," Mr. Hob orders, dragging me out of my memory. "Walter will be here at eight. I want him on the cash register by himself today. He's been here long enough that he should be able to handle it."

"Yes, sir." I stick my bag behind the cashier counter, grab a green employee apron, and make sure all three floors are in order. Then I take my temporary post behind the cash register and find my boss still lingering.

"I heard something funny about you," he says, still licking crumbs from his fingers. "Apparently, you were in a bit of a row at the Time Between on Friday night."

Wonderful. Just what I need, to be a hot piece of gossip in the Faerie Realm.

"Oh, don't be so cross," Mr. Hob says, elbowing me as I roll my eyes. "I'm proud of you, lass, for standing up to him. Good thing Fuloch was plenty drunk, though. Might have ended none too pretty otherwise."

"The look he gave me when he got thrown out was none too pretty," I mutter, opening my sketchbook.

Mr. Hob cackles. "So? It's not like the bastard can touch you. I heard someone told the queen, however. She wasn't too hard on you, was she?"

My stomach flips, making me stop midsketch. "No. She was fine."

Mr. Hob scowls. "That's the saddest lie I've ever heard. What happened?"

"Nothing. She was just...upset. Her daughter showed up, thankfully."

The goblin's ears perk up. "You met our princess? Lovely lass, isn't she?"

"She's certainly interesting. And quite the talker."

"Probably because you're human. She misses this realm something terrible."

"Why'd she go back to court then? I know I wouldn't if the queen was my mother."

Mr. Hob strokes his chin. "Duty called, I suppose. Or it will. Her Majesty can't stay queen forever."

Seeing as faeries are practically immortal, that certainly seems like a possibility.

A very real, very depressing possibility.

"But let's speak of more interesting things." Mr. Hob places his hand to his mouth and whispers, "I heard you left the Time Between with a girl."

Good God, faeries are gossipy.

"I just sat outside with her," I explain. "Her friends forgot her, thanks to a spell I asked someone to cast. It missed her."

"Well played, my girl," the goblin snickers. "Surely you used that time to your advantage?"

"We just talked."

My boss deflates a bit. "Well that's dull. Did you at least ask to see her again?"

"I didn't get her number."

Mr. Hob groans. "What am I going to do with you? You're far too introverted for your own good."

"Pot, meet kettle."

"I'm more like a meat tenderizer. You, on the other hand, are a seventeen-year-old human. You need to spend more time with people. How else do you expect not to get sucked into Faerie? It's a wonder you haven't been already."

No joke, especially considering how my last trip to court went.

The bell above the door rings, saving me from a longer lecture. In walks Walter, the other part-timer. "Good morning!" he calls, strolling in the door like the untamable ray of sunshine he is. "Lovely day!"

"It *was*," Mr. Hob grumbles under his breath. In his place stands a pudgy old man. In his human disguise, Mr. Hob only looks slightly less frightening than normal. He continues to glare at Walter's back as he takes off his jacket and slips on an apron.

Walter joins us at the counter. He's gangling, scruffy, and always slightly spacey. When I first met him, I figured he had to be in James-Child's philosophy department. Imagine my surprise when he told me he's a premed student.

"Really feels like autumn outside, doesn't it?" he says.

"It sure does," I reply.

"Walter, you're on the register today," Mr. Hob explains. "By yourself. Think you can handle it?"

"I'm on it," the newbie replies with a salute. He plops down in front of the register, watching the surrounding shelves with a stern glower.

Mr. Hob rolls his eyes, and I try not to snicker at the two of them.

"Jocelyn, do you think you can handle taking inventory and stocking?"

"Sure thing."

"Good. I'll check on you two in a few hours." As he waddles past me, he adds, "And for goodness's sake, Jocelyn, go do something fun later."

I shake my head and go to work.

I didn't exactly move to Grand Harbor for fun. I need to finish that last painting to save my mom and fix my family, but Hob might be onto something. Faerie drove me to smoking, after all. And then there's the fact I couldn't produce any decent artwork this weekend. Going out somewhere other than the Time Between might get my wheels turning.

I keep an ear out for Walter as I shelve newly acquired books and return those left out to their rightful places. He's oddly quiet for an hour and a half. Just as I'm beginning to worry, I hear his voice and footsteps echoing off the stairwell.

"—but who knows? Writers are weird." He rounds the corner and gives me a wave. "Hey, Jocelyn. Just helping a customer find a book all on my own." He puffs out his chest and grins.

I hold my breath as the customer steps out of the stairwell. She has dark skin, ebony eyes, and curls as big and beautiful as the night I met her.

"Asterina Fischler."

She does a double take and cocks her head to the side with a cautious smile. "Jocelyn Lennox. Fancy meeting you here."

"You too," I reply, leaning against a bookshelf like this serendipity is no big deal. The Universe is blessing me with a second shot, perhaps, but it's no big deal.

"What brings you here?" I ask.

Rina holds up a small note. "My morning class got canceled. Figured I'd get a little birthday shopping done since Brook was coming here anyway. My brother has this weird preference for used books over new."

"You definitely came to the right place then," I say. "What book?"

She looks down at the note. "*Earls of the Gauntlet: Book One.* Know it?"

Know it? It's only my favorite book series in the whole world and the best epic fantasy written in the last fifty years, but I try to keep my cool.

"Totally," I answer. "I have the series." And the movies. And the soundtracks. And several character figurines, but I shouldn't nerd out too much.

Rina's eyebrows perk up. "So does my brother. Well, he did until he lost the first one somehow."

Walter looks back and forth between the two of us, then smirks. The counter bell rings downstairs, and he hands me a slip of paper. "Why don't you take care of it? I'll go see who's at the register."

"You sure?" I ask, checking the book's information on the slip. "I don't want to take such a monumental occasion from you."

He shrugs and backs away. "It's cool. I didn't crash the computer searching for the book, so I'll count it as a success."

I'm nominating Walter for employee of the month.

Rina waves to him as he leaves.

"Did you get home okay?" I ask, scanning the numbers on the bookshelves.

"I did, actually," Rina answers, walking close behind. "Luckily, Brook didn't forget me at the side of the road. And, get this, Megan and the others don't even remember getting back to campus. When I confronted them about it, they were really freaked out, saying that everything was a blur."

I try to feign surprise. "That's crazy."

"Yeah," Rina repeats dryly. "Crazy."

I catch her intense gaze from the corner of my eye and do my best to play dumb. She can't possibly think I had something to do with what happened, can she? The truth is too insane for her to ever guess.

I change the topic just in case. "So, have you read *Earls of the Gauntlet*?"

"Nah. I watched the movies, though." Rina answers. "I've thought about reading the books, but I already have plenty of reading, thanks to my classes."

I find the shelf we're looking for and pull down the store's only hardcover copy of *Earls*. As I hand it to her, I take a deep breath and say, "I could give you a rundown of what's different in the books, if you're free sometime."

Rina furrows her brow as she takes the book from my hand.

My heart hammers against my ribs.

C'mon, I can do this.

"What I'm trying to say is, want to get coffee sometime?"

Her eyes widen and she blinks a few times before looking down at the book. "Oh! Um, I'm sort of swamped with school right now, so..."

Strike one.

"You have to take a study break eventually, right?"

Her eyes dart over the shelves with her bottom lip between her teeth. "I don't know, Jocelyn..."

Strike two.

"Nothing serious," I insist. I trace an X over my chest. "Cross my heart."

She begins to speak, but frowns over my shoulder. "What was that?"

I look down the empty aisle. "What was what?"

Rina slips past me and walks to the end of the aisle. "Something just flew by."

It must have been a sprite. They're usually good about staying out of sight due to Mr. Hob's constant threats. Every once in a while, though, they try their luck.

"A bug must have gotten in." I study the rafters with her, grateful to find only empty shadows.

"I don't think so," Rina muses, looking left and right. "It *glowed*."

"Trick of the light." I point back toward the opposite wall. "See? The sun lines up with this aisle at this time of day. It must have hit whatever you saw."

Rina folds her arms around the book, eyes narrow as she studies the dark ceiling.

"If it makes you feel better, I'll look into it after I check you out."

Rina turns back to me, expression bemused.

I realize why with a wave of dread.

No. No, no, no, I did not just say that.

"Oh my God—I meant down at the register!"

Rina raises an eyebrow. "Got a better angle down there or something?"

"I meant the book!"

"Sure you did," she snickers.

The register bell rings, giving me a way out.

"I'm really sorry," I say. "I need to go help Walter."

Rina nods. "Go ahead. I want to look around a bit before you *check me out*."

My face burns while I walk down to the register. Dad always said jokes like that would be my undoing.

Except he called it my "*pun*-doing."

Downstairs, Brook waves at me from the counter. "Hi, again. Jocelyn, right?"

"Yeah," I mutter. "What's wrong, Walt?"

"I forgot how to ring up a discount," he admits, scratching his head. "Sorry."

I punch in my code, then ring up the purchase. "No problem."

Rina joins us as Walter gives Brook her change. She stays silent, which makes my palms sweat. When I finally force myself to look at her, there's a smirk on her face that I can't read. To make it worse, Walter slips away to Mr. Hob's office and Brook goes to wait in the car.

All I can say to her is "Your total is seven twenty-three."

She just keeps smiling as she hands me her debit card.

As she takes the paid-for book from the counter, she sighs. "Listen, I need to put some cards on the table. This whole liking-girls thing is still new territory for me. I'm even still contemplating killing Brook for telling you. My family knows, my friends know, but the whole dating part is still…a lot right now. I don't want to get your hopes too high by saying yes to coffee." Before my shoulders can droop in disappointment, she adds, "However, my friends and I are going out for pizza and a movie Friday if you want to come. Maybe we can see where to go from there?"

My brain short-circuits. "Really?"

She shrugs and leans over the counter to scribble on her receipt. "Sure. It's not a date but—"

"Pizza's cool. Friends are cool. Everything's cool," I reply, folding my arms in a sad attempt to look nonchalant. I rub my chin to keep the goofy smile off my face.

Rina hands me the paper and tucks away the pen. "If you're sure, call me Thursday?"

I fold the receipt and slip it in my pocket. "Definitely. Thanks."

Rina shrugs again. "Thanks for waiting with me on Friday. Adios."

I wait until she's been gone for a solid minute before triumphantly punching the air and letting myself grin like a big dork. I can't believe it. I got her number *and* a date! Well, not a *date* date, but I get to see her again.

Best. Monday. Ever.

As I put Rina's number in my phone, the day catches my attention. It's October nineteenth.

Mom's birthday.

Seven

THE REST OF the day passes in a blur. Mr. Hob and Walter badger me about the stupid grin on my face, but I decide to keep my not-date with Rina a secret. After living among faeries for four months, jinxes seem all too real. I don't want to risk it. When I clock out, Mr. Hob swears that he'll fire me if I don't tell him tomorrow what I'm so happy about, but I know he won't. He'd be stuck with Walter all the time if he did.

I swing by a flower shop and pick up a vase and a bouquet of multicolored roses down the road from the hospital. Mom always liked getting a bunch of colors. She said they looked more festive that way and hospital rooms need all the festivity they can get.

Even after months of visits, the silence of the room is still unsettling. There's only the beep of the heart monitor and the distant white noise of the hospital to offset the muted paint, dimmed lights, and sterile air. At least Mom can breathe on her own now. The hum of the ventilator always gnawed at me, like a condescending whisper.

She's fragile, she's fragile.

Look what you've done, look what you've done.

I knock on the doorframe before entering just to feel something close to normal. "Happy Birthday, Mom," I announce, flicking on the lights. "Brought you some flowers." I avoid looking at her for as long as possible by filling the vase and arranging the flowers in excruciating detail. Once they're perfect, I have no choice.

Mom looks thinner every time I visit. She has more gray hairs, too, regardless of how time has stopped for her. Her skin looks like porcelain against her freckles. The version of Mom in the photo at home seems more real than the woman in front of me.

Not for much longer, though. Just one more painting.

"Good news," I say, pulling up a nearby chair. "I got the sixth painting done. One more and my commission is up. I'm not sure when I'll have it done, but it shouldn't take long. A few weeks if I work fast and my commissioner likes it. I could be home in time to start the next semester back at Northland High." The doctors can't confirm if Mom can hear us. We like to think she can, which is why I'm careful with how much I tell her. "I met someone pretty cool today. Well, I actually met her Friday, but she gave me her number today."

A pair of hands slam down on my shoulders, scaring me half to death. "You got a girl's number?" exclaims a familiar voice. "Ooh la la, do tell."

The girl perched over me stands much taller than the one in the photo at home, but she still has the same blue eyes and blonde hair that match mine. A mischievous smile replaced her innocent one years ago. Come to think of it, I don't think she's ever been innocent.

"Hello, dork," I tease, batting her hair out of my face.

"Hello yourself," Anna replies, setting a second bouquet of flowers on the nightstand. "Thanks for giving us a heads-up, butt-face."

"Sorry. I remembered last minute. Where's Uncle Rick?"

A heavy, calloused hand musses my hair. "Right here." My uncle grins down at me. "Hey, kiddo."

"Hi, Uncle Rick. What's up?"

"Well, you know..." He sighs, removing his favorite Northland Lions baseball cap. "Same old, same old." He leans down and kisses Mom on the forehead. After one glance around the room, he frowns. "Where's David?"

Good to know Dominic's enchantment is still sticking.

"He's got a cold," I lie. "He said he didn't want to put other patients at risk."

Rick strokes his short dark beard and plops down in the chair on the other side of the bed. "That's too bad. I was hoping to say hi. We see him even less than we see you. He sure is a busy fella."

I shrug. "Yeah, well, you know how it is."

"How's that fancy art program of yours?"

"Okay. Same old, same old there too."

"Jocelyn's got a girlfriend," Anna teases, poking my cheek.

"She's not my girlfriend," I argue, swatting her hand away. "I just met her."

A mischievous twinkle comes to my uncle's dark eyes. No wonder he and my teenaged sister manage to get along.

"Okay, so a potential girlfriend," he says. "Where'd you meet her?"

"School. She's in my graphic design class."

Anna folds her arms and leans against the nightstand. "You've had her in class all semester and you've just now met her?"

Whoops. Time to backtrack.

"She's a new student," I amend, scrambling for anything else to talk about. "How's practice for the Christmas concert, Anna?"

My sister rolls her eyes and yanks off her backpack. "You're no fun." While she unzips it, she adds, "It's all right, though."

"She refuses to try out for the solo," Rick interjects.

My sister cringes. "And throw up on stage again? No, thank you."

"You were eight," I remind her. "No one remembers that."

"Don't care. Never again. I'd rather swim across a lake."

Wow. Given my sister's paralyzing fear of deep water, that's saying something. She almost drowned me one summer in her attempt to get out when our cousin threw her in his pool as a prank. That's how scared she is.

"Aha!" Anna pulls out a wrinkled blue sheet of paper, does her best to flatten it, then hands it to me. "Here's the concert info. You should bring Uncle David. That recluse needs to get out almost as much as you do."

I look it over. "Kinda early for flyers, isn't it?"

Anna shrugs. "It's a rejected prototype. Figured you'd like it. I drew it."

I grin from ear to ear, newly in awe of the cute snowmen and intricate snowflakes. "This is beautiful, Annalise. I didn't know you were this good."

My sister shrugs and zips up her backpack. "It's nothing like your stuff."

"It doesn't have to be. It's beautiful in its own right."

Anna looks down and tucks a lock of hair behind her ear. "Yeah, yeah."

"Speaking of art," Rick interjects, "Have you heard back from any of the schools you applied to?"

Oh, yeah. College. That thing normal kids my age worry about.

It's mid-October of my supposed senior year, but thanks to the paintings, I haven't given college much thought. Even with the fake transcript Dominic and I put together—ensuring there isn't a big gaping hole in my record—I've put it on the back burner. Uncle Rick doesn't know that, obviously.

"Both of them rejected me." I sigh, feigning disappointment.

Rick winces. "I'm sorry, kiddo."

Anna twirls a lock of hair and studies my face. "I don't believe you," she says. "Who would be crazy enough to reject you with your portfolio?"

"Um, anyone who looks at my grades in my other classes? Besides, I've thought it over, and with Mom's medical bills, I can't justify going to art school next fall. I'll go to community college first and knock out some general credits. My program will still look good on my transcript if I transfer sophomore or junior year."

The community college part is true at least. Of course, I don't know *when* I'll be going, but I'll cross that bridge when I come to it, assuming I survive my last trip to the Faerie Court.

Rick take's Mom's hand, stroking it with his thumb. "I think you're being practical, but I don't want you to worry about your mom. I've got it under control." Given that Rick's a software engineer, I don't doubt that. "And she wouldn't want you to hang around town on her account."

"Yeah, but...I'm her kid, you know? I need to help, seeing as I—"

"Jocelyn." Rick's eyes flash to me. His voice hardens. "Don't."

A pressure settles over the room that makes me swallow my words.

We've made an unspoken pact: don't talk about the accident in Mom's room. She doesn't need to hear us fight, and talking about the accident always leads to that.

Rick refuses to let me take responsibility for it. To him, it doesn't matter that I was driving. It doesn't matter that I was arguing with Mom about college, of all things. It doesn't matter that I promised Dad to look out for her and Anna. "An accident's an accident," he always says.

It isn't, though. Not for me.

Anna tenses but tries to laugh it off and pokes me again. "If you spent more time studying and less time chasing girls, maybe you'd have more luck getting into art school."

I let Anna change the subject. This isn't her fight. If Rick would just let me own up to it and help make it right, there wouldn't be a fight at all.

Poking her back, I joke, "I'm sorry, but how many boys have you fawned over in the last few years?"

Anna catches my hand. "I can fawn over whoever I want. *I* keep my grades up."

"Whatever, nerd," I shoot back, switching tactics by tickling her.

With the storm avoided, the rest of the visit proves pleasant. I try to keep the conversation on Rick and Anna as much as possible. The fewer lies I have to make up now, the fewer I have to remember later. At six o'clock, Rick reluctantly announces that he and Anna need to leave. She apparently has a mountain of homework and a piano lesson at seven.

I need to head home, too. That last portrait isn't about to paint itself, and Dominic is no doubt getting ready to blow up my phone, wondering where I am. The three of us kiss Mom goodbye and ride the elevator down together.

"Don't be such a stranger in your own home," Rick says, tousling my hair one last time. "And bring that uncle of yours along with you. I'm starting to think you made him up."

"Ha-ha. Wouldn't that be something?" I mutter.

Rick begins walking toward the car, giving Anna and me a moment alone.

"I hate it when you two argue." She grumbles. "Especially about the accident."

"I'm just trying to take responsibility for my actions." I explain. "Be an adult, you know?"

She locks gazes with mine, as if she's trying to read my soul. "Do you have to try and do it all at once?" she demands. "And do you have to do it all the way in Grand Harbor?"

I massage my neck and try to squirm out from under my sister's gaze. "Life doesn't always let you choose when or how you grow up, Anna."

Anna's expression morphs to worry. "That's not all that's going on. Uncle Rick won't listen but..."

My heart starts to pound. I stick my clammy hand in my pockets, praying that Anna isn't deducing anything that could complicate things. "What do you mean?"

"You've been weird," Anna answers. "Ever since you moved away."

I force myself to laugh. "You've always thought I was weird."

Anna chews her bottom lip. "It's not normal Jocelyn weird."

"Is it superhero-secret-identity weird? Because that's what I'm going for."

Anna gently punches me in the arm. "Ass-hat. I'm trying to say I'm worried about you."

Rick waves from the car. "Anna, come on."

"You better go," I say. "And don't tell Rick I'm a superhero."

Anna sighs and elbows me. "See you, big sister."

I elbow her back. "Bye, baby sister."

I watch her jog to join Rick. She's getting smart. Well, she's always been smart, but now she's starting to ask questions. I just hope she doesn't get too nosy. It's the danger she would be in that really scares me.

I could never forgive myself if she got tangled up in Faerie.

She's changed in more subtle ways too. Her hair's longer and she left it wavy today instead of straightening it. She's dressing less like a tomboy and she's taller. While I'm stuck in Faerie, life's still moving at full speed for her. As she and Rick drive past and wave to me, I get a punch to the gut: I'm not just paying for that accident with the paintings. I'm paying by missing out on my sister's life.

Best not to think about it. I need to get back to work. The sooner I get that portrait done, the sooner I can put all this behind me. Maybe going out with Rina and the others is a chance to start doing just that.

I'm not sure I've earned it, though.

It's strange what magic can and can't do. Warp the mind? Sure. Alter the very fabric of matter? No problem. Wake up a comatose woman? Piece of cake. Telling me how to move forward?

Nope. For that I'm on my own.

Eight

I HAVE ENOUGH faith in humanity to believe that, if we had magic, we would use it for good. We'd cure diseases, fight world hunger, and stop global warming. I'd want to save the world too, but first I'd use it to make a half-decent outfit for this not-date, seeing as Dominic refuses to help in that department.

"I'm not crafting a glamour for something so superficial," he chastises, looking over my latest ensemble. "Besides, you look fine." He goes back to cutting up an apple.

"Just *fine*?" I ask.

"Well, what else can I say?" Dominic snaps, waving around the knife. "I'd say you look lovely, but you'd complain that I sound like your mother."

"No, I wouldn't," I retort. "Just don't pinch my cheek or anything."

Dominic looks at me again, studying me longer this time. "You look lovely, but you need to do something with that hair."

I can't help but snicker. "*Now* you sound like my mother. And you could help me out just a *little* bit."

Dominic rolls his eyes, puts the knife down, and comes around the table. "I'm a faerie knight, you know," he grumbles, fussing with my hair. "I used to defend my queen in battle and helped secure countless victories. This is below my dignity."

"You volunteered for this job, remember?" I tease.

"Not for this part." He sticks his tongue out from the side of this mouth as he rearranges another lock of hair.

"You *literally* just—"

"Hush. How does that look?"

I look at my reflection in the window. It's not bad. My hair looks messy on purpose for once.

Dominic goes back to cutting his apple. "Now go make friends. I don't want to see you back here until at least eleven."

Eleven? That's a bit late for my liking. I finally managed to produce a decent concept sketch this week, so I was looking forward to putting it on the canvas later tonight.

"But, Dominic—"

"The only 'but' you should worry about is yours. Get it out the door."

Dominic sounds more like a faerie godmother than a faerie knight, but I don't dare say so out loud since he picked the knife back up. Instead, I just chuckle to myself and grab my keys.

In the car, I rehearse what to say to Rina and her friends. It's a little unnerving, how good I've gotten at lying. Then again, opening with, "I work for the Faerie Queen so she'll heal my mother" is a sure way to get committed to a psych ward. I need to sound normal.

I find the pizza joint easy enough. The warm smell of baked bread, meat, and tomato sauce reminds me that I skipped lunch; I had to cram in as much sketch time as possible.

Rina waves at me with a grin from a circular booth across the restaurant.

I never knew someone could look so dazzling in yellow.

The others turn my way and smile. That's a good sign, I think. It doesn't *seem* like they're analyzing my every move. I wave back and stride over, trying to look more relaxed and confident than I feel.

"Sorry I'm late," I say, sliding in next to Rina.

"You're fine." She hands me a menu. "We just got here." Turning to the rest of the group, she announces, "Everybody, this is Jocelyn, the girl from the nightclub I told you about." She points in turn to let me know who's who. "Jocelyn, this is Jun, Travis, and you've met Brook."

Travis extends his hand over the table to shake mine. "Thanks for having our girl's back." His other hand grazes over his buzzed black hair.

I try not to wince in his strong grip. "It was no big deal."

"Rina said you're into *Earls of the Gauntlet*?" Jun asks, shaking my hand as well. "Consider yourself already among friends."

Thank goodness. I was worried about what I'd talk about with people smart enough to get into James-Child.

"Before you start geeking out, let's order," Brook says. She brushes a red curl from her face to read the menu. "I'm starving."

Once we finally choose, the questions begin. As far as anyone knows, I moved to Grand Harbor after turning eighteen. I work at the Novel Spell part-time while also taking commissions, and I go to school online for graphic design. I only have to lie about school and my age. Shouldn't be too hard to remember.

After that, I start asking some questions of my own. Turns out Travis is a mechanical engineering major from Detroit, Jun is from Seattle and wants to be an art therapist, and Brook is a linguistics major from Small Rapids.

"You guys are all over the place then," I say. "How'd you start hanging out?"

They all look at each other and groan. "Professor Bern's literature class." It can't have been too bad, though, because they all laugh.

Rina lays her head on the table. "Can we not talk about Bern? That group project he gave us last month still gives me nightmares."

"It wasn't that bad," Jun argues.

"Easy for you to say," Rina retorts. "You did yours on Doctor When."

I sit up straighter and lock gazes with Jun. "You watch Doctor When?"

He smirks. "Are the Odd the oldest telepathic race in the universe?"

Just as I'm about to high-five him, Rina chimes in with "Nope."

We both stare at her.

After a long sip of her soda, she explains, "In the classic series, there was a race called the Lek-Dars, and *they* were said to be first life-forms to use telepathy, so they trump the Odd."

I think I want to marry this woman, and I want Jun to be my best man.

Travis and Brook look at each other with blank expressions as Rina and Jun debate the nuance of 'oldest' versus 'first to discover,' which Rina has in the bag. Thanks to Mom, Annalise and I grew up watching the Australian sci-fi drama, Doctor When, alongside Saturday morning cartoons. The argument ends in a draw once the food comes.

Brook and Rina dig into the veggie-pineapple pizza while the guys and I look on in horror. The thought of pineapple on pizza sounds weirder than the existence of faeries.

"Sure you don't want some real pizza?" Travis taunts, plopping a slice of meat-lovers on his plate.

"Maybe when I'm done using my arteries," Brook shoots back. She offers me the spatula with a look that says, "Choose your alliance."

I glace over at Rina, who raises an eyebrow. I'm not above going out of my way to impress her, but pineapple pizza is a bit *too* far out of the way.

"Thanks," I say, taking the spatula from Jun as he hands it to me. "But I'll take clogged arteries over pineapple any day."

"Suit yourself," Brook says, slipping the spatula under another piece.

I can't remember the last time I ate real food. And by "real food," I just mean something that didn't come straight from a box. The company's nice too. Mr. Hob was right. I should have been getting out months ago. Leaving the easel hasn't caused a fire or an earthquake. Yet.

When everyone reaches for their wallets to pay, Rina stops me from pulling out mine.

"I got it," she says, putting our portion of the bill on the little black slate. "I invited you, so it's my treat."

"It was my idea first, though," I argue.

Rina takes my hand as I reach for my wallet again, and I shiver from the jolt of energy she sends up my arm.

"Seriously, I got it," she says.

"Dude, just let her," Travis chuckles. "We'll never get out of here otherwise. Besides, we won't judge you."

She hands the slate to the waitress before I can do anything, so that settles that, I guess.

We leave the restaurant and head toward the movie theater. I'm the last one out the door, and Rina lags behind to walk beside me.

"Thanks for paying," I say. "I owe you."

"It doesn't weird you out too much?" she asks.

I shrug. "Nah. Though I'm a bit curious as to why you did it."

Rina slips her hands into her pockets and cocked her head to the side. "I owe you for waiting with me. That club was hella creepy."

"Can't argue with you there."

"And you go there why again...?" Rina asks, walking backward to face me.

"Like I said, the bartender is a friend of mine."

Rina snickers. "You don't go just to *check people out?*"

I pull up the hood of my jacket, trying to hide how red my face must be turning. "I'm never living that down, am I?"

"Not a chance," Rina laughs. "At least it was better than that terrible joke you told at the club."

I clutch my chest, pretending to be shot. "Terrible? I beg your pardon—"

"Pardon's all yours."

I have to pause and rethink what to say. "I'm starting to think you just brought me along to tease me."

Rina shortens her steps so that we walk closer together. A playful grin spreads across her face, lighting up those ebony eyes so that my heart catches. Whatever she's planning, with a look like that, she's not playing fair.

"As fun as that is," she says quietly, "I'm also rather curious."

"About...?"

Jun calls from farther down the street, "You guys coming or what?"

"Yeah, we're coming," Rina replies. She looks back to me, her expression still mischievous. "Let's finish this conversation later. We don't want to keep the others waiting."

If it means getting to flirt with Rina, I'd make them wait all night.

"Everyone still game for *Scornful Robin*?" Travis asks once we join them.

"Define *game*," Brook says with an apprehensive look. "If you mean 'willing to watch it,' then yes. If you mean 'excited for the roaring sea of emotion,' then no."

Apparently, *Scornful Robin* is the last installment of movie series based on a book series that I haven't read. I don't want to be a downer, so I go along with the unanimous choice. We get in line for tickets, and I slip in front of Rina so that I can buy hers. When I hand it to her, she looks down at it in confusion, then back at me, then back at the ticket.

"For letting me tag along," I explain as we step out of line. Under my breath, I add, "And to help you forget what I said on Monday."

That smirk comes back as she takes it from my hand. "Well played." Lowering her voice, she adds, "It'll take more than that, though."

"Well, maybe an actual date would do the trick? Tonight seems to be going pretty well, after all."

Rina's expression turns to surprise, but the rest of the group catches up before she can reply and Jun starts asking about my commission gig.

"You said you do freelance work?" he asks as we file into the theater. "How did you get into that?"

"Well, I was just sort of at the right place at the right time is all," I answer.

Jun sighs, his artistic dreams probably slightly dashed. "Getting work like that at eighteen. That's a great opportunity, man."

"Yeah," I agree flatly. "Great."

The lights dim, the commercials run, and the movie starts. I instantly regret not telling them that I don't know anything about it. I could ask Rina what's going on, but judging by the elation on her face, she's enjoying herself. I wouldn't want to distract her. Luckily, there are enough explosions and bad guys getting beat up for the movie to be fun anyway.

But then cold fingers rake against my neck.

I whirl around. The seat behind me is empty, and I don't know the people sitting on either side of it. It doesn't look like anyone got up to exit the row either.

"You okay?" Rina whispers.

I tear my eyes away from the black spaces beneath the seats and force them back on the screen. "Yeah," I reply. "I'm fine."

The movie loses its appeal. I'm too busy reassuring myself that I'm well within the Human Realm. The paranoia that the queen sent someone after me competes with rest of the movie.

She can't care that much about me staying out of trouble, though. Can she?

The unease fades a bit as the lights brighten and the movie ends, but I eye the crowd suspiciously as we exit.

"So glad that's over." Brook sighs, wiping her eyes.

"They certainly upped the effects for this one," Travis comments. "So, that was one thing to be happy about. They looked a little lazy in the others."

"I guess," Jun mutters. "Could have done some cooler stuff with makeup and models with the aliens. Not *everything* has to be CG. What did you think, Jocelyn?"

"What?"

Right. I'm supposed to be normal, not searching for faerie spies.

"They were all right," I answer. "I don't watch many movies these days, so I wouldn't be—"

A man cutting through the crowd knocks me backward.

"So sorry, dear girl," he says, steadying me. "My apologies."

I start to apologize too, until I look up.

The stranger is inhumanly handsome. Strong jaw, perfect cheekbones, neat dark brown hair, and smoldering eyes, though his face is a bit long. His eyes have the crafty, knowing calm of every faerie I've ever met and he smells like cloves.

"No, it was my mistake, sir," I reply coldly.

The faerie smirks and turns to the others. "I see you've made some friends."

They smile back but shift awkwardly.

"Good," the man continues. "A young lady like you needs friends like these nice people." Clasping me on the shoulder, he leans forward and mutters, "Rather than your *usual* crowd. Who knows what kind of trouble they might drag you into?"

My blood boils. This is not happening. No faerie is going to mess with me in the Human Realm, the queen's spy or not. This is my turf.

I smack his hand away and snap, "Do I know you?"

The stranger takes a step back, wide-eyed. There are too many witnesses to do anything about my attitude, but judging by his glare, he would love to. "I suppose not," he surmises. "My mistake."

With that, he melts back into the crowd. A security guard follows close behind. At least I'm not the only one who gets a bad vibe from him.

"What was that about?" Rina asks hesitantly.

"No idea," I say, making my face as blank as possible. "That loony thought he knew me, I guess. Never seen him in my life."

"You seemed to handle it okay, though," Travis says, massaging the back of his neck. "Looked him right in the eye and everything. He creeped me out."

"Me too," I second. "Let's go before he thinks he knows anyone else."

"Good idea," Brook agrees.

We file outside, and I follow the group back to their car. It's only ten thirty. Hopefully, under the circumstances, Dominic will let me back in the house early.

"Looks like I was right," Rina says as we round the corner. "Weird stuff does follow you around."

"Is that what you were curious about?" I ask, trying to laugh it off.

Rina starts listing on her fingers, "My friends left me at that club, there's something weird flying around that bookstore, and that weirdo just now."

"Oh, so *that's* why you invited me," I tease. "And here I thought you were starting to like me."

She tilts her head and thinks for a moment, then smiles. "I just might be."

My heart flips, freezes, and flutters all at once. I didn't even know that was possible.

This girl is something else.

Trying to keep cool, I look to make sure the others are a good distance ahead of us. "Well, there's a new Indian place down the street I want to check out. It's not exactly coffee, but..."

"Indian food trumps coffee. Pick me up at six on Wednesday?"

I try not to grin too big or jump for joy. "Sounds good."

Wednesday just became my favorite day of the week. I might pull a few all-nighters to make up for the time spent not painting, but it just might be worth it.

Their car sits across the street while mine is around the corner, so we part ways.

"See you Wednesday at six," Rina says with a wink.

"Wednesday at six," I repeat, returning the gesture. I must not look nearly as cool doing it because Rina giggles as she catches up with the others.

I walk extra slow to my car to make sure no one follows them as they get on the road. When they're all clear, I check the backseat of my car, lock myself in, and head home, checking the rearview mirror every few minutes.

No one follows me home, and Dominic isn't there when I arrive. I'll have to talk to him tomorrow. In the warmth and safety of the farmhouse, I try my best not to let the encounter with the stranger ruin my mood. Rina's friends seem fun, and it's nice to know I can still socialize like a normal human. Maybe there's still hope for me after I sort this mess out after all.

Or, maybe, cold fingers will always be scratching on the back of my neck.

Nine

THE NEXT MORNING proves surprisingly pleasant. I even manage to nail Dominic in the head with a pillow when he guerilla-attacks me out of bed, which I've never managed to do before. Over breakfast, I tell him about Rina and her friends. He says there's hope I might turn back into a normal human after all, because a morning without a single jab would be weird. As I explain what happened with the weirdo after the movie, his mood shifts from agreeable to furious.

"I shouldn't have let you go unprotected," he huffs, slamming his mug on the table. Tea splashes everywhere. "I should have sent you with a charm or something."

"It's not like he attacked me," I explain, handing him a pile of napkins. "Does he sound like someone you know?"

Dominic mops up the spilled tea with more force than necessary. "No one I'm on familiar terms with. He must be a solitary faerie."

I munch on an apple and silently list the solitary faeries I know. Mr. Hob, Iver, a few acquaintances at the Time Between, and Calista, whose necklace I still have...

Uh-oh.

"Dominic, are kelpies solitary fae?" I ask hesitantly.

He tenses and his expression turns stormy. "What did you do?"

"I made a deal with a friend at the club the other night. She helped me get rid of the girls Rina was with. In exchange, I agreed to hold onto a necklace for her. She said some kelpie wanted it. That must have been him."

Dominic pinches the bridge of his nose. "Jocelyn Mae—"

"I couldn't just leave them there," I exclaim. "There was this redcap—"

Dominic raises a hand to stop me. "There's no point in arguing about it now. It looks like she sold you out."

"I don't think she would," I argue. Calista is a lot of things: crafty, promiscuous, ditzy, but she doesn't strike me as a snitch.

He raises an eyebrow and rises from his chair. "Well, however he found you, tell your friend to collect her trinket. Make sure she comes here to get it. Don't leave the house with it and don't leave the house unarmed. I'll put something together for you before you go to work."

While Dominic works on that, I send Iver a text message, hoping he knows how to get ahold of Calista. He replies that he hasn't the slightest idea. Lovely. I might have to camp out at the club to find her. Iver says he'll let her know I'm looking for her if she comes in.

I dig my dad's old pocketknife out of my desk drawer and slip it in my pocket. Mom gave it to me for my fourteenth birthday, figuring I'd like to have it. It's my favorite birthday present to date.

With one of Dominic's charms around my neck, I head to work, glancing over my shoulder every few miles. It doesn't *look* like there's anyone following me, but I can't shake the feeling of those fingers on the back of my neck.

Mr. Hob seems to have just as much on his mind. He's standing at the counter tapping his foot and checking his watch when I walk in.

"How was your date?" he demands.

"How did you—oh, never mind." I sigh. "It wasn't a date."

"Whatever. How was it?"

"Fun. Ate pizza. Saw a movie I hardly understood. I'm seeing Rina on Wednesday."

"Mmhm. Good."

Something's off. Mr. Hob was pushing so hard for me to have fun, but now he seems to just be asking as a formality. He begins pacing in front of the cashier counter with his arms folded.

"Is everything okay?" I dare to ask.

"Fine. I'm just expecting some visitors."

"Who? The Faerie Mafia?"

Mr. Hob gives me a dirty look. "Just make sure the store's ready for business." He shuffles toward his office. "Do you think you can handle it on your own? We might be closing early today, so I asked Walter to take the day off."

"Yeah. Sure."

With that, he shuts the door behind him.

Thankfully, the customers are in a better mood, and for most of the morning, I manage to forget about both the kelpie and Mr. Hob's visitors. I even manage to work in a little time to sketch. Around noon, however, things go back to their usual weirdness.

Two men enter the store, both clearly faeries. They're as eerily attractive as the kelpie from last night, only these guys don't know how to blend nearly as well. Their outfits scream "Faerie Court" with their strange blend of elaborate clothes, gaudy jewelry, and fauna. One man sports several piercings in both of his pointed ears and the other has a blond streak in his otherwise dark hair. Thankfully, there's no one in the store to gawk at them or ask questions.

The guy with the piercings leans on the counter. "Excuse me, young lady," he says. "Is your boss around?"

I hop off my stool and head toward Hob's office. "I'll go get him."

The goblin has the door open before I even knock.

"I heard them," he grumbles, making his way to the newcomers. He shakes their hands and invites them into his office.

A few of the sprites come out to investigate the strangers. They perch on the faeries' shoulders and play with their hair, but the men don't seem to mind. If the sprites like them, I can't imagine they're bad news, but Mr. Hob still seems uneasy.

He checks around before following them in. With one hand on the door handle, he tells me, "I think it would be best if we closed for the day."

He doesn't have to tell me twice, seeing as that gives me more painting time.

I close up in a flash since the store's empty. When I take the cash drawer to Mr. Hob's office, he cracks opens the door and snatches it from my hand.

"Good talking to you," I mutter. "See you Monday."

As I drive home, I try to think of what Mr. Hob could be hiding. Now that I think about it, I know even less about the old goblin than I do about Dominic.

My eyes wander to the shop windows of Main Street as I roll up to a red light. All the questions disappear when I spot Rina sitting inside one of the cafés. Her gaze scans a table covered in textbooks and papers. She's dressed down in a gray hoodie, jeans, glasses, and her hair is in the poofiest bun I've ever seen.

Closing early and pondering all these mysteries have sapped me of my energy. Maybe I should grab a coffee before driving home. If I happen to say hi to Rina, it'll be a total coincidence.

Her table sits off to the right of the pickup counter. I pretend to do a double take as I wait for my order.

"Rina?" I call, feigning surprise.

She pulls out her earbuds and looks around. Her mouth spreads into a heart-stopping grin when our gazes meet. "Jocelyn! Hi!" She begins straightening up the table. "What are you doing here?"

I pick up my black coffee and walk over. "My boss let me off early. Just grabbing a drink before heading home. I'm not bothering you, am I?"

"No, not at all." Rina gives up on organizing the notes. "I could use a break. We just finished midterms, but my professors have already piled on the work again."

I plop into the chair across from her. "What are you studying?"

"A little bit of everything."

"Can I see?"

She passes me her textbook. I give an impressed whistle as I read the subject heading. "*Detecting the Atmospheres of Extra-Solar Planets.* Sounds...science-y."

Rina's smile widens a bit. "Good. I'd be worried if it didn't."

"*Interpreting the Chemical Makeup of Atmospheres.* Also science-y."

Rina gently lifts the book from my hands. "It is. And difficult, given that chemistry isn't my strong suit."

"Have you taken it to a tailor? They might be able to help you out."

Rina blinks a few times, then shakes her head. "After the *check-out* incident, you're still trying to make jokes?"

"What can I say? I have a gift." The conversation lulls. I can't think of another pun. "Is this astronomy stuff how you got into Doctor When?"

"That was my father, actually," Rina says before taking a sip of her own drink. "He had the box set when I was growing up, and we didn't have cable, so I watched it quite a lot. What about you?"

"My mom got me and my sister into it. She watched it growing up, too."

"How old is your sister?"

"Fourteen."

"How big is the age difference?"

"Only three years."

Rina abruptly stops writing. "But you're eighteen."

Shit, that's right.

"Dang it." I snap my fingers. "She turned fifteen last week. It'll take me six months to remember, I bet."

Rina smiles, so the crisis must be averted. "My brothers can never remember how old I am either. Graduating early messed them up, I think."

"Maybe. Getting into a school like James-Child and picking an intense program probably makes you seem older, too." Wait. Cute girls don't like seeming older. "In a good way! In a kick-ass accomplished way."

Rina's smile wilts and she goes back to writing. "I guess." There's a wistful tone in her voice I didn't expect.

"Don't you like your program?" I ask.

"Yeah, but..."

I lower my voice and ask, "Does the whole 'liking girls' thing have something to do it?"

Rina shakes her head. "No. That just boils down to the fact that I've never dated a girl."

Given how smart, fun, and cute she is, even in sweats, I have a hard time believing that. "How come? If you don't mind me asking."

Rina scoffs and motions to herself. "Do I strike you as 'gay enough' to date girls at this point?"

"I asked you out, didn't I?" I remind her. "And there's no such thing as 'gay enough,' Rina. You're you. If that's not 'enough' for someone, then kick 'em to the curb. You've got better things to do than listen to that nonsense."

She nods along with my words, but stays quiet. Her gaze lowers. "Cool necklace," she says, pointing at my chest with her pencil. "What's inside?" She must be talking about Dominic's charm rather than Anna's cross.

I try not to laugh at her lack of subtlety. If she doesn't want to talk about it, I'm not about to push her. I can sympathize with the sentiment. Everyone has to figure this stuff out in their own time. I got lucky with how quickly I figured it out. Some days, I wonder if I figured out anything at all.

"Good question," I say as I gingerly hold up the little bottle and squint to make out the garden of unnaturally tiny plants. "I'm not quite sure."

"Can I see?"

It can't hurt to let her look at it for a second, so I take the cord from around my neck and hand it to her. She holds it up to the light but looks more puzzled the longer she looks at it. "These look so real," she whispers. "But they can't be..."

My phone rings, saving me from any sort of explanation. My gratitude quickly turns to confusion as I look at the caller ID. It's Calista. Iver must have gotten ahold of her?

"Sorry, but I gotta take this," I say, standing up.

"It's cool," Rina replies, still studying the charm. "Take your time."

I slip outside and make sure I'm alone before taking the call. "Hello?"

"Jocelyn, please, help me," Calista begs, voice shaky and high-pitched. The usual lofty confidence has been replaced with terror.

"What's wrong?"

"He won't stop following me," Calista cries. "He says if I don't give back the necklace, he'll—" Any further explanation is lost in quick, panicked breaths. "It's so much worse than I imagined. Please, you must help me."

"Hey now, calm down," I tell her, taking a quick look around. I wouldn't be surprised if the kelpie had someone watching me too, but the coast looks clear.

"I can't calm down! Listen, Essen was there that night in the club and thinks it was all an act. He doesn't believe you have the necklace."

It *was* him at the movie theater.

"I haven't been wearing it," I explain. "It's at the farmhouse."

"You have to tell him that," Calista begs. "If you do, he'll stop this. You have the Queen's mark. He wouldn't go against it."

I take a deep breath and massage my temple to ease my own rising panic. This sounds so much worse than Calista led me to believe. "Where are you now?"

"In some human park," Calista answers. "I thought all the iron would keep Essen at bay, and it has, for now. He'll come, though. I know he will."

"What park?"

"I don't know. It has a statue of a man on a horse. It reeks terribly of iron. I don't know if I can hide here much longer, Jocelyn. It's making my head spin."

Abraham Park. That's not too far away.

"Okay. Hold on, Calista." I put the receiver to my chest and rush back into the café.

"Is everything okay?" Rina asks, eyebrows pulled together in worry.

"Not really. A friend got into a fight with her...brother. She left home and is really upset. Sorry, but I need to go."

Rina shakes her head. "No, don't apologize."

Halfway out the door, I call, "See you Wednesday."

I hold the phone back up to my ear as I run toward the café parking lot. "Calista? Hold tight. I'm on my way."

"Good," she says, "Because I imagine Essen is too."

Ten

I FIND CALISTA curled up under a tree near the statue she described. She rocks back and forth, her head between her knees. Has she always been this small? She can't have been.

I kneel beside her. "Calista, are you all right?"

She flinches and blinks her wide terrified eyes. A smile breaks over her face, and she throws herself into my arms, nearly knocking me on my butt. "You came for me!" Happy to see me or not, she's still trembling. With her head pressed against my chest, she stutters, "For the past three days, Essen hasn't let me be. No matter where I go, he follows. He doesn't believe you have it. Our plan didn't work."

"Where is he now?" I ask.

Calista pulls away and scans the park, her eyes fixed on things only she can see. "I don't know. I set up a protective barrier. It's all I could do."

I look around too, suspicious of every shadow and shift of dim light, trying to see what Calista sees, trying to figure out what to do next.

The house will be safe, even with the necklace there. Thanks to Dominic's charms, the kelpie won't be able to get in. Then we can figure out what to do next. But how do we get there? Calista already looks pale and nauseated. The car is only going to make her worse. Even with all his spells and elixirs to ward off the effect of iron, Dominic stays as far from it as possible.

"Calista, how do faeries usually get around?" I ask.

"It depends," she answers. "Nymphs like myself have always been close friends with the wind. It gives us rides whenever we wish."

Well, that makes even less sense than I expected, but okay.

"If I describe a place to you, could you get us there?"

"I could take us halfway, if we're lucky," Calista answers, clinging to my arm as I pull her to her feet. "Traveling with a human is hard enough without being in your wretched, draining realm. No offense."

I shrug it off and take her hand, squeezing it to comfort her. Calista gives me a smirk that says she's misreading the gesture on purpose.

"You'd better hang on," she whispers, wrapping my arms low around her waist and wrapping hers around my neck. "I don't want to leave you behind." She twirls a lock of my hair.

"Really?" I snap. "You're doing this *now*?"

Calista gives me a coy grin. "What can I say? It's in my nature."

I try to keep my temper in check and explain the geographical location of the house along with the interior. I don't know how precise Calista's method of travel is. The second I finish the description, we're moving. I think we are, anyway.

The wind around us turns into howling gales and everything blurs to mere impressions. Then they disappear from sight. New distorted landscapes appear, only to dissolve seconds later. One haunting sight lingers.

A dark horse stands sharp against the background. It's the color of deep, muddy water, and its mane flows like gentle waves as it watches us with depthless black eyes.

The kelpie.

It rears and gallops our way.

I reach for Dominic's charm and grasp only air. My stomach plummets. Rina still has it.

I try to tell Calista to change course, but it feels like all the air has been sucked away. I can't take in enough breath to speak. Calista turns and sees him anyway. Her face pales and she clings to me tighter.

We speed up so fast that I can't keep my eyes open. I don't think I want to.

A tidal wave hits us and knocks what little air I have from my lungs. We both go sprawling. Somewhere in the spinning dark Calista screams my name.

I slam into sand. The world halts.

The park's replaced with a familiar strip of beach. I pass it every day, but it's never looked so menacing before. The lake's never sounded so angry. At least Calista was going in the right direction.

Wait. Where is she?

I scramble to my feet, only to be knocked back down by vertigo. My head pounds from the impact with the ground.

"Calista, where'd you go?" I call, voice slurred.

"Here," she coughs in response.

I spot her slumped against the rocks leading up to the road. Blood blooms from her forehead and she's covered in bruises, but she's in one piece. With a sigh of relief, I get to my feet again. Since I can stay up this time, I gingerly walk over to Calista.

The lake roars louder.

Calista screams and points past me.

A giant wave rises up from the lake, suspended like the grim reaper's scythe. I shove Calista up the rocks. She scrambles toward the road and wraps one arm around a tree, then reaches for me. Our fingers brush. Then, darkness. Ice-cold darkness. Spinning. Painful pressure builds behind my eyes and in my chest. Directions don't exist anymore.

Just as I swear I'm about to explode, the water spits me back out, sending me into a face full of sand and twigs. I prop myself up on my elbows and knees, gulping for air and coughing up small trickles of water. Calista is nowhere in sight.

"So sorry, dear girl," calls a sickly sweet voice. "I was aiming for the nymph."

The horse that followed us rises up out of the lake. It tosses its mane of foam and takes a few sinking steps onto the wet sand. As it comes near, the water falls away and leaves a human figure barefooted and bare-chested in soaked jeans. His long, inhumanly handsome face contorts into a sneer. It's a face I know.

"You're the man from the theater," I wheeze. "You're Essen." I wipe sand from my eyes and clamber to my feet, feeling around for dad's knife. Shit. Did I drop it in the water?

The kelpie cocks his head to the side with a gloating grin. "That's right. I'm flattered you've heard of me. My reputation must precede me."

I feel the knife in my pocket, but I don't linger on it too long. Can't draw attention to it just yet. "You could say that," I mutter.

"Then you should know protecting that nymph is a horrible idea."

"Leave her alone," I hiss, hoping a glare can compensate for my raspy voice.

Judging by Essen's sinister laugh, it doesn't. "What *is* it with you and heroics?" he snickers. "First your comatose mother and now this nymph, who, from what I hear, hasn't given you anything." He looks me up and down. "Unless you're not interested in women after all. I'll let you use her to find out before I finish her off, if you tell me where the necklace is first, that is."

Red tints the corners of my vision. "Fuck off and find another necklace," I spit, drawing the knife.

Essen pauses at the sight of it, eyes narrowing into a glare.

"It's a piece of junk," I say. "I'm sure you can find another one."

Essen grins again. "So, you do know where it is." Putting his hands to his hips, he begins pacing. "Unfortunately for you, I can't 'fuck off.' It's the principle of the matter. I let one bratty nymph steal a trinket, word gets out, and folk start walking all over me left and right. Gnomes start drinking from my streams. Mermaids start vacationing in my lakes. It's a slippery slope."

"You can slip on your slope all the way to hell. I'm not letting you hurt her."

The kelpie's expression shifts to boredom. With a flick of his hand, another wave rises up. "You're in no position to 'let me' do anything, young lady."

The wave sharpens to a whip and lashes forward.

I tumble out of the way and lunge at Essen. He falls back and snarls as I come down on top of him, the knife still in one hand.

"It's not yours anyway," I snap. "It belonged to her friend."

Essen gives a nasty sneer. "And where do you think her friend got it?" Water wraps around my neck, cutting off my air and yanking me back. Balancing on my toes keeps me from outright strangling, but just barely. Thrashing at the water does nothing, even after I drop the knife. My hands pass through it like a puddle. The pressure on my windpipe tightens.

"It was a gift," Essen muses as he gets to his feet. "A hook to get that stupid little pixie to come back to me time and time again. Since she's dead, it's mine again." He looks me square in the eye. "Drowning her was incredibly satisfying. Almost as satisfying as drowning humans."

Rage pushes the black dots from my vision.

He stands a little too close as he mocks me. The water holds me up as I kick him square in the chest. With Essen's concentration broken, I stumble away and heave for breath as I look for the knife.

"I'll give you one more chance," Essen hisses, "because you're the Queen's pet. Tell me where the necklace is, or I'll make you wish for death."

Pet? Being kicked around and bewitched by the queen is one thing. That's all par for the course. But a monster like Essen trying to do the same? Not today.

The glint of the knife catches my attention in the shallow wake.

"Keep your chance, Essen."

I dive for the knife.

Just as my hand brushes the handle, my feet fly out from under me. The water swallows me again.

It's too deep to push myself up. Too dark to tell bottom from surface. Too heavy to try. Hands secure themselves around my neck and the weight of a body pushes me down farther. As I go numb, it gets harder and harder to fight. What little light I can make out through the dark water begins to fade.

Giving up sounds nice. The burning in my muscles and lungs would stop. No more lying. No more weight on my shoulders. No more mind games with the queen.

But I'm dragging Calista down with me.

And I have to save Mom.

There's something cold against my chest. Colder than the water.

Anna's cross.

Pushing past my pounding skull and exploding lungs, I grope for the blessed iron and rip it from its chain. Holding tight to Essen's shoulder with one hand, I slam the cross against whatever skin I can find.

Through the water comes a muffled screech of pain. The weight holding me down disappears and the water flings me away. My body acts on its own, gasping for air and taking in some water in its hurry.

There's no time to get all my breath back. I need that knife.

While Essen recovers, both hands cradling the scalding skin on his chest, I crawl toward the knife, grabbing the blade. I ignore the bite against my palm and flip it. A wave threatens to take me again.

I turn and lash out for any flesh I can find.

The knife slices just below Essen's collarbone.

The kelpie screams in rage, turning back into the horse, ready to trample me.

I can't fight with my limbs crushed.

There's only more chance.

I thrust the knife out as he crashes over me, hoping to hit anything.

I never imagined it would plunge into his chest.

The water falls away, running red as the kelpie's humanoid body falls limp on top of me. The waves stop rolling. I crawl out from under him with his blood streaking my wet clothes.

"It burns," Essen whimpers, his body twisting and contorting as he tries to turn over. "It burns." He pulls weakly at the knife.

Blood trickles from his mouth as he cries again, "It burns! It burns!" His wide eyes bore into me. There's no hate. No pride. Just desperation.

This isn't real. It can't be real.

Essen goes limp. His eyes glass over and it all registers.

I just killed someone.

My mind stops. Nothing processes. There's too much. What little coffee is in my stomach comes up, acrid and bitter. Even with nothing left, my body continues to heave violently, as if it can rid itself of what I've just done.

This feels a thousand times worse than that car accident, but it shouldn't. Should it? Mom's in a coma, but she's not dead. I never meant to hurt anyone when I swerved and hit that tree, but Essen was a monster. He was going to drown Calista. He's drowned plenty of other people and was no doubt going to drown more. I had to stop him.

But did I have to kill him?

I hear footsteps on the sand. The scent of blood hits me like a wall and the wind becomes breath on the back of my neck. Hot, moist, bloody breath.

It whispers with a nasty chuckle, "I told you so, Jocelyn...I told you—"

"Jocelyn!" Dominic's voice sounds like shattering glass.

The breath disappears.

I look up to see him leap from the road, over the boulders, and land on the sand as if he'd only stepped off a staircase. Calista follows suit. In Dominic's hand swings a crystal sword as bloodthirsty as the look in his eye.

I try my hardest to steady my shaking body and wipe the sand and blood from my clothes, the evidence that I killed Essen. The thought threatens to make me sick again.

"Jocelyn, what happened?" Dominic demands. His face morphs into a nasty snarl as he studies my injuries.

"I'm fine," I cough, my throat sore, aching from the effort.

"Liar," Dominic hisses. "Essen's a dead man once I—"

I motion to the kelpie's body. "Too late."

Dominic's face pales, and his body goes limp with shock.

Calista throws her arms around my waist and squeezes me harder than I imagined possible for her. "I'm so sorry, Jocelyn," she cries. "I never imagined this would happen. Please forgive me."

Dominic's blade flicks to Calista's throat in one small swift motion. I stop breathing. She lets me go and the color drains from her face.

"Do not touch her," he orders, his voice dangerously quiet. "No amount of apologies, accepted or not, will be enough. You know who she is. You know what was on the line if she died. You should have never involved her in this."

"She's right, though," I explain, gently pulling the blade away. "This got out of control. He was supposed to forget the whole thing. Neither of us thought I would..." My stomach churns at the memory of my knife biting into skin and the way Essen thrashed in agony. "Neither of us thought I would kill him."

Dominic lowers his sword and paces around the body, shaking his head. "What a pity. I had so hoped to run the bastard through. My blade hasn't tasted blood in quite some time." His nonchalant tone hits me like a punch to the gut. He doesn't sound like my quirky tea-obsessed housemate anymore.

He's always been more than that, though. He's a faerie knight.

"What happens now?" Calista murmurs.

Dominic nudges Essen's body with his foot. "Now, I get rid of this."

"What about the queen?" I ask hesitantly. The greater implications of what I've just done catch up. I can't breathe. "She said if I attack another faerie the deal's off and I just killed one."

"By her own authority, you had the right to," Dominic says. "This isn't some petty bar fight. He put your life in jeopardy and his was, therefore, forfeit. He committed a crime against the crown by trying to kill you." He pauses for a moment to look at Calista. "As did Calista by involving you, but I was originally planning to overlook that."

Calista goes stiff and inches behind me.

"If she takes you home while I take care of this, I might still let her live."

I step up to Dominic. I'm a bit taller, but it always feels like I'm standing in his shadow. "You don't mean that," I say. "You wouldn't kill Calista for this. I volunteered—"

"You don't want to find out what I would and wouldn't do, Jocelyn," Dominic snaps. "Now, go home while I take care of this."

Calista latches onto my arm and drags me out of Dominic's way. "Let's go before someone drives by," she mutters.

With steps as heavy as stone, I allow her to drag me back toward the road.

Dominic glares at Calista as we go. "Try anything and you'll live just long enough to regret it."

"Stop it, Dominic."

He scoffs, then turns back to the body.

I pause and turn to him again. "Right before you showed up, I heard someone. I didn't see them, but they spoke to me. They said, 'I told you so.'"

Dominic scans the surrounding forest and the distant road. "I'll be sure to investigate. For now, get cleaned up and get some rest. We'll talk when I get home."

Getting cleaned up should be easy enough. Rest, however, won't come as simply. Not with the uncertainly of what will come next.

And with the question of who saw it all.

Eleven

CALISTA HAS TO coax—and possibly bewitch—me to take a shower because I don't want anything to do with water. The scalding water burns away the chills and tremors that threaten to shake me to pieces and each cut and scratch is set on fire under the pelting stream, but the pain hardly registers. A pile of clothes and a towel wait for me on the counter when I get out.

My reflection looks like it belongs to someone else. Someone older. The bruises and cuts make me look like I've just survived a battle rather than a single faerie. Lines sink into my forehead and around my eyes that I swear I didn't have before.

Once dressed, I clean and wrap the cut from grabbing the knife by the blade. Doing it one-handed proves to be a challenge, but I don't want help from Calista. Before going downstairs, I grab that stupid necklace from my desk. She's taking it back whether she wants to or not.

She sits at the kitchen table, massaging her temple with her brow scrunched. Her head shoots up at the sound of my footsteps, and she jumps up from her seat. "Here," she says, pulling out the chair across from her. In front of it sits a large bowl of chicken noodle soup and a mug of what I assume is tea.

I blink at it. The idea of a faerie making chicken noodle soup throws me for a loop. I sit anyway and pick up the spoon.

"I've heard that this is a popular home remedy among humans for a variety of illnesses," Calista says, taking her seat again. "Of course, this is not the most conventional time for it, but..." She bites her bottom lip nervously.

"It's perfect." The salty broth, meat, and soggy vegetables are more soothing than I expected. "Thanks."

The corners of Calista's mouth turn up a bit only to wilt as I slide the necklace across the table toward her.

"This is your problem again," I say. "Essen's dead. Our deal's finished."

Calista scoops it up and holds it to her chest. "Of course. I wouldn't expect you to hang onto it." She looks down at it like it's her child. "It's such a stupid thing to put both our lives at risk for."

"Essen told me what he did," I mutter.

Calista's hand closes around the necklace into a fist. "Did he tell you that this is all I have left of her?" she hisses. "That he never even gave her body back? She's lying at the bottom of a lake somewhere, alone."

I hold the mug to keep away a chill that threatens to creep back into my bones. "He didn't tell me that, but that necklace isn't just a 'stupid thing,' if that's the case."

"It was a chance to *do* something," Calista growls. "He's hurt so many people and yet…" Her eyes darken, the rage behind them sharpens, and her face hollows out. I've never imagined she could look threatening.

"Someone had to stand up to him… but I'm just a nymph and Her Majesty would never do anything. I just wanted to…" Calista sighs and her fury drains away, but there's still pain engraved on her face. "Never mind. It's over."

What little anger I had worked up toward her fizzles out. Taking the necklace from Essen was a stupid move, but when someone feels like they're out of options, stupid moves start looking pretty good. It kind of sounds like a certain someone who made a deal with the Faerie Queen.

"Just don't try something like that again, okay?" is all I can say. "For everyone's sake. Get more creative. Maybe more devious. Faeries are supposed to be good at that."

Calista sighs. "I'm not good at being a faerie then, am I?"

"Eh, that's all right. I'm not good at being a human."

Calista scoffs. "Says the girl who almost died today and protects strangers in nightclubs. If that's not 'good at being human,' you don't need to be." Her eyebrows pull together. "Why do you do it anyway?"

That's a good question. My dad only told me to look out for Mom and Anna. Somewhere along the line, my net got bigger. I can't say for sure why, though, so I shrug and drink my tea.

Calista stares out into space. "This wouldn't have happened if Titania were still queen. Killing for sport, human or faerie, was forbidden, and the laws were enforced. She couldn't do anything outside her realm, of course, but inside we were safe."

I've heard that name before. "Who was Titania, exactly?"

"She was Her Majesty's sister," Calista answered. "She ruled this region, the old Seelie Court. The current queen ruled the lands to the south, the former Unseelie Court."

I remember the trashed artwork the queen showed me. Her talk of sacrifices. Titania must have been one of them. And then there was her breakdown at the sight of Shaylee.

"Did the sisters look alike?"

Calista blows on her mug of tea for a moment. "Incredibly so. Why? Did you happen to witness one of the queen's breakdowns? Thinking she sees Queen Titania? That her ghost is coming for her?"

"Everyone knows?"

"Everyone gossips about it, if that's what you mean. The only people to have seen it firsthand are Lyle, Princess Shaylee, and you, apparently." She takes a long sip of her tea. "We don't need to witness it to know. This happens every time someone gets it in their head to unite the Seelie and Unseelie Courts. The hallucinations, the paranoia, the heightened Hallowed Offering. It's like clockwork."

Calista glances out the window toward the line of trees that lead to the court. "Her Majesty has held up longer than any other ruler, unfortunately. But let me assure you, the Hallowed Offering works less and less as a buffer against the magic each time. One day, it won't restore her defenses. When that happens, balance will return. That or complete and utter chaos. It's a fifty-fifty chance either way. I hear some people have started placing bets."

I slowly process Calista's words, impressed by the fact that I'm not mad myself by now. "Killing Essen is eating at me enough," I mutter, raising my mug. "Killing your own sister..."

"Oh, Her Majesty didn't kill Queen Titania," Calista corrects. "Dominic did."

I choke and spit tea everywhere. As I mop up the mess, I rasp, "There's no way."

"If it makes you feel any better," Calista continues nonchalantly, "it's all rather speculative. Apparently, very few people actually saw her body."

"But why Dominic?"

"The queen couldn't bring herself to do it. She didn't *always* have a heart of ice-cold stone. Dominic served them both, so it must have been a test of loyalty."

"Dominic served both queens?"

"Oh, yes. He was a spy for Her Majesty." A sly smirk creeps onto Calista's face. "Or was he a spy for Titania and something went wrong?"

That must be why Her Majesty trusts Dominic to watch me away from the court. Killing someone who supposedly had your undying loyalty would be a pretty good test, if you ask me.

It would also be a good reason to never let them out of your sight.

Calista leaps from her seat and dashes to the window. "Speak of the devil. Dominic's on his way home." Looking over her shoulder, she adds, "You should scurry off to bed. I don't want you two squabbling over me in your current condition."

I don't have the energy to object. I'm beginning to suspect there's more to this tea than herbs. It's getting hard to stay awake.

"He won't hurt you, will he?" I ask, getting to my feet.

"No. I've been on my best behavior," Calista says, gently coaxing me toward the stairs. "Besides, he knows how upset you'd be. If nothing else, he wouldn't want to risk that. Despite his bad mood, he genuinely cares about you, Jocelyn."

He also supposedly cared about Queen Titania and that didn't work out too well.

I'm too drowsy to straighten it all out. By the time my head hits the pillow, my thoughts are nothing but a jumble of words and images. As I fall asleep, they fade to less than that. My dreams are made of tense, harsh conversations. Angry muttering and hissing. It rises to shouting.

A booming crash tells me that it's all too real.

It feels like I've only been asleep for a few seconds, but my room is pitch black. I look around the room in a panic, waiting for Essen to spring from the shadows. As reality settles, I remember that he can't.

The voice from downstairs is worse than any nightmare.

"You told me you could handle her! You assured me she would stay in line!"

The queen.

I tiptoe toward the stairs and hear Dominic's hushed argument. "The girl was within her right. Essen threatened her life. And, while my assumptions might have been slightly skewed, I *have*, in fact, handled it. There were no witnesses and the body has been disposed of."

"There shouldn't be a body in the first place," the queen screeches. "I gave that girl very clear instructions. I have half a mind to cancel her contract and let her mother waste away."

I bolt down the stairs. "Your Majesty, no!" I skip the last two steps and stumble to my knees. Maybe it could work to my advantage. Judging by the way she grabs me by the hair, it doesn't.

She towers over me, yanking my head back with her nails digging into my scalp. A snarl contorts her face, like a succubus morphing into a creature from a deeper layer of hell.

Dominic gives her an equally terrifying glare behind her back.

"Give me one good reason why I shouldn't," the queen hisses. "I don't *need* your paintings. Desperate artists are easy to fine and they usually don't give me this much trouble."

"I didn't want to kill Essen," I assure her through gritted teeth. "I was defending myself. Like Dominic said, I was within my right. You're the queen. Don't you honor your own laws?"

The queen's grip tightens and her right eye twitches. Before I even see her move, her dagger presses into my throat.

Dominic inhales sharply, and my heartbeat pounds in my ears.

"Honor does not rule the Faerie Court, Jocelyn," the queen spits. "I do with the laws what I please." The blade presses harder, threatening to slice into my skin if I breathe too deep.

I have to think fast. I notice the amulet swinging around her neck. It looks duller, as if its polish has worn off.

Focus, damn it!

"Of course, Your Majesty, but you couldn't very well let Essen do the same, could you? I did you a favor. Death at the hand of a human is a befitting death for someone who ignores your mark, don't you think?"

My own words make me sick.

"Besides, no one knows except for you, me, and Dominic." I'm not dragging Calista into this if I don't have to. "You don't want word to get out that a *solitary* faerie dared to ignore your mark, do you? This is a bit more serious than a bar fight."

The queen twitches again, and the knife bites into my neck. I can feel blood trickle down to my shirt collar.

"One of those will be easy enough to be disposed of," she threatens.

"I'm not so sure," I say softly. "It might look like the pressure of ruling two courts is too much for you. Like maybe you wouldn't have been able to heal my mother once our contract was fulfilled. You can't want that this close to the Hallowed Offering. You're too vulnerable." I lick my dry lips, trying to think of more bullshit to spin. Judging by the way the queen's face lights up, she knows I'm running out.

"Give me until October thirty-first," I offer. "I'll have the painting finished by then, and I'll be gone. You'll get your portrait, my mom will be healed, and you'll never hear from me again. We both get what we want."

The queen's gaze darts over my face, weighing my words.

"Please?" I tag on desperately. "Do it for my sister. She's just a kid. She already lost our father. What if Shaylee lost you?"

A glint comes to the queen's eye. It's a moment of calm recognition I prayed for but didn't really expect. Her expression softens for a moment. The pendant around her neck catches the light and the moment passes.

Her eyes go wide with terror.

"You've seen her," she whispers. Her hands begin to tremble. "Roaming the court. Haunting my halls." Her voice gets louder and more hysterical with every word. "Whispering. Always whispering. Always accusing me, but it's her own fault. She wouldn't listen. She knew that they'd come looking for us one day, but she wouldn't listen. I had to act on my own. She forced my hand. Don't believe a word she tells you, Jocelyn. Does she scratch on the inside of your skin? I wouldn't let her out of mine!"

The queen gives me a violent shake. Pain shoots down the muscles of my neck.

"Majesty, you're hurting her," Dominic shouts.

His voice brings her back. Her eyes shrink down to their normal size and she lets me go. She watches with confusion as I get to my feet and trace the cut across my throat. It runs just below the bruises Essen gave me.

The queen looks from me to Dominic like she's never seen us before. Then she shakes her head and tucks back a few curls that fell out of place. "Let me see what you have so far."

I scramble to my feet and run up the stairs. When I return with the unfinished painting, I'm out of breath. I was afraid she would change her mind while I was gone. The queen looks at it from several different angles, her expression calculating. It really won't be hard to—

The queen slashes the canvas from the top to bottom.

The tearing fabric sounds like an earthquake.

My legs feel like they might give out. I can't carry much more of this.

"I don't like it," she snaps, putting away the dagger. "Start over." Her voice is a flat, cardboard calm. "You only have two weeks, so I suggest you get working."

She turns to Dominic. "Don't make me regret trusting you," she threatens. "It would be a shame if it turned out I made a mistake after all these years."

The two lock eyes with expressions so harsh that sparks might fly.

Dominic backs down. "It would indeed, Your Majesty," he replies. "And you won't. I promise."

A series of small popping noises make me jump. The overwhelming smell of burnt chives makes my head pound. I close my eyes as they begin to water. When I open them again, the queen's gone.

When the smell finally fades, I drop into a chair. The ruined painting clatters to the floor as I hold my head in my shaking hands, trying to remember how to breathe. My closing throat doesn't make it any easier. I can't break down. I don't know if I'll be able to pick myself up if I do.

"That was too close," I mutter. "Too damn close, Dominic. If the queen doesn't kill me, the stress will."

"Don't talk like that," Dominic replies harshly. He lifts my face and looks at the cut across my neck. Despite my rising panic, I can't help but notice how close he stands to me. "This mess is my fault. Calista found me while I was in a meeting at court. Lyle spotted me leaving and reported me to Her Majesty, the rat."

He crosses the kitchen, rinses his hands off, and begins pulling out jars filled with herbs and elixirs. "We need to get you patched up. You look like hell."

Right. Can't have anyone finding out faeries are trying to kill me on a regular basis. The thought sounds so ridiculous in my head that I laugh out loud. That's not a good sign, but I'm just getting started.

"You guys should make Shaylee queen," I suggest.

"Wouldn't that be nice," Dominic sighs.

"The queen's weak right now, right? It wouldn't be hard. I'd help."

Dominic stops working and looks at me in horror. "You need to rest. You've been through too much to start working on that portrait now."

I look down at the ruined painting. "I'm not saying you have to kill her."

"Jocelyn—"

"You've staged a coup before, right?"

A jar shatters on the floor.

I look up to find Dominic inches from my face. His glamour dissolves. All his humanity melts away, leaving his features eerie and harsh. It feels like the first time I've seen how other faeries truly are. I should be scared, but I'm too numb.

"I don't know what you've heard," he growls, "But you are on a Very. Dangerous. Road. One that's been around long before you were born. I suggest you get off it. Understand?"

I nod once.

"Never speak like this again. *Ever*. Keep your head down, finish that damn painting, and get out of Faerie."

I nod again.

Dominic slowly returns to the counter. "Go get some sleep. I'll prepare something for your injuries."

Without a word, I get up from the chair, pick up the torn canvas, and drag myself up the stairs. Instead of my room, I go straight for the studio and set up the spare canvas I stretched and primed just in case.

I have to get to work, exhaustion be damned. The conversation with Dominic plays in my head and fear finally catches up with me, pushing me to work into the early morning. It's not just about fixing my mistake anymore. It's not even just about saving Mom.

It's about saving myself.

Twelve

THE TEXT MESSAGE chime startles me awake. I peel myself from the chair in front the easel and pick my phone up off the floor, massaging my sore muscles. Fold-up chairs aren't the best places for naps.

The message reads, *Is your friend okay? —Rina.*

She's okay, I type back.

Seconds later she replies, *Are YOU okay? I still have your necklace, by the way.*

I write, *Hold on to it for me* and stick my phone in my pocket.

My stomach growls, ordering me to get up and go downstairs. Food, coffee, one cigarette, and then back to work.

Just as I sit down to a bowl of cereal, Dominic comes out from his room, careful to shut the door as always. He doesn't look like he's slept too well either. He silently goes about making himself some tea as if it's a normal morning. Midafternoon, actually.

As the kettle boils, he places a small wooden box in front of me. I open the box and find a balm that smells of lavender. This must be what he wants me to use on my bruises.

"Thank you," I say.

He only nods.

Man, did I mess up.

"Is it true what you told the queen?" I ask. "Everything's taken care of?"

"It is," Dominic answers. He snaps his fingers and the kettle whistles.

"Did you find anyone else?"

Dominic shakes his head. "No. There were traces of magic, but they were too weak to determine who left them. I imagine they belonged to Essen." He stroked his chin in thought, then lifted his eyes to me. "Have you considered that your mind was playing tricks on you? You were quite vulnerable at the time, after all." He turns and opens a cupboard.

That makes sense, but it doesn't sit well with me.

Neither does the question eating at the back of my mind.

"Dominic...would you have really killed Calista?"

His hand lingers above a mug. Taking it and beginning to fill it with herbs, he says, "Jocelyn...we do not operate the same as humans. I am no exception, as human as I may appear for your benefit."

"So, that's a yes?"

"Correct. If Her Majesty had asked about the nymph's involvement and ordered her execution, I would have had no choice. My own body would have turned against me and struck her down, such is the power of a faerie's true name, which the queen alone knows."

The silence begins to creep back into the room, heavier than before.

Dominic pours the hot water and takes a seat across from me. "Are you frightened of me, Jocelyn?"

"Of course not," I answer. "You're my friend."

Shaking his head, Dominic swirls his mug, watching the spinning herbs. He stops abruptly. "We're friends?"

"Well, yeah. I thought that was obvious."

He sighs. "You have a strange level of comfort with things that could easily kill you. It's a wonder you've survived this long."

"It's for my family. I can take it."

"Says the child who was almost murdered by a kelpie and the Faerie Queen."

I glower. "I'm seventeen, thank you very much."

A wry smile comes to Dominic's face. "Is that supposed to impress me?"

I roll my eyes, but I'm relieved. Bringing back a sense of normalcy wasn't as hard as I thought it would be.

The smile wilts from Dominic's face. "If we're friends, why didn't you call me when Calista contacted you yesterday?"

Good question. It never crossed my mind. These things never seem to until long after they're important. Even if I thought of it, I don't think I would have called. Calista might have started that mess by giving me that necklace, but I was the one who made it worse by making Essen think she still had it.

"I thought I could handle it," I finally answer.

Dominic's eyebrows rise as he repeats, "You thought you could handle it?"

"I held my own against that redcap at the club, didn't I? It's not like I knew the guy could manipulate water like that." I focus on the rest of my cereal to avoid Dominic's gaze.

"You should let people help you, Jocelyn," he says quietly.

"And let them get caught in the crossfire? Absolutely not. When I mess up, I'm the one who needs to fix things."

Dominic goes back to swirling his tea. "Your need to fix everything is bordering on obsession. Do you realize that?"

I shrug. "If that's what it takes to make things right, then—"

"That's not what you're supposed to—"

My phone rings. The caller ID reads, "Annalise."

I can't decide if she has the worst or the best timing ever.

"What's up, baby sister?"

"Jocelyn? You haven't been down to the beach lately, have you?" Anna asks in a panic.

Dominic slumps back in his chair and gives me a dirty look.

I shrug at him and his glare gets more severe.

"No. What's wrong with the beach?"

"There were reports that the tides were acting weird yesterday. Local authorities are warning people to stay away," Anna explains.

"Define *weird*."

"Really low. Like, one radio station said twenty feet, I think. A bunch of nearby rivers dried up too, only to come back hours later. No one's been able to explain it."

I look at Dominic, silently pleading for an explanation.

"It must have been Essen," he mutters. "He was after Calista for some time before coming after you, from what she told me. If he was angry enough, I wouldn't be surprised if he threw caution to the wind and went after her with any means necessary."

That wasn't quite the kind of explanation I was looking for. I had hoped for a story to feed my sister.

"Who's that? Uncle David? " Anna asks.

"Yeah. He says he hasn't heard anything weird either."

"Hi, Uncle David," Anna shouts, nearly blowing out my eardrum.

Dominic chuckles and replies, "Hello, Annalise."

"He says hi," I reply.

"So, you haven't been down to the water?" Anna continues. "I know how you like to paint pictures of the lake."

Dominic pauses as he lifts the mug to his lips. "You like to paint the lake?"

Okay, time for a cigarette. I put my bowl in the sink and step outside to sit on the rickety porch swing.

"Let's talk about something else. How's school?" I ask, cigarette between my teeth.

"Same as always," Anna answers. "Oh, I get to rewrite a fairy tale for extra credit in English class, so that's cool."

"Since when do you need extra credit?" I ask after taking a puff.

"I don't. It's for fun."

"Ha-ha. Nerd."

"Oh, go huff some paint," Anna fires back.

"All right, all right." I chuckle. "I'm sorry. I won't call you a nerd anymore. So, what's your fairy tale going to be about?"

"I don't know yet," Anna answers.

"Stay away from stories about faeries, all right? Rewrite *Rapunzel* or something."

"Why? Faeries seem interesting."

My chest tightens. "They're not," I hiss. "Write about something else."

Anna pauses. "Geez, it's just an English project.... Are you okay?"

Right. Annalise doesn't know. I shouldn't take any of this out on her.

"Yeah, sorry. I'm exhausted from school, that's all."

"It's deeper than exhaustion. You sound...off."

A figure with chestnut hair emerges from the woods. I panic, thinking the queen is back for round two, but a closer look reveals the figure to be Shaylee.

"Hey, hero," she greets, hopping up the stairs. "Dominic home?"

Covering the mic, I say, "He's inside."

She gives a small salute and lets herself in.

"Look, Anna, I got to go," I say, bringing the phone back. "I'll be by soon."

"Good. You're alone too much."

"I'm not, I promise, but thanks for worrying. Love you." I hang up and linger on the porch, savoring the moment of stillness. The longer I stay, the less I believe it's real. The air itself seems plastic and two-dimensional, like it all stopped yesterday. Strange how the world keeps spinning with or without us and we have to choose which one it's going to be. Well, most days anyway.

The cigarettes in my pocket tempt me, but that painting won't finish itself.

I go back inside to the sound of voices in the basement through the cracked-open door. While Shaylee's visit is unexpected, it doesn't merit eavesdropping, until I catch the conversation.

"She won't last until the Winter Solstice. You've seen it yourself, Dominic. We need to act now."

"Our orders were very clear: wait until Her Majesty is between Seelie and Unseelie lands. Why is that so hard for you, Shaylee?"

"Because it's a bad idea. That's nearly two months when someone could take her out and crown themselves monarch. Lyle ain't tough shit like he thinks. He can't protect her from herself *and* the rest of the court."

"Then we do away with whoever is foolish enough to take the opportunity," Dominic hisses back. "Or you stick to Her Majesty like glue, like you're *supposed to be doing right now*, and make sure that doesn't happen."

"What about the Offering? She'll be stronger once the sacrifice restores that amulet of hers. That'll just make her harder to fight at the Solstice."

"Not by much. She's been queen of both courts for too long."

"What if she uses Jocelyn?"

Dominic takes a long time to reply. My blood runs colder with each moment he waits. "She won't. The paintings will be done, she'll be gone, and the Offering has to be willing. Jocelyn's still enough in her right mind that she wouldn't agree. She just needs to keep her head down."

Shaylee chortles. "Jocelyn keep her head down? Yeah, right. Should we see what Essen thinks about that idea?"

"Jocelyn *won't* be the Offering. I'll make sure of that myself if I have to."

"Your job is to watch her and drag her to court if she backs out of the deal, not protect her. We can't have you getting attached—"

"And your job is to watch the queen, yet here you stand, bold as brass," Dominic barks. "Let me do my job the way I want, or your mother is going to hear about how poorly you're doing yours. Is that clear?"

A tense silence hangs in the air.

"Yes, sir, Mr. Champion, sir," Shaylee finally mutters.

"Any other orders you want to question, or are we done here?"

"Chill out already. Damn." Shaylee gripes. "I came to see Jocelyn, too. Yesterday probably really messed her up."

I take that as my cue to scramble up the stairs. The sound of Shaylee's steps covers mine, and I stick a clean paintbrush in a puddle of white just as she knocks on the doorframe.

"How you holding up?" she asks, tucking her hand in pockets as she ambles into the room.

"Oh, well, you know," I say, trying to steady my breath.

Shaylee stops and studies the canvas. "I don't, actually. That's why I asked."

I raise the brush and begin on the queen's dress. After a few strokes, I give up. Hiding the truth from Anna over the phone is one thing, but Shaylee's standing right next to me. I'm too tired to lie convincingly even if I wanted to.

"I don't know either," I finally answer. "Essen was going to kill me and Calista. He's killed who knows how many others but…"

Shaylee smiles sympathetically. "But someone's still dead because of you."

I nod. "I keep playing it over in my head, trying to figure out what I should have done differently."

Shaylee puts a hand on my shoulder. "We all do sometimes, but you have to get out of your own head. You did your best when both choices were shit. Sometimes that's all you can do. That and move forward."

"Yeah, but I'm supposed to be better than this," I snap. "I try to take care of my family and now my mom's in a coma. I try to help Calista out and someone winds up dead. What do I keep doing wrong?"

Shaylee ticks up an eyebrow. "I hardly think Essen is worth an existential crisis, girl." She lets me go and studies her mother's image on the canvas. "You're seventeen and facing some seriously messed-up shit, so start by keeping that in mind and cut yourself some slack. Second, it wouldn't hurt if you asked for help every once and a while."

"So I've heard," I mutter.

"For good reason," Shaylee replies. "And third, like I said: move forward. Think while you walk, if you have to. Standing still for too long is bound to drive you crazy."

As she heads toward the door, she adds, "That goes for while you're painting too. All work and no play will burn you out before Halloween. Call up that girlfriend of yours some time."

"How did you—never mind." I sigh. "She's not my girlfriend, but we are supposed to have dinner Wednesday night. I should probably cancel, though."

"No, don't," Shaylee exclaims.

What the...?

She composes herself and slips her hands back into her pocket. "I mean, what did I just say? You can't just lock yourself away in here." She looks down and nudges a loose floorboard with her foot. "I never got to be a human teenager. If I wasn't running wild on my own, I was at court being a princess. I'd hate for Faerie to take that experience away from you, too."

After what happened with Essen, I think it might be too late. The idea of Shaylee being a normal teenager makes me laugh, though. "You mean the queen doesn't let you date?"

She rolls her eyes. "She'd skewer anyone who asks. Literally." With a shrug, she meanders out of the door. "But, who knows? Things might change once I'm queen."

She sounds so sure about that. Not to mention the way she was just talking to Dominic... And he *did* freak out when I suggested putting Shaylee on the throne.

"When do you think that'll be, exactly?" I ask.

Shaylee reaches out to shut the door as she leaves. "I could tell you," she says, "but I'd quite literally have to kill you."

There's no doubt in my mind about that.

Dominic's words from last night haunt me again. They remind me that I need to get this painting done and get the hell out of Dodge. Something big is brewing in the Faerie Court, and I don't want to be around when it boils over. I can't say for sure what it'll look like, but I know it won't end well for Her Majesty.

Because the Faerie Court isn't as unified as she thinks it is.

Thirteen

Mr. Hob won't hear of me coming into work on Monday or Tuesday. When I call, he argues that he ran the store long before I started working there and he will do so long after I leave. He also promises to be extra nice to Walter since I won't be there as a buffer. All I need to worry about is the painting.

On Wednesday, however, Walter calls in with the flu.

With a guilty conscious that bleeds through the phone, Mr. Hob asks me to come in for a few hours. Truth be told, I'm happy to do so. Shaylee was onto something. Staring at a canvas for twelve hours straight messes with your head.

"I wouldn't ask, but I need to step out for a while," Mr. Hob explains when I arrive. "And I'll be damned if I let those sprites run the place."

"It's fine," I say, plopping down behind the counter. "I need a break anyway."

A yawn distorts my words, earning me a disapproving scowl from Hob.

"This probably isn't the kind of 'break' you need," the goblin grumbles.

I take out my sketchbook. "Relax. Like you said, it's just for a few hours. Scurry off and do what you need to do. I'll be fine."

"Have you seen that girl of yours?"

"We're having dinner tonight, but she's still not my girl."

Mr. Hob groans. "It's one step forward, two steps back with you."

"Do you want me to watch the store or not?" I sigh.

Finally, Mr. Hob leaves, but not without a series of worried glances over his shoulder. He's probably right to worry.

My phone buzzes with a message from Rina.

Can't make it tonight, it reads with a frowning face. *I'll let you know when I'm free again. Sorry.*

Well, so much for that. It's probably for the best. Coming into work seems like a long enough break.

No problem, I reply. *Everything okay?*

Three dots appear under her name to show she's replying. They sit there for a solid minute or so, then turn into two words: *Everything's peachy.*

So, something is obviously wrong.

Are you sure? I ask. Rina doesn't reply, but I don't ask anything else. I don't want to pry.

The store picks up, then quiets down again, so I go back to doodling to keep my mind busy. The drawings consist of friendly cartoons of memorable customers, Mom, Anna, and a few sketches of Rina. It's nice to work on something that isn't just a bargaining chip.

"You're really good," says a familiar voice.

I look up to see Jun leaning over the counter, looking at the sketchbook.

He backs up when his eyes meet mine. "Sorry. Didn't mean to spy on you. Can I have a look?"

"Sure," I tell him as he begins to study the pages. "I don't get to draw much these days, so I'm a bit rusty." I brush off the eraser shaving and hand it over. Growing up, Anna would always watch me draw, so it doesn't bother me too much, even if none of it is very good.

Jun gives a whistle as he flips through the pages. "If this is rusty, I'd like to see you on top of your game."

"Thanks." I try not to squirm self-consciously under the praise. Talking about something else would help. "So, how's it going?"

"In spite of today's campus-wide midterm return, pretty good." Jun sighs as he continues to flip.

"Uh-oh." I chuckle. "How bad is the damage?"

"I got out unscathed."

"How were Rina's?" I ask hesitantly. Maybe that's why she canceled.

Jun stops on one of the sketches of her. "Not sure. She wouldn't tell me when class got out, but she didn't look happy. I spied her heading off toward the astronomy tower before I headed over here."

What a bummer. She looked like she was studying so hard when I saw her in the café the other day. That certainly explains the "Everything's peachy" comment.

"I hope she's okay," I mutter as a customer approaches the counter.

Jun waits for him to leave and says, "Well, you could go check on her. It might cheer her up."

I sputter a few awkward snickers. "What makes you think seeing me would cheer her up?"

Jun leans on the counter and smirks up at me. "Well, she *was* pretty excited about your little date. I'm sure popping by to say hi would do her some good."

My heart stops for a moment. "She was excited?"

"Totally." Jun chuckles. "Well, she wouldn't come out and say it, but it was obvious. She asked to borrow my art history textbook and checked out *The Earls* from the library. Don't tell her I told you."

I try to keep any signs of excitement off my face. "I might be able to swing by after work," I reply casually. "If I do, is there anything in particular that would cheer her up?"

"She's a sucker for ice cream. I'm sure that'll do wonders."

I drum my pencil on the counter. If Rina really is upset, I'd like to help her feel better, but I don't want to be intrusive. Besides, there's the painting...

"You didn't come here just to tell me that, did you?" I ask.

Jun sets three books on the counter and gives me a mock-offended face. "Of course not! I came by to see what retro sci-fi you have in stock and you happened to be at work."

That's believable enough. The Faerie Realm is making me paranoid. "You still didn't have to bring it up," I point out, ringing up the books.

"I've known Rina for a while now," Jun explains, gaze lowering to his wallet. "She's a great girl, but not very savvy when it comes to emotions. Especially her own." He shifts his mouth into a sly smirk. "Besides, why are you complaining? I'm handing you free brownie points."

I sputter out a few words of protest, but none of them are coherent.

Jun laughs. "It's all right, Jocelyn. You can help her out *and* try to get her to like you. No crime in that. You can't be one-hundred-percent hero all the time."

That hits a little too close to home.

"Your total is twelve dollars and fifty-three cents," I tell Jun. "And I'll try to check on her after work."

Jun beams from ear to ear as he hands me his card. "Thanks." He takes his bag and heads toward the exit, but then pauses. "Oh, and if you could *not* mention this conversation to her, I'd be grateful. I'd never hear the end of it if Rina knew."

"Your secret's safe with me."

Jun gives me a wave and heads for the door. "Awesome. See you around."

Mr. Hob nearly trips Jun as he strides in the door, but pays the human no mind. Instead, he waddles behind the counter and promptly begins shoving me off the stool.

"Off you go," he orders. "I've got my business taken care of, so go finish yours."

I spot the goblin-sized sword hanging from Mr. Hob's belt.

"What sort of business?" I ask, eyeing the weapon.

Cursing under his breath and scowling up at me, Mr. Hob takes the blade from his belt. Glancing around nervously, he shoves it onto the bottom shelf of the counter for the time being. He then plops down on the stool.

"Mind your own business," he snaps, folding his chubby arms. "From what I've heard, you know too much as it is. I don't need Her Highness mad at me."

"You mean Shaylee?"

"No, I mean the queen's other changeling daughter."

His choice of words catches my attention. Even solitary folk like Hob refer to Shaylee as the queen's daughter, but I've never heard her refer to herself that way.

"Are you sure Shaylee's really the queen's?" I ask.

Hob narrows his beady eyes.

"After all, faeries steal infants left and right from the sound of it. She could have come from anywhere."

"The nature of their relationship is their affair and theirs alone," Hob answers, stroking his chin. "But it wouldn't be the first time a queen adopted a child, and no faerie is *completely* heartless. Not even Unseelie faeries, like the queen. At least she wasn't always. Given how identical they are, though, her adoption seems unlikely. Not like it's any of *your* business, unlike that painting."

"Okay, okay, I get it," I mumble. "I'm leaving."

"Good," Mr. Hob huffs after me. "And I don't want to see you back here until that painting is finished, do you hear me?"

"Loud and clear," I call back.

On my way out to the car, I check my phone. Rina hasn't said anything.

I should leave her alone. If she wanted to talk, she wouldn't have canceled.

But I could use a little more time away from the easel. It's a miracle I can see straight. A quick visit to check on her wouldn't take too long. Then I'll go right back to painting in twelve-hour increments.

Once I'm in the car, I head for the grocery store. As I drive, I repeat over and over in my head, *Say hi. Ask if she's okay. Give her the ice cream. Leave.*

It would be so much easier if I had asked Jun what flavor Rina likes. Too bad the idea doesn't hit me until I'm standing in the frozen food aisle. I don't have his number either. I do, however, have my sister's.

She picks up on the first ring. "What's wrong?" she demands.

"Nothing. I just need your help with something."

Silence on the other end, then a cautious, "Go on."

"If you did really poorly on a test, what kind of ice cream would make you feel better? It's for a friend."

Anna puts two and two together and lets out an elated squeal. "Your *girl*friend, you mean?"

My face gets hot. "She's not my girlfriend. Can you just help me out here?"

"Chocolate Cherry Cheesecake is your safest bet," she answers. "And why isn't she your girlfriend yet? What did you do?"

I hunt for a carton with that label. It sits on the far left and I grab one for myself, too. Can't deny that it sounds pretty good. "I didn't do anything. I don't think I did, anyway. She's just crazy busy with school, it seems."

"Or maybe she's playing hard to get."

That makes me laugh out loud. "I don't think so. If anything, she might be trying to get rid of me."

"She's not trying to get rid of you," Anna groans. "Dating or not, I'm glad to hear you're spending time with people. You artist types get weird and reclusive. I don't need you cutting off an ear or something."

"Rude. I don't get weird and reclusive. I get eccentric."

Anna snorts. "You're already eccentric. Wait, why are you buying ice cream?"

"I told you. This girl—"

"No, I mean why are you buying ice cream at *ten in the morning?*"

Whoops. It's only Wednesday. I should be in school, not on my way home from work. How could I be so stupid to forget that?

I try to think of a cover story as I fumble with my keys. "Well, uh, the thing is, I'm playing hookie. A buddy of mine told our teacher that I went to the office because of a migraine. We're just watching a movie today, so it's no big deal." But Anna's supposed to be in school too. "What's your excuse?"

"Me? I'm on my way back from the bathroom. Thought I'd take the long way around since you called. We're watching *1984* in English, so you're saving me from dying of boredom. Worse. Adaptation. Ever."

"Can't argue there," I reply, getting in the car. "I tried to skip out on that too."

"Like older sister, like younger sister, I guess."

I put the phone on speaker and stick it in the cupholder so I can drive. "Nah. Everyone tries to get out of that movie. You turned out way better than me."

"Oh, stop," Anna chastises. "You turned out fine. You're not even done yet. Cut yourself some slack and go back to class."

"I will if you will."

"The cutting yourself some slack or class? Because you—damn it." Anna's voice drops to a whisper. "Vice principal at two o'clock. She's yelling at Mark Robinson for the millionth time this semester, so I think I'm safe, but I gotta go."

"'Kay. Me too. Love you, baby sister. Stop swearing."

"Love you too, big sister. And I'll swear if I damn well please."

She hangs up, and I'm left shaking my head.

Cut yourself some slack, she said. She sounds like Shaylee and Dominic, but I'm not sure that's an option. I'll figure it out later. Right now, I'll cut myself about fifteen minutes' worth of slack by going to see Rina, then it's back to finishing that blasted painting and, hopefully, cutting the ropes altogether.

Fourteen

THE OBSERVATORY IS easy enough to find since the giant telescope gives it away. I expect someone to make sure I'm actually a student—check for an ID, ask if I have a class here or something—but I stroll into the building without even drawing a suspicious glance. I blend into the crowd, and for a moment, I see a glimpse of what my future could be once this is all over. At a much cheaper college, obviously. Still, it's not a bad view.

The observatory entrance sits on the fourth floor. It's a bland little hall decorated with framed photographs taken with the telescope. Swirls of color pop against the black void of space. Shapes eerily similar to things on Earth invite the viewer to find meaning in it all. Other photographs show students shaking hands with scientists I've never heard of in front of machines I have no hope of understanding.

Rina's nowhere in sight.

At the end of the hall there's a sign that reads, Closed Due to Daylight.

Closed or not, the door's unlocked.

Rina sits up on the risen platform, textbooks and notes spread out while the computers and telescope blink silently behind her. The closed dome above faintly echoes back her mutterings. She's dressed down: jeans and a Silver River High T-shirt, her hair up in that poofy bun I'm beginning to love and a few curls framing her beautiful, determined face. She sighs, takes the pen from behind her ear, and scribbles some notes.

"We're closed," she says, attention still on her books. "Come back tonight."

"And here I was hoping to look directly at the sun," I reply.

She looks up with a scowl, then laughs when she realizes it's me. "How'd you know I was here?"

"I just had a hunch," I answer, joining her on the platform.

Rina rolls her eyes and looks back down at her books. "Um-hm. Something tells me that hunch took the form of a particular Korean friend of mine."

"I don't think you know how hunches work." I plop down beside the sea of study material and open the grocery bag. "But we have more important matters to discuss, like ice cream."

Rina stops writing and looks up as I pull out the cartons. Her eyes go wide at the sight of the Chocolate Cherry Cheesecake label. When I hand her a carton and a spoon, she cradles them like I've just handed her the Holy Grail.

"I can't decide whether I should kill Jun or hug him next time I see him," Rina grumbles, popping off the lid. "Thank you, Jocelyn."

"Why would you kill him?" I ask, opening my own. Staying a few minutes longer wouldn't hurt, I suppose.

"I *really* need to focus," Rina answers. "I need to redo the problems I got wrong on my midterms. The professor said he'll give us a few extra points if we find our mistakes and correct them."

"Looks more like you're getting ready to retake it," I observe.

"Yeah, well, I'm doing a little extra studying so I don't make the same mistakes again. And I need to review the mistakes on my programming midterm. There were a ton."

"Define *a ton*."

Rina tenses as she raises a bite of ice cream to her mouth. "I don't discuss grades." After eating it, she adds, "Besides, you don't want to hear about that boring stuff. What's up with you? How's the commission?"

Suddenly, I'm not so hungry.

It must show on my face because Rina frowns. "Uh-oh. Something wrong?"

"N-Not really. My commissioner just didn't like my last painting and made me start over. It was supposed to be the final one too."

Rina winces on my behalf. "That sucks. I'm sure it was awesome, though."

"You haven't seen any of my work yet," I remind her.

"Well, I'm still sure it was awesome." She takes another bite. "Do you have anything I can look at?"

"I left my sketchbook in the car."

She smirks. "Isn't that convenient?" With one hand, she turns a few pages of her textbook and scribbles a few notes on the bottom of her test paper. I get a glimpse of her grade as she flips to another section.

It's a B.

I can't help but blurt, "You're doing test corrections on a B?"

Rina freezes, glances down at the paper, then shoves it her textbook and slams it shut, as if she's angry at it for betraying her. "I said I don't discuss grades." She focuses on her ice cream, chipping at a particularly frozen patch.

"There's nothing wrong with a B," I say. "It's pretty awesome, actually, considering you're a freshman, right?"

"Not awesome enough," Rina mutters bitterly.

"You're not getting kicked out of your program, are you?"

Rina stabs at the ice cream a bit harder. "No."

"Are your parents mad?"

"They say as long as I don't sink any lower, they'll let this semester slide since it's my first, but I know they're disappointed. I am too." She slowly takes another bite of ice cream. It clearly isn't helping the way I had hoped.

"You're awfully hard on yourself for seventeen," I point out.

"I have to be. My oldest brother's a big-shot lawyer in New York City and the younger one is a year away from being a heart surgeon. My parents wanted me to be an engineer. They said it would be more 'practical.' I had to fight for them to let me study astronomy, seeing as they're paying for it."

I just blink in response. I didn't think it was possible for smart people to be born in that high of concentration. Rina's parents would have disowned me practically out of the womb.

Rina takes my silence as a cue to keep talking. "On top of it, they never let me forget that I'm a black girl in a scientific field at a very challenging private school, like I don't know it well enough." She rolls her eyes at that last part. "So not only do I have to prove to them astronomy is a good field that I can excel in, I have to prove that I deserve to be here."

She's lost me.

"What do you mean?" I ask.

"I'm sick of people thinking students like me are here to fill some quota," she hisses. "I mean, no one's said anything *directly* to my face, probably because they know I'll kick their ass, but...I worry. I hear stories from other students here, and I wonder when they'll come. The judgmental comments. The assumption that I'm not working as hard as everyone else. I feel like if I keep straight As, I can prove to everyone, including myself, that I deserve to be here."

With a sigh, she pushes around a few notebooks in an attempt to organize. "Of course, it's not that easy. People are going to think what they want, but...I just need to feel in control, I guess."

That I can understand all too well. If I can get the paintings done, I can force life to go back to normal. Mom will wake up. Our family will be whole again. Well, as whole as it can be without Dad.

I can't put that into words, though. All I can manage is, "I'm sorry you feel that way."

She chuckles and flips a few pages of her book. "And you know the worst part? Just being smart doesn't feel like enough for me. I mean, I like school, but..." She shakes her head and goes back to the ice cream. "Outside of it, I'm not sure I am. I feel like I haven't done enough to know. I feel like all I've ever done is study and participate in extracurricular activities that my parents thought would help me get here." After another bite, she forces a smile. "Sorry. You probably didn't want to hear all that mess. I'll shut up."

"No, its fine," I answer. "I think it's pretty normal. If you just let one thing define you, it can swallow you up and leave you with less than you started with..."

Jeez, I'm starting to sound like Dominic. The realization catches me off guard.

Rina waves a hand in my face. "You still there, Jocelyn? Did I finally bore you out of your mind?"

I shake my head and come back to earth. "No, I just thought of someone else that should hear that." I'd rather not talk about who that someone is, though. "Anyway, whoever you are, I know you're pretty cool. You're fun to be around, you stand up for your friends, and you've got a mean right hook. Your taste in pizza could use some work, though."

Rina looks up from her ice cream and gasps. "I beg your pardon—"

"Pardon's all yours."

Rina opens her mouth to speak, then shuts it. "Well played," she mutters.

I shrug. "I do what I can."

Rina scrapes the bottom of her carton and gives me a sheepish grin. "Sorry I bailed on you."

"Don't worry about it," I assure her. "This beats small talk over Thai food."

Rina raises an eyebrow. "Really? Even Doctor When small talk?"

"One does not simply 'small talk' about Doctor When," I correct. "But yes. Though I am rather curious about who your favorite doctor is and why."

"Eleven. I liked how whimsical and lighthearted he was. He had the only decent character arc in season seven."

"What? You didn't like the Lakes?"

That gets Rina smiling again. "I tolerated the Lakes, but that's it."

"Amber was hilarious!"

"Amber was annoying."

"But, the episode with the crying cherubs!"

Rina chews on the end of her spoon. "Okay, fine. She was good in that one."

She studies me again with her smoldering ebony eyes. It would be kind of hot if I wasn't so worried about what she's going to say next.

"What's your angle?" she finally asks.

"What do you mean?"

"I mean you're weird. Waiting with me at the club. Checking on me with ice cream after I bailed on you. Listening to that whole mess. You're weirder than the stuff that keeps happening around you. You've got to have an angle."

She's not wrong about the weird part, but not for the reason she thinks. I don't think I'm clever enough to devise an "angle." Seeing Rina is one of the few things I really look forward to these days.

"We had a date tonight, remember?" I remind her. "Seems pretty self-explanatory. And you know I couldn't just leave you at the club."

"Yeah, but you're going above and beyond here."

"What were you expecting?"

She tenses and lowers her eyes. "I don't know."

Something tells me she does, but I've pried enough for one day.

"And that makes me feel worse about canceling," she mutters.

I inch around the pile of notes and sit next to Rina so that I can open her textbook. It's hard to ignore the heat radiating off her and her signature scent of ginger and citrus.

"Well, how about instead of dinner, you teach me about—" I scan for a section title. "'*Black Holes and Gravity*.' That way, you're reviewing, but you don't have to feel bad."

After reading a few paragraphs silently, I change my mind. "On second thought, maybe we should start with something easier."

Rina gives me a playful shove, letting her hand linger on my arm and slide down to my hand. Her touch sends a jolt up my arm. I hope she doesn't notice how my breath catches.

"Yeah, black holes are a little much," she says, flipping a page in the book.

"I probably wouldn't understand the *gravity* of such a topic." I snicker.

Rina freezes mid page-flip. Her mouth crinkles as she tries not to laugh. Leaning closer, she whispers, "Keep those terrible jokes up, and I'm never letting the 'check out' incident go."

"Worth it," I mutter, meeting her gorgeous eyes.

Everything about her sends my heart racing. I never realized how warm people are. I can't remember the last time I was this physically close to someone. Someone who wasn't trying to kill me, anyway.

We're both frozen. I don't know if I'm waiting for her to move or she's waiting for me. I can't think straight enough to guess. I need to figure it out, because waiting like this is torture.

Turns out I don't get the chance. Rina's phone rings, startling us both.

She pulls away and begins to throw everything in her backpack with one hand. Her other hand holds up her phone. "Yeah, I know. I'm sorry. I'll be there in a second.... No, I can still make it. Bye." Hanging up she adds, "I forgot I had a meeting for a group project. That would have messed up our date anyway. Why am I so bad at this?"

"You've been stressed lately," I say, gathering the ice-cream trash. "No harm done."

Rina throws her backpack over her shoulder. "You're something else. You know that, right?"

"No. What am I exactly?" I ask, following her out the door.

She doesn't answer as she locks the observatory door. Since we take the stairs two at a time, I don't really mind. I have to concentrate on not breaking my neck. Once we dash out the front door, she stops abruptly and I nearly run into her.

"You're more patient with me than I ever expected someone to be," she blurts. "I figured you'd disappear after the movie. If not then, now after that little..." She waves her hand toward the telescope. "Emotional outburst."

I try not to laugh. "That wasn't an outburst, Rina. That was just talking."

Rina cringes as if that's just as bad.

"Do you want me to disappear?" I ask cautiously.

She kicks at a loose clump of grass, then looks up at me. "No. That's one thing I don't want." Adjusting her backpack, she sighs. "Look, I'm sorry I still don't completely have"—she points back and forth between us—"this figured out. I'm trying, though."

I bite the inside of my lip to keep from laughing. I never thought that I'd be the one more comfortable with heart-to-heart conversations, especially considering how hard Anna has to work to pull them out of me.

"No big deal," I say with a shrug. "Besides, it's nothing serious, remember?" I make an X sign over my chest. "Cross my heart."

"And you're okay with that?"

"I don't see why not."

Rina bites her bottom lip and taps her foot. "Do you want to go haunted-house hopping this weekend with everyone? We could eat afterward. My treat."

It's tempting, but I need to get that painting done. This little break has already gotten much longer than it was supposed to be. If I can manage to finish it, turn it into the queen, and figure out when I'm going home, maybe I could spare a few hours.

"I'll keep you posted," I say.

"Sounds good." Rina sighs. "Though I'd really like it if you could come. Someone's got to stop me from punching the poor saps in costumes. Travis and Jun will just laugh at me."

I'm not quite sure if she's joking or not.

"I'll try to be there," I say. "For *fight-or-flight* duty."

"Thanks." Rina shifts from foot to foot, looks around at the empty sidewalk, then abruptly leans forward and kisses me on the cheek. Then she's gone, jogging across campus to her meeting.

I'm left stunned, unsure what to do, and floating on more air than I'd like to admit. I consider texting her about it but decide against it and head off toward the parking lot. I need to get that painting done. After that, I can try to understand Rina.

Fifteen

THE AIR STANDS still early Saturday afternoon. The remaining autumn leaves hang limp without the usual light breeze. I can't hear a single bird outside the window. The world seems as tense and anxious as I am.

I dip my thinnest brush in the white paint and ever so slowly, add the light to Her Majesty's eyes in steady, minuscule strokes. Satisfied, truly satisfied, I lift the brush and carefully step back.

A giant weight lifts up off my shoulders and the room brightens. The final portrait sits finished on the easel. It's as beautiful as any priceless piece in a museum.

Relief washes over me and threatens to lull me to sleep, but I can't rest yet. This isn't over until the queen gives me the okay. First, I should probably deal with the nausea and dizziness setting in. I can't clearly recall the last time I ate. Constant cups of coffee don't count. Taking the painting to Her Majesty in this state might be suicide. I can't imagine collapsing in Faerie is much safer than her try to kill me.

The smell of toasted bread settles it: eat, then take it to court.

I head down the stairs with the painting and find Shaylee at the stove.

She's certainly made herself at home, judging by the way she whisks a pot of tomato soup with a spatula in her free hand. There's three spots set at the table with a plate stacked high with grilled cheese sandwiches, mostly burnt, in the center.

At the sound of the creaking stairs, she turns and smiles. "Hey there, Picasso," she greets me, transferring the last sandwich to the table. "I was just about to call you."

"What are you doing here?"

She scoffs and turns off the burners. "Nice to see you, too."

"Sorry. I didn't mean it like that. I just didn't expect the princess of Faerie to pay us a visit."

Shaylee begins to pour the soup into mugs. "I came to check on you." Satisfied with her work, she looks me over and frowns. "You look terrible. How long have you been painting? I told you to pace yourself."

"Too late," I say, holding up the canvas. "I finished."

Shaylee's eyes widen, and she grins from ear to ear. "You're really done?"

I nod, smiling in spite of the exhaustion as I gently lean the painting against the table and take a sandwich from the pile. "Yep. I just need to have Dominic dry it real quick and I'm home free."

The princess slaps me on the shoulder. "Good for you, girl. I knew you were talented, but *damn*. You're just in the nick of time, too. The queen's losing her mind."

"She has a mind left to lose?"

Shaylee's expression turns grave. "I guess so. She's killed three servants in the past week, calling them Seelie spies. She's removed every mirror in the keep because she thinks Titania is talking to her through them. She can't even look at me anymore since we look so alike. The Offering can't come fast enough."

"Why not just do it now?" I ask, dipping my sandwich in the soup. "Why wait for the thirty-first?"

"You know how Halloween used to be called Samhain?"

I take a sip of soup as I strain my memory. "Nope."

Shaylee rolls her eyes. "Typical American. No tie to your ancient roots."

"That's not my fault," I argue. "Besides, my family's French and Dutch. *Samhain* doesn't sound like it comes from either."

"Fair enough. Samhain has Celtic roots," Shaylee explains. "It marked the end of the harvest and the beginning of winter. People also believed that the veil between this world and the Other World, the realm of the gods and spirits, thinned during Samhain. They weren't wrong.

"To this day, we faeries have a feast on Halloween in the Other World's honor. Every seven years, however, the veil between our worlds is particularly thin. That's when we perform the Hallowed Offering, which gives faeries their magic. We offer up blood and the Other World gives us our powers. The queens—sorry, *queen*—acts like a bridge between the two."

"And the bridge is wearing out," I conclude.

"Exactly," Shaylee confirms.

Footsteps thump up from the basement. They can only be Dominic's.

Shaylee cups her mouth and calls, "Except some people are too scared to seize an opportunity like that. Wouldn't know opportunity if it slapped them in the face."

"Let it go, Your Highness." Dominic squints in the bright kitchen light. Or maybe it's a glare. "I'm not in the mood."

With the circles under his eyes and how scruffy he looks, that much is obvious. I didn't know faeries could even look scruffy.

"Fine. Jocelyn finished the painting," Shaylee blurts.

Dominic freezes, stares at me, then snatches up the painting. "This is incredible," he gasps. "There might be some fae in you if you can finish something this beautiful this fast. I'm rather curious about what made you decide on such a theme, though. It hardly seems like the queen."

He's got a point. In the painting, Her Majesty sits beside a lake wearing a clean white gown and a tranquil expression. A human child sits asleep in her lap as a pixie plays a pan flute at her side. From the lake, a mermaid offers her a wreath of seaweed. Her amulet hangs around her neck, bright and beautiful.

"Well, she's always going on about unifying everybody." I yawn. "So, I figured playing on that might get me back in her good graces."

Dominic strokes his chin and nods. "Not a bad idea." He holds the canvas in both hands for a moment, gaze focused in concentration, then shoves it into my hands. "Take it," he orders. "I'll let Her Majesty know you're coming."

"Jeez, let the girl finish eating," Shaylee argues. "Look at her. She's too skinny."

"Could you *try* not to backhand me with your concern?" I snap.

Shaylee shrugs and takes a few bites of her own food. "Besides, the queen's away at the moment. There's a little border skirmish brewing up north. Apparently, a pack of shapeshifters is trying to take advantage of Her Majesty's weakness and muscle in on faerie territory." She raises her gaze to Dominic's. "Can't say I blame them, seeing as they've got *the perfect opportunity—*"

Dominic growls, "So help me, Your Highness, if you don't—"

"You mean I can't take her the painting?" I exclaim. They can fight all they want later. First, I need to figure out what I'm going to do.

"Afraid so." Shaylee sighs. "But if it helps, she sent word that she should be home within the next couple of days."

Dominic scowls. "I was told nothing about such an endeavor."

"That's because you're still in hot water for the Essen fiasco," Shaylee replies. "I'd watch it if I were you. We can't have you losing your good standing now."

Lips pursed and eyes narrowed, Dominic replies, "Duly noted, Your Highness."

"You're her daughter," I remind her. "Can't you end the contract?"

Shaylee shakes her head. "Nope. No one can understand the queen's magic but her. That's, like, Magic 101."

I slouch in my chair, appetite gone.

Lovely. The dumb painting's done and I'm still stuck. "A few days" isn't that long, but given my current track record, I'm not convinced that I can last that long. Faerie might not let me. Maybe I'll call Anna and Rick and tell them I'm coming home. I need to focus on the light at the end of the tunnel, not the dark walls.

"You should take this time to rest," Dominic suggests. "Her Highness is right. You look worn out."

"Go see that girl of yours like I told you," Shaylee interjects. "She'll take your mind off stuff."

Dominic gives her a quizzical look.

Well, Rina did say she was going out with her friends tonight.

"Let me call my family first."

"Sounds like a fine plan," Dominic concludes. With a lazy wave, he heads back toward his room. "And keep that painting somewhere safe." With that, he shuts the door and is sure to lock it as always.

"What does he have in there that's so mysterious anyway?" I ask.

"A computer database of faerie spies," Shaylee says around a mouthful of gooey cheese and bread.

I flash her a dirty look.

She swallows. "All right. You caught me. I don't have the slightest idea."

With our meal finished and Dominic still locked in his room, I head upstairs. Shaylee hangs back, probably so she can keep fighting with Dominic.

I dial Anna's cell.

"Okay, how bad did you blow it with ice-cream girl?" she groans.

"Hey! Things went great, I'll have you know," I snap. Behind Anna comes chatter and the distant drone of a crowd. "Is now a bad time?"

"Nah, it's cool. Just give me a second." There's a rustle and the noise quiets down. "What's up?"

"Well...I was sort of thinking about moving back home. I mean, if it's cool with you and Uncle Rick. If you two would rather not have me—"

"Jocelyn," Anna laughs. "Of course we want you to come home! Why on earth would we not want you to come home, dork?"

I drop onto my bed. It's like the realization that I'm almost home knocked me over.

"Why the change of heart? Don't you like your art program? Is something wrong?"

"It's not proving to be worth it. Besides, I'm considering a career change. Also, being away from you guys has been really draining."

Understatement of the millennia.

"Mom will be glad to have you home." Anna sighs.

A smile creeps onto my face. "I imagine she will."

"What does Uncle David think?"

"Eh...he'll miss me, but he thinks it's for the best too."

"Have you called Uncle Rick?"

"Not yet. I'll call him next."

"I'll let you go then," Anna says. "See you soon! Love you."

"Love you, too. Bye, baby sister."

She hangs up, and I dial Rick's number. It goes to voice mail, so I leave him a message. Then I hang up and lie back on my bed. As I close my eyes—just for a second, I swear—my phone beeps with a text message.

It's Rina. *What's the haunted-house verdict?*

Shaylee's right. A few hours with Rina would probably be good for me.

I can come. What time?

I almost fall asleep before she replies.

Six. Here's the place. She sends a second message with an address.

'Kay. See you tonight. With my last bit of consciousness, I set an alarm for five and pray I don't sleep through it. That prayer goes unanswered.

Dominic pokes his head in my room and watches me scramble to make myself presentable. "No need to rush. Just let her know you'll be late." He leans against the doorframe. "Besides, you needed the sleep. Did you contact your family beforehand?"

"Yeah. Anna seems excited. I couldn't get ahold of Rick. You might have to play Uncle David a few more times so no one knows I've been squatting in a farmhouse for the last four months."

"I figured as much." His calculating gaze drills through the back of my head. I can feel it. "Are you going to be okay once you go home?"

I pause as I hunt for a clean shirt. "Sure. As soon as I see Mom awake, I'll be fine."

"You honestly think it's that easy?"

"It has to be."

"Incorrect," Dominic replies. "You seem to have no reservations about taking hits in order to be the hero, but those hits leave scars, Jocelyn. Ones like Essen especially—"

My stomach flips. "Can we not talk about him? Like, ever?"

"We don't have to, but you should."

"I already talked with Shaylee."

Dominic scowls. "She doesn't count." His expression lightens again as he asks, "But that does remind me, did Calista take back that trinket of hers?"

"I gave it to her when she brought me back to the house."

"And she didn't try anything?"

"Luckily, no. Would have made things with Rina kind of awkward."

Dominic raises an eyebrow as an amused grin spreads across his face. "Staying true to a woman you've yet to call your lover? My, my, Jocelyn, such chastity. I take back what I said earlier—you're far too pure of heart to be one of us."

My face gets hot as I sputter, "I—she just—who asked you?"

Dominic tousles my hair as I make a break for the stairs and he snickers. "Nothing wrong with that. Though it begs the question: How old are you, again?"

I yank away from him and walk down the rest of the stairs. "Oh, shut up."

With a sigh, Dominic muses, "I'm going to be so lonely without you to tease once this is all over."

I nearly forgot. Once I move back home, Dominic's gone. Watching me won't be his job anymore.

The thought slows down my escape. I had been so focused on what I'll gain from getting this painting done that it never crossed my mind that I might actually lose something as well. I didn't think I could ever miss anything from Faerie.

"What will you do when you're done here?" I ask as I hunt for my car keys. "You're not going back to the queen, are you?"

"For a time," Dominic gripes. "Fret not, though. It won't be for long."

"Should I even bother asking what you mean by that?"

Dominic weighs the question for a moment, tilting his head back and forth as he thinks. "I'd rather you didn't. Faeries can't lie, but we can weave quite confusing truths."

As I head out the door, I give Dominic a thumbs-up. "Good communication. Glad we're so honest with each other."

Dominic chuckles, "What friendship could survive without it?"

So, he thinks we're friends after all.

That's just going to make leaving all the harder.

Sixteen

THE HAUNTED HOUSE sits at the end of a dirt road surrounded by a muddy makeshift parking lot. Corn rises up around the property like an impenetrable fence, framing signs adverting a maze, hayrides, and fresh apple cider. The nearby barn glows with a safe, warm light while the house stands dark and ominous with skeletons and menacing jack-o'-lanterns in the yard. While I'm walking to the barn, shapes shift and morph in the dark windows.

Rina and the others stand huddled just outside the barn with donuts and cups of steaming cider. She throws her head back as she laughs at something Travis says and her gold earrings catch the light. Even from here, I know her eyes are sparkling.

Good God, Jocelyn. Get a hold of yourself.

Brook notices me first. "Hey, you made it."

"You ready to get scared out of your mind?" Jun asks with a pompous grin.

"As if," I scoff. "If you think I'm scared of some silly roadside attraction, you're *gravely* mistaken."

Travis high-fives me while the others groan.

"You're hopeless," Rina teases. "Let's go."

As we all head toward the house, Jun elbows me and gives me an approving nod. I can only assume he knows I went to visit Rina and appreciates it. I nod back, grateful that he told me to go.

Rina slips between us, unaware of our silent conversation. "So, how's the makeup painting?" she asks.

"I finished," I answer. "And the test corrections?"

"Wow, congratulations. And I got just enough points to get a B+."

I sigh and shake my head. "You're way too smart for me. Sure you don't want me to bail?"

Rina gently elbows me. "Nope. You signed up for fight-or-flight duty. Besides, if I'm going to teach you astronomy, you have to teach me how to paint."

"Sounds like a good deal to me."

We join the others on the creaking, rotting porch. Brook squeals as the scarecrow sitting by the door springs to life, nearly giving us all heart attacks. With shaking hands, we pull out our wallets to pay the man, but he holds up a hand to stop me when I hand him the money.

"Are you Jocelyn Lennox?" he asks.

Everyone looks at both the scarecrow and me with confusion.

I'm just as confused. "Yeah. Why?"

"The last guy who came through said you'd be by, so he paid for you. 'It's on me,' he said."

I look at the others, but they're still lost. It's not as if we have any mutual friends, and until very recently, I hadn't had any friends nearby to speak of. Not any human friends anyway.

"Did you get the guy's name?"

"No. But he was a really short fella. Black hair. Early twenties, maybe?"

So not Dominic, Mr. Hob, Iver, or Calista. Who could it have been?

"Maybe it was someone who shops at the Novel Spell a lot," Rina suggests, pulling me toward the door as it creaks open.

"Yeah," I mutter. "That must be it."

The man grins as we pass with a smile too wide for his made-up face and teeth filed to a point. "Have fun," he says with a wink.

A chill shoots down my spine.

Faeries wouldn't hang around here, right? They'd find this sort of place boring next to the world they live in. It's just part of this guy's job to be scary and he enjoys it. That's all it is.

We find ourselves in a long dark hallway shrouded in fog and eerie blue lights. On the wall hang holographic pictures that shift from sweet, innocent portraits to sinister, menacing monsters as we pass. A family of four becomes a pack of werewolves. A pretty young woman decays into a zombie. A pair of siblings becomes an ax murderer and his next victim. Disturbing, but not exactly terror-inducing.

And yet Rina cowers behind me.

"You can sucker punch a random guy in a nightclub, but you're afraid of a haunted house?" I whisper.

"I'm not scared. Just cautious," Rina whispers back.

I try not to snicker and follow the others down the hall. Jun tries the door at the end of it, but it's locked. Unfortunately, the other ones aren't very appealing.

Something violently throws itself against the door to our left and frantic, unintelligible mutterings come through the door to our right. We try the doors closer to the entrance. The left one's unlocked, but the flashing lights coming from the keyhole are far from inviting. Brook leans down and looks inside. She jumps back after a second and hides behind Travis.

"Do we want to know?" I ask, unsure whether to laugh or start worrying.

"Let's just say *Alien* looks like a family film next to what was crawling out of those unfortunate souls," she says, inching away from the door. "Jun, I think we should have started with a tamer house."

Jun rolls his eyes and leans down to look through the keyhole. "It can't be that bad," he says. Seconds later, he goes pale.

Behind the last door comes a timid knock interrupted periodically with a small voice asking, "Mommy? Mommy? Are you there, Mommy?"

"Well, what do you think?" Travis asks, folding his arms and studying one of the portraits. "We got the Incredible Hulk, the asylum patient, Alien, and the kid with abandonment issues."

"They all sound so appealing when you phrase them that way," Rina scoffs.

All the doors go silent.

Then, a tiny click.

The door at the end of the hall inches open, pulled by a pale hand streaked with blood.

The color drains from everyone's faces.

A blood-curdling screech rips through the walls. A ghostly, blood-streaked figure comes lumbering down the hall, one leg mangled and an eye dangling from its socket.

"Abandonment issues," I declare, grabbing Rina's hand and diving for the door handle. "Definitely abandonment issues."

"Good idea," Rina cries, pushing me. "Go, go, go!"

We tear into the next room and the door slams shut before the others can follow. They bang on the door and we pull at it until the actor scatters them. I keep trying, but it won't budge.

"Is that supposed to happen?" I ask.

"Hell if I know," Rina answers, voice shrill with terror.

My pulse pounds against my eardrums, and my whole body shakes. Even though I feel like I might drop dead, I'm laughing.

Holy shit, I'm really laughing. I honestly thought I never would again.

"I'm starting to think studying black holes is a better de-stressor than this." I chuckle, wiping the sweat from my forehead.

My laughter dissolves when I look across the room at the little girl sitting on a moth-eaten antique sofa. She rocks back and forth in a torn dirty outfit, muttering to herself. It looks like she just crawled out of a grave. Rina and I freeze, waiting for her to attack, but she doesn't seem to realize we're here. Let's leave it that way.

Rina latches onto my arm. We tiptoe past the girl toward an ascending staircase on the other side of the room. Once we're close to her—too close for comfort—I can make out her words.

"Where's Mommy? Where's Mommy?" she chants under her breath. "Where's Mommy? Where's Mommy? Where's Essen?"

What did she just—

She snatches me by the shirt. Rina screams.

The little girl looks up, eyes pitch black and a nasty sneer on her gray wilting face. "He'll get you for this." She cackles. Her gaze flits above me.

I glance up.

A woman clings to the ceiling wearing a bloodstained nightgown. Her neck contorts in an unnatural angle and her hair hangs in thick matted clumps. She stares down at us with bulging expressionless eyes.

As Rina begins to look up, I push her toward the stairs. A skittering noise up above sends us sprinting and we take the steps three at a time. *Mommy*'s bulging bloodshot eyes meet mine as she crawls along the ceiling right before I slam the door.

"What? What is it?" Rina exclaims.

"Found Mommy," I pant. "We need to get out of here."

Taking Rina by the hand, I jog down the hall, ignoring the skeletons and vampires that jump out of the bedrooms. I hardly hear the scientist inviting us for brain-infused tea. I'm too scared of whatever that girl was to bother with them.

At the end of the hall sits a staircase that leads to the kitchen. Dirt cakes the counters. Fake limbs stick out of pots and dangle off cutting boards. I can think of a few kinds of faeries who might like a kitchen like this, but none of them would come after me for killing Essen. The only way out is down into a cellar. I begin pacing and wringing my hands. There's got to be another way out of this death trap. Walking into its depths can't end well.

Rina takes me by the arm to steady me. "Are you okay?"

"I don't know, I... Something's wrong about this place."

"That's the point," Rina reminds me. "It's a haunted house. This is all par for the course." She studies my face. "This isn't about the house, is it?"

"I'm just claustrophobic is all." I pant.

Rina's eyes go wide. "Why didn't you tell me? We could have—"

The stove bursts into a blazing inferno.

A man crawls out of the oven, charcoal black and smoking. With one hand outstretched toward us, he screeches, "I'll get you for this!" and chases us into the basement.

He stops when I slam the door.

The hanging lights above flicker and sway, revealing an old musty wine cellar. We wait in silence for some sort of monster to show itself, but there's only silence. It winds my muscles tighter.

"Let's go," I mutter, dragging Rina between the shelves, hunting for the exit.

"We didn't have to do this," Rina said. "We could have met up afterward. Why didn't you tell me?"

"I wanted to impress you." That part isn't a total lie at least.

"Why? You already took punches for me and my friends."

A zombie leaps into our path, sending us sprinting the other direction and reminding me there are more life-threatening issues to deal with. Another zombie cuts us off, sending us down a new aisle. We take a few more left turns, and I spot the exit: a series of steps leading up into the inky black night.

I push Rina ahead of me and she bolts up the stairs. We're home free if—

The door swings shut in my face and the lights go out.

I turn to face the zombies, but I'm met with empty air and silence.

Above, Rina pounds on the door. "Jocelyn, you all right?"

"I'm fine," I lie. "It's probably part of the house. Just have to wait it out." So, I wait and wait and wait. All the while, I dig my nails into my palms to keep from shaking and force myself to breathe slowly. I gingerly walk back down the steps and call, "Hello? Anyone there? I think there's a malfunction. Can you let me out?"

Nothing.

I roll my eyes to convince myself that everything is fine. "Okay, zombie dudes. I'm scared. Terrified out of my mind. You did a good job. Now, let me out."

With a whoosh of air, I feel a face appear a few centimeters in front of mine.

A face with hot sticky breath that reeks of blood.

"We both know you're not afraid, Jocelyn." It snickers. "But since you killed my kelpie, you should be."

I stumble back and trip over the stairs. The door still refuses to budge despite the banging and shouting of the crowd forming on the other side.

"That knight of yours didn't clean up as well as he thought he did." The voice laughs, now a few feet away. "He had more than a body to worry about."

"I never meant to kill Essen," I call, slowly getting to my feet. "I just wanted him to leave my friend alone."

"It wasn't your affair to meddle in," hisses the voice in the dark.

As my eyes adjust, I can make out the fuzzy shapes of the shelves. Beside one of them looms a figure. I can't place it as human or faerie. Not that I need to.

"It was just a necklace. It meant a lot to my friend. He should have let it go," I explain, attention locked on the figure. It disappears when I blink. I take a few cautious steps toward the shelves, but the figure doesn't reappear.

"Well, weren't you just a saint?" the faerie cackles in my ear.

I panic and swing a fist, barely missing one of the shelves. Then I take one of the decorative bottles from its rack. Here I am ready to bash a faerie's face in and yet I'm the saint. Then again, judging by the smell of blood on his breath, the bar for sainthood is on the ground.

"What did you ask for in return, hmm?" the voice croons. "Something quite good, I hope."

"Just for her to stay out of trouble," I say, taking a few cautious steps forward.

"You'll end up dead if you keep up that heroic nonsense," the voice sneers from the other side of the room. "Then again, I don't think you're much of a hero at all. Between your mother, the girls at the Time Between—"

It's that redcap. Fuloch. He was the one who saw me kill Essen.

"—and the nymph, you must be compensating for something. Something before Essen. Why else would you keep throwing yourself in the line of fire?"

My grip tightens. I hope Fuloch can't see that he's struck a nerve.

"I'm telling you, I never wanted to kill him."

A sharp nail rakes up the back of my neck.

"And yet you did anyway."

I swing the bottle and it grazes the brick wall.

"And you're trying to kill me. All I've done is talk. Humans are so full of it."

"Essen was an accident," I repeated. "I don't want to hurt you either, but I can't die."

A snicker comes from the exit stairs. I follow it with the bottle at the ready. "Oh, I'm not going to kill you, Jocelyn. That would be such a waste."

Just as I expected, the stairs are empty.

Fuloch's voice comes from behind me again. "Essen served a very important purpose, and you murdered him. You'll have to replace him, I'm afraid."

"What do you mean?" I already know I'll regret asking.

"You see, Essen got to drown all the poor saps he liked and I got the bodies afterward. I took care of all the evidence so long as he gave them to me fresh and full of blood. It was quite a nice setup. You get to be my new delivery girl."

"Go to hell," I snarl.

Fuloch cackles. "Well, if that's how you feel, I guess I'll just have to break something of yours to settle the debt. Your mother's a vegetable, so that leaves your darling sister or uncle."

My heart stops and my stomach turns to ice.

"Rick works with computers or something, right? And Annalise is what you call a *freshman* in high school, if I'm not mistaken."

How does he know that?

"You stay away from my family," I growl.

It doesn't sound like me. It's something primal, born out of terror and fury.

Fuloch cackles again. "I will, so long as you bring me a supply of blood by tomorrow at midnight. If not, I'll have to go out looking myself, and I know exactly where I'll start."

As his voice fades, I'm left alone. The heavy air of magic dissolves, but it leaves behind a sense of dread that threatens to bring me to my knees. After all the time I've spent on the paintings and everything I've endured from the queen and her court, my family is in danger again.

And I'm the one who put them there.

Seventeen

THE DOOR FLIES open behind me and the lights flicker on. I drop the bottle and shield my eyes against the flashlights bombarding the exit.

Rina bounds down the stairs and throws her arms around me. "Are you okay?"

I take advantage of the opportunity and hold her tight. Her warmth begins to melt the ice in my chest and the sharp smell of her perfume clears my head. "I'm fine," I mutter, "just weirded out."

"God, that was scary." She sighs, letting go and straightening my jacket for some reason. She catches herself, stops, and shoves her hands in her pocket. "I told Jun this was a bad idea."

The scarecrow from the entrance squats down and peers down at us, a crowbar in one hand. Jun, Brook, Travis, and a small gathering of visitors, many with cell phones ready to be dialed, look down with concern and curiosity.

"You all right, kid?" the scarecrow asks.

"I'm okay," I answer, following Rina out of the cellar and holding tight to her hand. "You guys really know how to put on a haunted house."

"That wasn't the house, Jocelyn," Rina explains with a frown.

"A fuse blew or something," Travis offers. "We were about to call the fire station."

Good thing they didn't. That would have slowed me down.

"No need. All good. Gotta go," I say, pushing through the crowd.

The scarecrow follows, fumbling with dollar bills and change. "Hey, don't you want a refund or something?"

I wave the money away. "Nah. It just added to the experience. Besides, someone paid for me, remember? No harm done, but I really need to leave."

The scarecrow stops and reluctantly turns back toward the house. "All right. If you're sure."

"You're not hurt, are you?" Brook calls as I get farther and farther away.

"Nope," I answer, pulling out my keys. "I did, however, get a very urgent text, so I gotta bolt." Waving to Rina and the others, I add, "I'll be in touch. Have fun."

The others hang back, but Rina follows on my heels and grabs the open car door.

"Jocelyn, are you really okay?" she demands.

The concern is touching, but I don't have time for it. "Of course."

"Given how much weird stuff keeps happening around you, I don't believe you," Rina huffs. "The nightclub. The guy at the theater. That door just now. It just flung itself shut, Jocelyn, and it wasn't exactly a screen door."

It's not like I can deny any of that. With a sigh, I get out of the car and look down at Rina, trying to figure out how to salvage this.

"It's my turn to put some cards on the table." I sigh. "Weird stuff *does* happen around me, but I can't tell you why. Not yet. Right now, I have to go deal with it. Afterward, if you don't think I'm a dangerous freak, I'll explain everything, okay?"

Rina bites her bottom lip as she thinks it over. "I don't think you're dangerous. I just want to know what's going on."

"You're awfully concerned for this being 'nothing serious,'" I tease.

Rina glances around and kicks at a pebble. "Yeah, well...maybe, now that I know you a little better, I'm rethinking that." She offers me her hand. "I'll let you know when I get an explanation. Deal?"

I take it and squeeze tight. "Deal." With Rina's hand still in mine, I quickly glance around, pull her closer, and kiss her on the forehead. As she stares up at me with a mix of shock and confusion, I say, "I owed you from earlier. Now, I really have to go."

Her friends cheer from the edge of the parking lot and she turns on them.

"Mind your own business," she shouts.

They just laugh harder. Even I manage to crack a smirk as I get in the car.

She looks back at me, mouth crinkled into a reluctant smile. Through the glass, I can make out, "Don't encourage them." I pull out of the parking lot with a wave and watch Rina watch me in the rearview mirror.

Faeries aside, I think she's the strangest thing to ever happen to me.

On the road, I get my head in the game and call Dominic.

He answers on the first ring. "What did you do?"

"First of all, don't be rude. Second of all, one of Essen's buddies is after my family."

There's a series of crashes, then Dominic sputters, "I'm heading to your former residence. I'll meet you there. Tell me everything."

I relay what happened in the basement as I fly down the highway. Once Dominic has all the information, he hangs up. Driving alone with all the possible outcomes swimming around my head is torture. There are too many cops on the road to speed, and the radio is just annoying background noise.

If Fuloch gets ahold of Anna...the idea and all it entails is too terrible to think about. Or what if he goes after Rick? What if Mom wakes up to find her daughter or brother—? I have to shake the thought out of my head. It'll make me sick if I dwell on it. To distract myself, I call Anna to let her know I'm on my way.

"You're coming home *and* calling twice in one day?" she teases. "Did you get abducted by aliens recently?"

"Anna, are you and Rick home?"

She stops short. "Yeah. Why?"

"I'm on my way over. I, um, need some of my art supplies."

"Well, we'll be here," Anna replies slowly. "Are you okay? You sound stressed."

"Group art project. One of the members has been slacking off, so I'm scrabbling to get it done," I lie. "No big deal."

"Oh, that sucks. See you soon."

Once Anna hangs up, I'm left with the worst silence imaginable. It presses in on me from all sides and makes me check the rearview mirror every few seconds, like I might find Fuloch sitting in the backseat, driving him to my family's doorstep.

In a way, I already have. I just hope it's not too late to keep him out.

The weight doesn't lift until I pull into the driveway. My headlights rest on Dominic and Calista, of all people. They melt into the shadows once I shut the car off. Even while standing right in front of them, it's hard to make them out against the dark paneling of the garage.

"What's she doing here?" I demand.

"*She* came to your aid due to the great debt *she* owes you," Calista huffs, lifting her hands to her hips. "You're welcome."

"Sorry. You're just not the fighting type."

"She won't be fighting," Dominic explains. "She'll be keeping tabs on your family once we set up a few protective charms."

"I don't want anyone in danger who doesn't need to be," I argue.

Calista rolls her eyes. "Too late. Since I'm the one that took the necklace, Fuloch would have come for me eventually. Might as well get some use out of it."

"Dominic and I can handle this."

"Damn it, Jocelyn, will you stop—"

The front door creaks open, flooding the driveway with light and dissolving the shadows where Dominic and Calista hide. Annalise pokes her head out, looking puzzled.

"Jocelyn? What are you doing?"

I face the bumper of my car and give it a quick scan. "Thought I hit something, but everything looks fine. False alarm."

Anna sighs. "Maybe you should slow down a bit."

I hop up the stairs and wrap my sister in a bear hug to distract her. "Nah. Then it would take longer to come see you."

She hugs me back, then pulls me into the entranceway of the house. The familiar smell of vanilla mixed with the scent of home-cooked food and the pictures on the wall throw off my sense of time. Even the furniture is exactly where I last saw it. For a moment, it feels like I never left home.

Little clues bring me down to earth. Mom's giant basket of yarn and knitting needles sit tucked behind her recliner instead of in it. The green-and-yellow summer throw pillows still decorate the sofa. Mom would have changed them to the red-and-orange autumn ones by now. Her bookshelf looks a bit dusty.

I take a deep breath and remind myself it's just a little longer. Soon, I'll take the painting to the queen, Mom will wake up, and everything will go back to normal.

"Rick's in the backyard, grilling," Anna tells me. "Why don't you go get your art supplies, and I'll go get him?" She heads for the back porch, and I slip into my old room.

I forgot how clean I left it. With everything neat and orderly, it doesn't look like my room. At least I don't have to hunt for the pastels I supposedly need for school.

A faint knock at the window makes my blood run cold. Seizing my old wooden bat, I turn, ready to take out Fuloch. Instead, I meet Dominic's eyes peeking over the windowsill, narrow with annoyance. I sigh and pull open the window.

"I know you're on edge," he chastises, "but that's no reason to bludgeon me."

"Sorry," I mutter, dropping the bat. "Everything okay?"

"Surprisingly, yes," he answers, surveying the strip of grass that leads to the backyard. "There are a few traces of magic, but none of it's malevolent. If Fuloch has been here, it's only been for surveillance. Once Calista and I get these spells up, he won't be able to touch any of you, queen's protection or no."

I drop on my bed with relief. "Thank God. Just be careful."

Dominic's mouth curves into a smug smirk. "Who do you think I am?"

Rick calls me before I can answer. "Jocelyn? Where'd you go?"

I pull the window shut and slip back out of my room just as Anna sits at the dinner table and Rick slides the porch door shut. "Hey, Uncle Rick."

"Hey, kiddo," he greets, setting the small plate of steaks on the table. "Still no David, huh?"

"He had to work late. Besides, I just needed to grab a few things."

"You'll stay for dinner, though, won't you?" Rick asks. He takes his usual seat at the table, and Anna sits across from him. Mom's spot sits vacant, but set, on the left. My place next to Anna is set too.

My sister looks up at me with puppy dog eyes, which I can never say no to, so I slide my chair out and plop down next to her. Maybe this will give Dominic and Calista more time.

"Thanks. I already ate, but I guess I could stay a minute."

"Good," Rick says, passing Anna the salad, "because I wanted to talk to you about this whole moving thing."

Should have seen that coming. Luckily, Rick waits for everyone to get food before starting with the questions. That gives me some time to gather my thoughts.

"What brought this on, exactly?" he asks, cutting up his steak.

"That art program wasn't that great after all," I reply, pushing around my green beans. "Besides, I'm not even sure if I want to go into an art-related field anymore. It doesn't seem practical."

Rick's expression goes somber. "You're not in trouble, are you?"

"No, of course not. When have I ever been in trouble?"

Anna snickers. I gently kick her under the table.

"How do you think that'll look to colleges, jumping around like that?"

"Community colleges won't mind. Besides, if they ask, I'll just explain what's been going on."

"The registrar offices haven't said anything?"

"Nope. Besides, it happens. Life circumstances change. I'm sure I'm not the first person to change schools during senior year."

Rick pauses midcut. "Jocelyn—"

"Besides, I'm still thinking about working a bit first to save up some money," I explain. "I've been doing some freelance art stuff and it's been going really well."

Rick puts down his fork and takes out his phone. "I'm calling David."

"No! Listen, Uncle Rick, I've got it under control."

"Really? Because it doesn't sound like it," Rick grumbles, attention still on his phone. "I should have been checking up on you more. What kind of uncle am I? And what the hell has David been doing? He should have been guiding you through all this."

"I can handle it."

"No, you can't. You're seventeen. You need someone to help you—"

"I don't want any help!" Somehow, I'm on my feet, fists on the table.

Rick lowers his phone. Annalise drops her fork.

"I don't *deserve* your help," I snap. "Don't you get it? I broke this family the day I hit that tree and hurt Mom. Just let me try to fix things on my own, okay?"

"And what would that look like exactly?" Rick fires back. "Your mother waking up? All her medical bills paid? Even if that happens, life won't be exactly like it was, Jocelyn. It doesn't work like that. Are you really going to let that chain you down for the rest of your life?"

His words stab me in the gut. The fact that I can't answer just twists the knife.

Movement outside catches my attention. Calista pokes her head up from underneath the porch. She gives me a dirt-covered thumbs-up.

"I'll get back to you on that." I grab the pastels and head for the door. Annalise follows.

"Why are you being such a jackass?" she shouts. "Rick's worried about you. *I'm* worried about you."

"I know that," I snap. "That's why I'm coming home. Things will get better."

Anna lets out a bitter guffaw of laughter. "Oh, yeah, sure," she spits. "Everything will be hunky-dory. The four months that I've had to spend dealing with Mom being gone *without you* will just evaporate!"

All I can do is stare at my sister. I can't give her the explanation she deserves. "I had to go away—"

"Just to give up your art program? Other than that, what exactly has abandoning us accomplished, Jocelyn?"

Anger flares up in my chest. I have to bite the inside of my lip to keep from spilling everything. Through my teeth, I manage to say, "I'll see you later, Anna."

She's not about to let up, though. "This is because of that stupid thing Dad always said, isn't it? About you needing to look out for us? You were thirteen, dumbass. How the hell are you supposed to—"

"What else do I have left from him, Anna?"

Those words weren't supposed to come out. Not ever.

The fury drains from Anna's face, leaving her wide eyes filled with tears.

That's how I have to leave her.

I can't bring myself to look at her as I get in the car and peel out of the driveway. I can't even look in the rearview mirror. The only thing that keeps me together is focusing on the road in front of me, but that only works for three blocks.

I pull into a grocery store parking lot and park hundreds of feet from the nearest car. A punch to the steering wheel breaks the dam, and I hold my head in my hands as months of frustration, anxiety, guilt, and hurt finally flow freely.

I've been bewitched, assaulted, blackmailed, and nearly killed repeatedly. My mother is in a coma from an accident I caused, my sister is furious with me, and my uncle is probably about to track me down and blow my cover sky high, and I've got blood on my hands. Rick's right. I'm not handling it. Not at all. I never was.

A tiny tap at the window drags me back to reality. I wipe my eyes and take deep breaths so my face isn't red, but I'm sure I still look a mess.

Dominic taps the glass again and beckons me out of the car.

"Hey, sorry." I step out of the car. "Things at the house got a bit heated so—"

Dominic grabs me by the shoulder and pulls me into a hug so tight I can't breathe. It throws me for such a loop that I'm not sure what I'd say if I could speak. He's as cold as Calista and the queen, but Dominic has a gentleness that neither of them had.

"I heard everything," he mutters, "and I think you're doing your best. I think that's all your father ever wanted."

My throat threatens to close again. I take deep breaths until it fades.

Letting me go, Dominic smiles and playfully punches me in the shoulder. "Now, chin up. Our work's not done yet."

"Right." I sniff. "If you're up for it, we should set up charms where my family spends most of their time. Anna's school, Rick's office, the hospital... And you need to be on the lookout for a call from Rick. He's starting to realize something's not right."

Dominic nods. "Right. I'm sure I can throw him off easily enough. And I'll make sure Shaylee alerts us as soon as Her Majesty returns."

"Good," I reply, hopping back in the car. "Because I needed to give her that painting four months ago."

Eighteen

BY THE TIME we finish Fuloch-proofing half of Northland, it's four in the morning, five by the time I drive up to the house, six thirty by the time I take Dominic's advice and fall asleep. Noon when Shaylee calls and tells us the queen is home.

"She's ready when you are," she says over the phone.

I jump out of bed and rake a comb through my hair. "How is she?" I ask.

"Not too bad, actually," she replies cheerfully. "That confrontation with the shapeshifters wiped her out, so you should be okay. I was going to ask Dominic to come with you, but she seems safe enough."

Turns out Dominic's not even awake. Setting up protective charms and spells must've taken so much out of him that he crashed on the couch instead of dragging himself to bed. I drape a quilt over him and leave a note on the kitchen table.

"If you don't think she's dangerous, I'm sure I'll be fine," I whisper to Shaylee. "I won't be there long anyway."

"That's true," Shaylee replies. "I'll catch up with you afterward. Bye."

I hang up, grab the painting, and go.

The horror of damaging it keeps me from running, but walking feels like moving in slow motion. The keep can't come into view soon enough. When it finally does, I find myself paralyzed with fear. What if the queen doesn't accept it? What if she finds some other way to hang Mom over my head? What if she tries to trap me again? There's no way of knowing until I stop panicking and just go.

A short, wispy faerie in ragged clothes greets me at the entrance.

"I'm to take you to Her Majesty," she squeaks. "She's feeling a bit under the weather and isn't holding audiences today, but she made an exception for you."

Strange. I didn't think faeries could get sick, especially the queen.

The keep stirs with its "morning" routine. Staff dashes here and there with fresh laundry, food, and knickknacks. Patrons roam the hall looking sleepy and spent from the night before as they prepare to do it all over again. It's unsettling how quiet and calm the place is. I didn't even realize quiet moments were possible in Faerie.

The servant leads me to the familiar jewel-encrusted door. It's as beautiful as I remember with its swirling patterns and lifelike movements, but something seems off. The jewels don't sparkle as bright. They're dull, as if covered with a fine layer of dust. Everything moves slower, like a wind-up toy losing momentum.

The servant gives a hesitant knock, distracting me from the door. "Your Majesty," she announces. "I've brought the human girl. She has the painting."

A faint "Let her in" barely makes it through the wood.

The servant looks from me to the door, gesturing with a small pushing motion. I take the hint and slip inside.

The room smells sour and stagnant, like illness. The only light comes from two candles on either side of the enormous bed where the queen sits with a steaming earth-colored mug in her hands. Her hair sits untouched in a dull ratty mess and her face looks worn. She wears nothing underneath her robe. Normally, I would assume that's on purpose, but judging by the rest of her, that's not the case today.

In the corner, Lyle busies himself at a small table covered with jars and small wooden boxes filled with herbs, spices, and fresh plants.

He turns off a small burner underneath a black kettle and says, "It's ready whenever you need it, Majesty."

"Thank you, Lyle," the queen says softly. "Leave us for a moment, please."

The champion tidies up a bit, then glares at me as he leaves. The queen's gaze falls on me, but I don't risk speaking until Lyle shuts the door behind him.

"I've brought the final painting, Your Majesty," I say softly, afraid to disrupt the strange stillness.

The queen makes it more unsettling as she sighs. "I'm so sick of being called that. My name is Mab."

Did she hit her head while she was gone? Or is it whatever is in that mug?

"Um...okay. Well, I've brought the last painting all the same." I unwrap the canvas and bring it closer so that the dim light can catch it.

The queen, Mab, lets out a small gasp as she reaches out to it. She traces her painted copy's white dress with distant eyes, then brushes over the pixie, human child, and mermaid in turn. With a wry smile, she looks at me.

"This is your best painting yet. I should have threatened you months ago." She chuckles.

I'm not stupid enough to argue, but I don't laugh either.

Under her breath, so quiet that I almost miss it, she murmurs, "This is who I wanted to be, you know?"

"What happened?" slips out of my mouth before I can stop it.

Mab sighs and brings her hand to the amulet hanging around her neck. "It grew to be too much, but it's too much to throw off now." She shakes her head and motions to a velvet armchair across the room. "Lay it there. I'll have someone put it with the others."

I do, then return to her side. She pats a spot on the bed next her, and I hesitantly take the seat. Months of experience tell me not to, but she seems so frail and small that I can't see her as a real threat right now. Mab sits up straighter and takes my hands in hers. I shiver at her touch. It's not the usual refreshing coolness. Her hands are like freezing, biting ice.

"Jocelyn Mae Lennox," she says, locking her gaze with mine. "You have done as I asked and fulfilled our agreement to my liking. You are released from our contract. Your mother is healed in both body and mind."

There's a spark of heat in my chest. It's far from the searing blaze that gave me the queen's mark. It's more like a hot spring rather than an inferno, washing away Mab's nightshade symbol and the anxiety that has eaten at me for months. I let out a breath I didn't realize I was holding.

I fixed it. I really fixed it. I can go home. Now to get out of here before Mab snaps back to her normal self.

"Thank you, Your Maj—Mab," I say, pulling my hands away and getting to my feet. "Now, if you'll excuse me, I'd like to get home and see my family. I hope you feel better soon."

"We both know that's a lie."

I stop with my hand on the doorknob, then turn back to face the queen. "Can you blame me if it is?"

She tilts her head to the side with a coy smirk. It makes a different fire burn in my chest. One I've tried to smother for fear of the damage it could do, but no more.

"You've threatened to let my mother waste away. You've tried to trap me here. You've tried to use magic to make me do God knows what. You've tried to outright kill me. You killed your own sister." My voice gets louder with every new offense and my hands start to shake. "Maybe I want you to suffer for a while."

Mab shakes her head. "You would have loved living at court after all."

"Shut up! You're a faerie. I get it. You think differently from humans, but does it ever occur to you how sick of an individual you are?"

"Every day for the last one hundred years."

I stop short of throwing another barb.

Mab brings one hand to her amulet, eyes distant and unfocused. The gesture reminds me of what Shaylee said about the queen's role and how the magic is wearing her down.

Whatever. I'm not wasting any sympathy on this woman.

With a sigh, Mab leans back against the headboard and lets herself stare out into the past. "As if magic itself didn't strangle me enough, the guilt of what I've done and what it's cost me threatens to swallow me whole..." She trails off and looks at me with a tired grin. "Surely you know the feeling?"

I don't give the question time to settle. "Why are you telling me all this?"

Mab chuckles. "Because, now that I can think clearly, I realize that we're the same." Her smile turns wry. "We both tried to save the world. We lifted it onto our backs because we thought it would be safer there. In return, it's trying to crush us."

My rage freezes into terror.

"I'm nothing like you," I snarl.

Something crashes outside the door. Mab goes pale. She scurries out of bed like a startled animal and pushes me aside.

Opening the door a crack, she peers into the hall. "Has she come for me?" she hisses, eyes narrow and shifting. "I don't see her. Do you? Or have they come for us? Have they come from the water? They always come from the water."

Mab's gone. Her Majesty has returned.

She pulls me down and makes me look through the crack. All I see is a maid looking around nervously as she picks up the pieces of a shattered vase.

"There's no one coming, Your Majesty," I answer.

"Figures," she scoffs, beginning to scratch at her forearms. "She crawled back into my skin. She wouldn't come down the hall. She's too clever for that. Always was too clever. It must be too soon for them. Lucky us. Too soon."

I try to harden my heart against the way she anxiously paces the room, but it's impossible. To be torn apart from the inside day in and day out like this must be hell on earth, even after everything she's done. She hadn't been sick moments ago. She had been the closest to healthy I'd ever seen her.

Still, this would be a good place not to be.

"Majesty, I have to leave. Get...better soon."

Mab slams the door shut, nearly catching my fingers.

"Is this really how you want to leave?" The queen giggles. Spreading her robe open with one hand, she pins me to the door with the other. "Lyle's little concoction didn't work, so I need another way to forget." She leans forward and whispers, "And I know you want to forget too."

It starts. The familiar dizziness, the need to have those hands on me.

Someone bangs on the door behind me. It sounds miles away.

All I can stutter is "I-I don't know w-what you—"

"Just because you fixed this doesn't mean it's gone. Everything's still eating at you. I can see it in your eyes," Mab whispers, sliding her hand down my chest. "Don't you want to forget?"

I do. I want to forget. I want to forget the fear of Anna and Rick finding out the truth. The worry that Mom might resent me for what I did to her. The way I killed Essen.

But if this is what it costs, I'd rather let it eat at me for the rest of my life.

I take Mab by both her wrists and shove her away. She sprawls back, trips on the hem of her robe, and lands at the foot of her bed. The queen stares at me with wide, panicked eyes, then cradles her head in her hands.

"Nothing works," she moans. "No matter what I do...no matter what I take, nothing lets me forget. Not for long."

"Maybe that's not what you need to do then," I mutter.

She lifts her gaze to me as Lyle bursts through the door.

He pins me to the nearest post of the queen's bed, sword to my neck. "What did you do?" he demands, fury burning in his eyes.

"Let her go, Lyle," Mab orders. "She didn't do anything. Your potion wore off. Go try another one."

Lyle lets me go with a scowl, then stomps back over to his table.

"You should leave," Mab tells me.

"Yeah," I scoff, heading for the door. "That sounds like a good idea."

"But, Jocelyn?" the queen calls, voice calm and controlled.

I force myself to wait.

"If you learn what I need to do, come and find me."

I just nod. I'm not wasting any more breath on the Queen of Faerie. Mom's healed and I'm free.

It's nearly impossible not to run out of the keep, but the last thing I need is more trouble. Even by quickly walking, I draw some attention. Or maybe it's the huge grin on my face. Once I'm out of the keep, Faerie becomes a blur as I dash through the woods.

Once the colors dull and the air takes on its normal mugginess, I sprint across the field outside the old farmhouse, propelled purely by excitement. I make it halfway across before my phone rings. It's a video call from Annalise.

"Hey, Jocelyn." She laughs, eyes red with tears. "Someone wants to see you."

I know what's coming and it freezes me. My brain can't find the words to tell Anna to wait, that I'm not prepared for this moment I've waited for. What am I supposed to say?

She takes my silence as a "go-ahead" and flips the camera view.

It blurs, then shows my mother in her hospital bed. She's as still as always, but her eyes are open and she's smiling. "Good morning, sunshine," she whispers. "Sorry, I overslept."

The legs I just used to sprint can't hold me up anymore. I fall into the tall grass, eyes blurry and throat closed.

"Uh-oh, did you break her?" Anna teases. She flips the camera, and her mouth falls open. "Oh, my God! Are you crying? You never cry."

"Shut up. I'm not crying, you're crying." I sniff, trying not to laugh. "Let me see Mom again." The camera flips. "Hi, Mom. Sorry about that."

Mom's smile widens, and she shifts to look at me better. "It's okay, baby." Her eyebrows pull together. "Where are you? Rick said you're living with your father's brother?"

"Yeah, but I'm coming home soon. Right now I'm just...out and about. What about you? How do you feel? How long have you been up?"

"About an hour or so," she answers. "And I've felt better. Muscular atrophy is a bitch."

Both Anna and I crack up, slaphappy with joy.

"So, that's where Anna gets it from." I laugh, wiping my eyes.

"I get it from you and you know it, butthead," Anna fires back.

"You both get it from me." Mom chuckles. "Sorry."

I take a deep breath. "No, Mom, I'm sorry. For everything."

Mom does her best to shake her head. "Honey, no. You—"

Rick's voice comes off screen. "Anna, the doctors need to get in here. They said they won't be long."

"Okay. Sorry, Jocelyn, but we need to pop out for a minute," Anna says.

I wave at Mom and wipe my face again. "See you soon. Love you."

"Bye, sweetheart," she says. "Love you even more."

Anna keeps me online as she slips out of the room and walks down the hall. Rick calls after her, but I can't make out his words.

"It's private sibling stuff," she replies. She stops once she reaches an empty stairwell, turns back to the phone, and looks me dead in the eye. "What did you do?"

"What did you mean?" I ask, playing dumb.

"I mean you had something to do with this," Anna says. "Mom's condition hasn't changed in months, but suddenly, after your little rant about fixing things last night, she's awake and acting normal."

I shake myself out of my emotional haze and focus on lying. "How do you know anything I did worked?"

"I don't know. It's this feeling I have like I'm missing something," she whispers, eyes filling with tears again. "Jocelyn, I'm so sorry I yelled at you last night. I just—"

I'm done feeling emotions for about a month, so I cut Anna off. "No, you were right. I'm a jackass. I shouldn't have left you and Rick."

The sound of footsteps puts a fake smile on Anna's face for a moment. As soon as they're gone, she sniffs and wipes her cheeks. "When you get home, we're going to talk, but thank you, Jocelyn, for saving our mother."

"I have no idea what you're talking about."

Anna rolls her eyes and hangs up.

Once the screen goes black, I fall back and stare up at the sky. The world looks brighter and the air smells cleaner. My body feels weightless. Mom's awake. I'm free.

My phone rings again, startling me out of my reverie. It's Rina.

I sit up and answer it. "Rina, hey. What's up?"

A dreadfully familiar voice snickers. "Oh, nothing much. She's had better days."

I almost drop the phone in shock.

"Why the silent treatment?" Fuloch cackles. "Did you think I was kidding?"

Nineteen

"GOOD IDEA HAVING that knight protect your family." Fuloch cackles. "I had fun thinking of an alternative. Good thing you've got a girlfriend, am I right?"

"What did you do to Rina?" I demand.

"Nothing yet. Frankly, I don't want to do anything to her. She's almost as big of a pain in the ass as you, but I meant what I said. I need blood and I need a new supplier, thanks to you."

"I'm not doing your dirty work, you bastard!"

"No? I guess I'll just have to drain her dry then."

"You so much as touch her and I'll kill you." My words scare me almost as much as Fuloch does. They can't be mine. This can't be my voice.

"Oh, I'm sure you'll try." Fuloch snickers. "But not before I get my fix from your girl. Here's a better idea: bring me a replacement by midnight like I told you."

I can't find the right words for my rage, both toward Fuloch and myself. My shaking grip threatens to crush the phone before the redcap finishes talking.

"You know that old paper mill on the other side of the railroad tracks? Of course you do. It's right down the road from that quaint little shop you work at. Bring a replacement for Rina to that mill by midnight, and I promise not to hurt her. Think you can handle that?"

"Yeah," I answer, my mouth like sandpaper. "Yeah, I can handle that."

"Good. Now, if I were you, I'd grab someone who won't be missed. You might have to drive over to a bigger city. Extra points if you can grab a runaway teenager."

I resist the urge to hurl the phone across the field.

"Twice the extra points if it's a girl. Ah, who am I kidding? You're new at this. I don't want to put too much pressure on you. See you tonight."

The line goes dead.

I take off for the farmhouse. My feet hardly touch the ground. The sooner I tell Dominic, the sooner I can get to Fuloch and wring his neck. I bound up the porch and burst into the kitchen. Shaylee drops her mug and it shatters on the floor. Dominic leaps to his feet.

I yank open the knife drawer. "Fuloch has Rina."

Dominic pales. "Are you sure? It could be a trick."

"He called me from Rina's number. I'm sure," I bark, starting a pile on the table.

"Jocelyn, stop." Dominic grabs me by the arm.

"I can't stop. I have to save her!"

"With your arsenal of kitchenware?" Dominic shoots back. "You can't do anything useful unless you calm down."

"Yelling at her isn't going to calm her down," Shaylee snaps, prying us apart. Looking to me, she says, "Breathe and tell us exactly what happened."

They're both right. All I'm going to do is get Rina and myself killed. Pacing the kitchen, I relay the phone call and how I have until midnight to find a substitute for Rina. Dominic perches silently on the counter, eyes fixed on the linoleum as he strokes his chin and listens.

When he finally speaks, his gaze shifts from the floor to me. "You can't go alone."

"If you come, he'll know I'm not bringing a replacement. He'll kill her."

"Don't worry. He won't see me," Dominic replies, getting up and walking toward his room. "The others might be a different story."

"Who do you mean by 'others'?"

"Hob, Calista, Iver, and a few friends who owe me favors."

"And me," Shaylee chimes in.

Dominic pauses just outside his door. "Highness, is that wise?"

"Fuloch is planning on killing a human on Seelie lands," she explains. "And if Jocelyn's story is true, he and Essen have been poaching humans for years."

"There are no *Seelie* lands anymore," Dominic mutters bitterly. "Her Majesty saw to that."

"But the laws are still on the books. The queen just never enforces them. If I can hold some sway, maybe everyone can walk away from this alive."

Dominic frowns. "It's been well established that the solitary folk care little for Her Majesty's authority. How do you think this whole mess got started?"

Rolling her eyes, Shaylee reaffirms, "That's why I said *maybe*. This guy might not be so tough once he finds out the crown is on to him."

Dominic gives a small bow. "If you insist, Your Highness. Go with Jocelyn to the Time Between. I will meet you there once I contact the others."

Shaylee follows me to the car, much to my surprise.

"Iron doesn't bother me. It's one of the many perks of being half-human," she explains as she fiddles with the radio. "Comes in handy quite a bit."

If I wasn't peeling out of the driveway, I might be interested, but there are more pressing things to deal with at the moment. "When I get ahold of that bastard..." I growl, leaving the thought open on purpose. There are too many appealing options. Too many of them startle me with just how violent they are.

"Hey, don't worry about him," Shaylee says. "Focus on getting Rina out. You should leave Fuloch to us. Essen was more than enough. Even with the paintings done, you shouldn't risk it."

She's right. It would suck to be out of the woods, only to trip and land in shark-infested waters.

By the time we arrive, Dominic and the others are already there. Along with the folk I know, there are four new faces: two green-skinned pixies and the two men that came to the Novel Spell to see Mr. Hob, one with a blond streak and one with a bunch of piercings. Now that they stand next to Iver, I figure they must be elves like him.

Everyone pauses their conversation as Shaylee and I join them. Calista breaks away and nearly knocks me over with a hug.

"I'm so sorry," she cries. "I should have watched your dear Rina as well."

"It's not your fault," I say, peeling her off. "This one's all on me."

"We can worry about blame later," Dominic says, handing out small woven strips of what looks like leather with vines and leaves twisted in. "Right now, we need to take care of Fuloch." As he hands the strangers the charms, he introduces them. "Jocelyn, this is Kole, Kellen, Brok, and Warren."

"Pleased to finally make your acquaintance," Kole, one of the pixies, says with a bow. "We've heard a lot about you."

"Also pleased to get rid of Fuloch," says Kellen, the other pixie. "Infuriating little git, isn't he?"

"Where is it you said he's keeping your Rina?" Brok, the elf with the blond streak, asks.

"The old paper mill," I answer. "Probably picked this side of town because of all the iron. He didn't think anyone could follow me."

"And that's what these are for," Dominic says, motioning to the charms. "Calista, Jocelyn, Warren, come with me. We need to see how hard it will be to get in and out. Where would be a good place to rendezvous once we're done?"

I rack my brain, trying to think of the layout of the area. "There's an abandoned lot just down the street from the mill on Posy Road."

"That should be far enough away. Hob, Brok, Kole, Kellen, meet us there. I'm not sure how long we'll be."

We all agree and head out. I offer to drive my party, but they all cringe at the idea of being in the car, even with their charms. Instead, Shaylee drives it to the rendezvous point while I set out on foot with the others.

"How much does the girl know?" Warren, the elf with the piercings, asks on the way.

"Not much," I answer. "I figured that would keep her safe, but I was wrong."

"If it wasn't for Fuloch, she would have been safe," Calista says. "And we could always erase her memory later."

"No one is touching Rina's memory," I argue. Silently I wonder if it may be a good idea. We'll figure that out later.

I come to a stop and block the others' path before they run out into plain view of the mill. Dominic and I peek around the corner and size up the building.

He motions to the broken window above us, and we slip inside one by one. From the windows, we survey the first floor as best we can. At first, it seems empty, but gradually tiny faces the color of wet soil become visible, poking through the windows. Their beady eyes scan the area from behind wispy, rootish hair before sinking back into the dark.

"Boggles," Dominic mutters. "That's a relief." Clapping me on the shoulder, he adds, "For once, I'm glad my kind underestimates you."

I let the potential insult slide. "What's a boggle?"

"A measly little solitary faerie," Calista scoffs. "They enjoy taking up residence in human homes and causing trouble. They usually get themselves mistaken for mundane hauntings, but with enough spite and anger, they can turn quite nasty."

"Not nasty enough to be threat," Warren mutters.

"Let's not assume that just yet," Dominic replies. "We need to be thorough."

The second floor doesn't have as many boggles, but we can see Fuloch as clear as day. He paces around the center of the gutted floor, occasionally glancing at the windows as if someone might swoop in at any moment. Rina sits nearby, leaning against a support beam with her head lolled to the side, unconscious.

My hands clench to fists against the dusty concrete. We should just take him out now, but the third floor has quite a few boggles. Only five patrol the roof with their long scrawny legs permanently bent and their clawed fingers brushing the floor. They look nasty enough, but like Warren said, not much of a threat. Still, the less mess we make, the less likely one of us gets hurt.

"So, what do you think, Jocelyn?" Dominic asks as we slip out of the building.

I do a double take and nearly trip. "Me?"

"It's your rescue mission."

Warren gives him a doubtful look that I have to agree with.

I take a few deep breaths and think it over. "The less we do, the better, I think. I want to see Fuloch pay, but like Shaylee said, I don't want to cross the queen again." I pace the sidewalk for a moment. "Shaylee and I go in and try to be diplomatic first. If that doesn't work"—Calista catches my eye—"we pretend to give him what he wants. Whoever pretends to be the victim has to be able to take Fuloch out as soon as we're out of there."

Calista raises her hand but tucks it behind her back as Dominic scowls at her.

"I'll take that job," Dominic says. "I don't want you in there any longer than you have to be and I'm particularly gifted with glamours."

"Can't argue with him there." Warren sighs. "But what if it goes wrong?"

"That's where everyone else comes in," I continue. "You guys take out surveillance above and give us a signal. We'll send another if things go wrong and we need you to break us out. Create a distraction and deal with the boggles while we get Rina out."

ЕЕ.

"Sounds like it could work," Calista says.

"I wish I could do more," I grumble.

Dominic pats me on the shoulder. "No worries. You're doing plenty."

"Let's just hope your friend is as resilient as you are," Warren says.

Rina is. I know she is. It's how she'll react afterward that really has me worried.

We find the others in the lot, pacing and whispering among themselves. They relax a bit when we come around the corner, but their faces quickly turn to alarm and confusion. When I turn and see Dominic lagging behind, I see why.

Where the faerie knight once stood now stands a tall blonde woman wearing next to nothing and a pair of heels. How that tube top and tiny skirt don't rip can only be explained by magic. They both clearly defy the laws of physics.

I can't help but laugh. "I think you went a little overboard."

"Go big or go home." Dominic sighs loftily, flipping his mane of blonde waves. "Isn't that a human saying?"

"You certainly went big," Mr. Hob mutters, mesmerized by the sway of Dominic's new figure.

Shaylee snaps her fingers. "Hey, pervs, focus. What's the plan?"

Everyone huddles in a circle while I relay the plan. We decide that the signal from the roof team will be a simple blinking light. If the plan falls apart, I'll light a cigarette. Mr. Hob will relay the signal for us, watching from across the street. They all seem on board with the plan but disappointed.

"It should work, but it's so boring," Kellen groans.

"We're not here to be entertained," Dominic reminds him. "Now, let's get into position. And, Jocelyn, do me a favor."

"Anything."

He scowls. "Drive with the windows of your accursed automobile down."

And so, seemingly alone, Dominic, Shaylee, and I drive toward the old mill and wait for the signal from down the street. As we sit in silence, reality begins to settle in. My hand shakes and steady breathing takes conscious effort thanks to all the disastrous scenarios running through my head. Fuloch could have done something to Rina already. He could kill her in the middle of the rescue. One of the others might get hurt or even die.

"Dominic, do faeries believe in an afterlife?" I ask.

With his head hanging out the window, he answers, "Most do. I've never given it that much thought, though." A tired smile comes to his made-up lips. "After a few hundred years, the idea of a life after this one starts to feel greedy."

Wonderful. Just the comfort I was looking for.

The last slice of sunlight fades in the west, and a light flickers from atop the mill. With a deep breath, I put the car into drive and pull up to the nearest door. Dominic stumbles out as if he's intoxicated. I can't tell if it's because of the iron or his high-heeled shoes.

"This is a strange place for a party," he slurs, startling both me and Shaylee with a stereotypical valley girl voice.

"Well, it'll be a strange party," I answer, taking him by the arm and guiding him to the door. "It's almost Halloween, after all."

"I love Halloween, don't you? It's so fun." Dominic giggles, leaning on me and making me stumble.

"Yeah," I gripe, steadying him. "Loads."

Dozens of tiny black eyes watch us as we enter the mill. Their small wiry bodies dart this way and that, whispering, growling, and cackling as they fade into the night and reappear in the weak light from the broken windows. Two grab me by my pant leg and drag me up the stairs. Their claws catch in the fabric. They poke at Dominic, but don't dare touch Shaylee. When I work up the courage to look one in the eye, it smiles back with a wide grin filled with jagged teeth.

Voices whisper from every dark hiding place. A few mutter Shaylee's name, curious about what she could be doing here. Pebbles dart across the floor and shapes move out of the corner of my eye. I can see why they're mistaken for ghosts.

In the middle of the second floor, Fuloch stands with Rina just behind him, her hands bound behind a support beam. She looks up at the sound of our footsteps. A dark bruise spreads along her left cheekbone. Cuts and scratches dot her body. The sight of them tints my vision with red.

If I'm not careful, I just might toss the plan and kill Fuloch here and now.

It would probably be easy enough. His skin looks ashen and his cheeks are hollow as if he's already wasting away, but a light comes to his eyes at the sight of us. He stands a little taller and straightens his beanie, which looks ragged and dull.

"Jocelyn?" Rina murmurs, her eyes still fuzzy and unfocused.

"This doesn't look like a party," Dominic whines.

"We're early," I answer.

Fuloch snickers. "Indeed you are. But, then again, I imagine you want to get this over with." He folds his arms and lets us get within a few yards. "That's close enough." His gaze darts to Shaylee. "Princess? To what do I owe such a pleasure?"

"You're currently threatening the life of a human within the lands of the Seelie Court," she hisses. "I had hoped to show you reason."

"The Seelie Court is dead, Your Highness, and a deal's a deal," Fuloch snaps, narrowing his eyes. "And I haven't touched a drop of the girl's blood, so you can't nail me for poaching just yet."

Shaylee glares at him. A lot of help she turned out to be.

"Jocelyn, what's going on?" Rina asks, voice shaking.

"Why is she tied up?" Dominic giggles, pointing at Rina and leaning against me. "Is it a game?"

As Fuloch looks over Dominic, his sharp-toothed grin spreads from ear to ear. "You could say that. Want to play?"

"Sure. I'm not much good at games, though."

"Oh, don't worry, love. You can leave everything to me."

Rina cringes and does her best to get to her feet. "Jocelyn, I asked you a question. What the hell is going on here?"

"I'll explain later. Just let me handle this."

"And what is *this* exactly?"

Fuloch raises an eyebrow. "It's not obvious? Your sweetheart here is making a trade. I personally think she's downgrading, but whatever."

"Keep running your mouth, and I'll be leaving with your tongue, too," I growl.

"I'd like to see you try, girly." Fuloch snickers. "But we can play that game another day. The sooner you hand over that girl, the sooner we can stop getting on each other's nerves."

I hold tight to Dominic. "Let Rina go first."

Fuloch's face falls a bit. "You're in no position to make demands, Jocelyn."

"Given your condition, neither are you," I snap. "Let. Her. Go."

Fuloch gives an absentminded wave. A boggle shimmies up the beam and locks its claws around Rina's neck. She gags and wheezes as she tries to breathe.

My heart nearly breaks through my ribs.

"Redcap, I would let the human go if I were you," Shaylee hisses. "You are standing dangerously close to a line you don't want to cross."

"Give me the girl, then," Fuloch demands.

I look up at Dominic, hoping for silent reassurance, but he continues to play the dazed drunk girl. He just cocks his head to the side. There's no time to look closer. I shove him toward Fuloch, who catches him with all-too-open arms. With a snap of his fingers, the boggle lets Rina go.

"When I get out of this, you're dead," Rina gasps.

Fuloch looks to Dominic, who shifts uncomfortably. "Good thing you're not going anywhere then." He snickers.

Time halts.

My mouth goes dry. "What did you say?"

"You heard me," Fuloch says with a sneer. "I'm not letting Rina go."

Twenty

MY PULSE POUNDS in my ears and my hands begin to shake. The only way to calm them would be to wrap them around Fuloch's neck. "We had a deal," I shout. "I bring a replacement, you let Rina go."

"Do it, Fuloch," Shaylee barks. "If you don't honor this agreement—"

"The agreement was that she would *stay safe* if Jocelyn brought a replacement. I never said I would let her go," Fuloch chuckles. "Clearly she left that part out." He passes Dominic off to a few boggles, and they keep him pinned where he stands. Dominic gives a few yanks as if trying to break free, but gives up.

"You finished the paintings, correct?" Fuloch says. "So, the queen doesn't have any hold over you. That gives you plenty of time to bring me more people like our friend here." He gestures to Dominic.

"Redcap, that is a very bad idea," Shaylee hisses. Her eyes darken and the softness of her face melts away. For the first time, she truly looks like a faerie. "You don't want this to go any further."

"You don't scare me, changeling," Fuloch snarls. "Even if you call the queen, what makes you think she'll help? When has she ever helped a human?"

"I'm the one you should worry about, not the queen."

"You wish." With a snap of Fuloch's fingers, a boggle shimmies up the support beam again. Rina pulls at her ropes, craning her neck to avoid the creature's eyes. "You want the girl? Bring me more people."

"Jocelyn, don't you dare," Rina orders, eyes sharpened with anger.

As Fuloch hushes her with a hiss, I take a deep breath and pull out a cigarette. The sight of it makes Fuloch scowl, but he doesn't protest me lighting it.

I breath deep, focusing on the heat and smoke in my lungs to calm down. I sigh, letting go of the smoke in one lazy puff. "Fine. You win. What do you want? More blondes? Brunettes? What's your type?"

"Jocelyn, do you hear yourself?" Rina exclaims.

Whirling with one hand raised, as if to hit her, Fuloch barks, "Another word out of you and so help me—"

"Touch her and you can get the rest of the victims yourself," I snap. Glancing around at the boggles, I smugly add, "Judging by all the hired help, that's getting harder for you, isn't it?"

Fuloch's eyes narrow into a scowl that threatens to turn me to stone. Before he can throw another threat, a giant *thud* from above shakes the ceiling, showering everyone in concrete dust. A chorus of shrieking boggles makes my blood run cold. Judging by the way Dominic goes stiff and Rina's face pales, they feel the same way.

"What's going on up there?" Fuloch bellows, face turning crimson with fury.

The mill goes silent. Every muscle in my body is wound so tight that I'm afraid something might snap.

Fuloch looks around at his boggles, their ears flat against their heads like cats.

"Keep an eye on them," he snaps, pointing to everyone in turn. "If they try anything"—he jabs his finger in my direction—"kill her. Be a bit more tactful with the others. I need those girls, and we don't want to hurt the queen's changeling brat."

Looking at me again, he says, "Wait just a moment, won't you?"

I nod and take another drag on the cigarette to calm my nerves.

With Fuloch gone, Rina dares to speak again. "Jocelyn, tell me this isn't real."

For the first time since we got here, I look her in the eye. Her strongest expression is disbelief. It shows through her wide eyes, her eyebrows pull together and her mouth turned down in a thin, pursed line.

"I would, but I'm a terrible liar," I mutter.

"But you're not really going to sacrifice people to this sicko, are you?" she pleads. "You wouldn't do that. That's not who you are."

"You hardly know me," I remind her, "How do you know who I am?"

Rina's eyes dart over my face and her expression eases. "You saved me and my friends from that club. You waited with me. You *listened* to me and you never demanded anything in return and you let me be me. You're incredibly kind, patient, and considerate. I've never felt as safe as I do when I'm with you, even if your jokes need some work."

The cigarette falls out of my hand. I have no idea what I expected her to say, but it certainly wasn't that.

"If you two are done—" Dominic sighs, his usual attitude bleeding through the valley-girl voice. "—could we get on with this?"

Instead of waiting for an answer, he draws a sword from his ridiculously short skirt. It's all glamour and magic, but that doesn't make the sight any less startling. I nearly miss the second sword he tosses to me. The boggles seem just as shocked. They stand around for a moment, unsure how to respond to such a bizarre development, which proves to be too long.

In one swipe, Dominic lops off the heads of three boggles. Their bodies crumple to the ground, splattering the floor with blood. The sight of their decapitated comrades send the others into a frenzy, claws and razor teeth bared. Shaylee draws her own blade and jumps into the fray. She and Dominic prove to be a good distraction, giving me enough time to dive behind Rina and begin sawing at her ropes with the sword.

"This can't be real," Rina whispers frantically. "There's no way this is real."

"Sorry, but it's very real," I pant.

The boggles turn on me, the easier target, which stops me from freeing Rina. Dominic hasn't tutored me in how to use a sword in weeks, but the boggles are easy enough to deal with. Thankfully, they back off once they're injured. As nasty as they are, I can't kill them. I can't take any more blood on my hands.

The sound of a similar struggle comes from above. Hopefully all the noise will keep Fuloch both busy and oblivious, but I can't worry about that now. I have to get back to Rina. My efforts meet the sharp pain of teeth and claws sinking into my skin. One grazes my throat from behind before being suddenly yanked away.

An angry grunt comes over the boggles. "Oh, no you don't. That's my best employee, you sots." Mr. Hob bashes the boggle into the floor and gives its limp body a kick.

"Where did you come from?" I gasp, sawing at Rina's ropes again.

"You're welcome," Mr. Hob wheezes. He swings his thick fists, taking out the few remaining boggles. "The others got the message, so I thought I'd check on you."

Just as I say, "Thank you," Rina's ropes snap. She propels herself off the support beam and knocks me over with a hug. Her grip is so tight that I can't breathe, but it's worth it.

"I knew you wouldn't let that creep win," she whispers.

"Guess I'm a terrible liar after all," I chuckle. "How'd he get to you anyway?"

"He showed up on campus looking like you," Rina explains, getting to her feet. "Said he wanted to talk. Like an absolute idiot, I went on a walk with him. Once I realized it wasn't you, he had a bunch of his little minions jump me."

"How did you figure it out?"

The others gather around us to listen.

With so many eyes on her, Rina begins to fidget. "Let's just say he came on way too strong. Promise you'll let me wring his neck before doing whatever it is you do to homicidal vampires."

"He's a redcap, a type of faerie, not a vampire," Dominic retorts, apparently insulted by the mix-up. "And I invite you to get in line." He looks like himself again finally.

"Can we please decide who gets to string Fuloch up later?" Shaylee asks. "We're dealing with a very small window of time here."

A crowd of boggles appears at the door and sounds the alarm.

"Looks like it's already closing," Dominic mutters, bracing himself for the onslaught.

Shaylee follows behind him with her sword at the ready and me and Rina behind her. Mr. Hob brings up the rear. Together, we charge the swarm of boggles and make it to the door with everyone relatively unscathed. Dominic disappears around the corner and down the steps, only to bolt back up.

"New plan," he shouts. "Other way."

As he shoves us up the stairs, I peek over my shoulder. A flood of boggles rises up from the shadows. There's so many that they fall over one another to get to us. Everyone takes the stairs two at a time, though Mr. Hob curses every step he takes. The pressure from Dominic's hands disappears from my shoulders. As I keep running, I hear a string of words in an unfamiliar language so quiet that I almost miss them. As we reach the third floor, the sound of the boggles grows distant and is replaced by the sound of another struggle.

We're on the floor long enough to spot Fuloch and what's left of his boggles taking on Iver and the others. Through the fray, he spots me. Judging by the bloodlust in his eyes, I have point two seconds before he comes for me, regardless of what or who stands in his way.

As we sprint up the final staircase, a cry of rage follows. We tumble through the door to the roof and wait for Shaylee and Dominic before slamming it shut and standing against it.

"What about everyone else?" I wheeze. If we make it out of this, I swear I'll quit smoking for good.

"They'll be fine," Dominic pants. "This beautiful mess behind us is the real problem. I never imagined he had this many boggles."

The door jolts against our backs repeatedly. Rina, Shaylee, and Mr. Hob pitch in as the door jumps again.

"Someone needs to get Rina out of here," I order.

"No, they don't," Rina snaps. "I owe that psycho a beating." Scrawny arms squirm through the doorway, clawing at her hair and clothes.

"We don't have time to argue. You can't fight these things."

"You need to leave with her," Dominic retorts. "Your family needs you."

"And we need her here," Shaylee argues.

"Why? She'll only get himself in trouble."

"You saw Fuloch," I remind him. My shoes grind against the floor as the boggles make some progress. "He's not going to stop. He'll follow me. I'm armed. Rina isn't."

"Then give me a sword," Rina orders. "I'm not moving."

Mr. Hob growls, "You two are perfect for each other. You're equally frustrating." and hoists Rina over his shoulder. He takes off across the roof toward the fire escape with Rina protesting and struggling the whole way.

"Put me down, you troll," she shouts. "Jocelyn, stop him."

"I owe you one, Mr. Hob," I call.

Rina shouts at him the entire length of the roof, and probably the length of the fire escape, but I can't hear her over the swarm of angry boggles that have practically broken down the door.

Dominic and I lock eyes. Instead of arguing, he nods. If he can't get rid of me, he'll at least have my back. I return the gesture. He counts to three, and then everyone leaps away from the door.

The swarm spills out into the roof like a thundercloud.

Even with the advantages of my height and the sword, I can barely fend the boggles off. For every one I manage to injure, five more bite and claw at me. Through the sea of black, I spot a flash of red and obsidian eyes.

"Jocelyn is mine," Fuloch bellows.

The boggles back off but still cloud my vision.

Fuloch breaks through the haze, a dagger aimed at my chest.

He misses, but only by a hair. He attacks again, this time faster. The boggles work to throw me off balance. I can't tell where the roof ends. I thrust the sword every which way and nick Fuloch's shoulder. He snarls in response. His next swings with the dagger are even faster and one catches my forearm. Flames erupt in my veins, spreading out from the bleeding gash. It spreads to the tips of my fingers, but I only feel it for a moment.

Because my feet go over the edge.

The world slows down, then speeds up again.

The wind rushes past my ears and I reach for the ledge. The force threatens to rip my arms from their sockets, and the dizzying view below makes my head spin. My sword clatters to the cement below and my injured arm threatens to give out any second as it goes numb.

A broken window stands to my left. If I can swing to the fire escape a few feet away, I can climb through it. I need to keep Fuloch here and away from whatever direction Mr. Hob and Rina could have gone.

Fuloch's crazed laughter distracts me. He stands triumphant with his hands on his hips as he sneers down at me. "It's a shame, really," he says. "If you had done what I told you, I would have considered letting your precious Rina go. Now, I'm going to drain her dry as slowly as possible."

He lifts his foot to smash my fingers into the tar. "So, you'll see her soon enough. Though I do hope you don't mind if she's not all in one piece."

His foot comes down.

I launch myself toward fire escape, catch the edge, and manage to hold tight. As Fuloch shrieks with rage, I pull myself over the bar, onto the fire escape platform, and leap into the broken window, sailing past the broken glass and grazing my left arm. I tumble to the floor, getting covered in dust and debris, then stumble to my feet. The few living boggles scatter, more interested in self-preservation than fighting. Pain shoots up my right leg from my ankle and I sprawl to the floor again. Shit. I must have messed it up when I came through the window.

Fuloch continues to shout from above.

I limp toward the shadows and hide behind an old rusty piece of machinery. An equally rusty crowbar sticks out from underneath. The burning in my right arm makes it impossible to grip it, so I take it in my left hand.

Fuloch comes flying through the window. His feet hardly hit the ground before he starts hunting for me. He turns over and tears apart anything that isn't bolted down, kicks at my hiding place and moves on. With Fuloch's back turned, I step out from behind the rusty junk with all my weight on my left leg and clutching the crowbar like a baseball bat. Amid the chaos I can still hear on the roof, I kick a piece of rubble with my bad foot. Fuloch's ears twitch. He spins, eyes wide with glee and bloodlust. I swing the crowbar. He catches it, heedless of the way it burns his hand. I'm doomed.

A sudden battle cry scares both of us out of our skin. Rina bursts from the shadows and swings a wooden plank at Fuloch's head. As he turns to inspect the sound, it nails him square in the face. He stumbles back, letting go of the crowbar and holding his nose as it gushes blood.

"You human bitch," he screeches, charging Rina with his dagger.

I take what small chance I have and nail him in the back of the head with the crowbar. There's a sickening crack. The redcap sprawls to the floor. Howling in agony, he stumbles back to his feet. He sways, his eyes roll back in his head, and he collapses to the ground in a crumpled, moaning heap.

Rina and I dare to breathe again. I lean against an old machine to give my bad foot a break. As Fuloch goes quiet, I slide down the floor.

"Jocelyn, are you all right?" Rina asks, dropping down beside me.

"Not really, no." I chuckle. "You?"

"I'm fine, but you…" Rina turns my right arm over to investigate the blood-soaked gash through my shirt. Her face goes paler at the sight of the cut from the window. When her gaze falls on the wounds on my face, they gloss over. "I'm so sorry, Jocelyn."

"Don't be," I say, wincing as I try to sit up straighter. "I might be dead right now if not for you." Above, the roof begins to go quiet. "Where's Mr. Hob?'

"Here," Mr. Hob pants, entering the room from the opposite entrance. He massages a decent-sized goose egg above his right eye as he waddles over to us. "Now that Fuloch is taken care of, learn how to control that woman of yours."

Rina glares at him, all the sympathy drained from her face. "You want another bump? Keep talking."

"Can you two save it for later?" I ask. "Rina, help me up. We need to get the others." She does, sending Mr. Hob one final dirty look as we get to our feet.

"Don't worry about this lout here," Mr. Hob says, giving Fuloch a nudge with his foot. "I'll tie him up nice and tight and keep an eye on—"

Dominic and Shaylee burst through the door. "Jocelyn!"

Just as I'm about to reassure them that I'm fine, a fury-fueled cry cuts me off.

Fuloch stumbles to his feet, knocking Mr. Hob across the face and snatching up his dagger. He charges me, face contorted into something demonic.

I shove Rina away. Dominic and Shaylee come running. Fuloch's blade meets my crowbar twice, then slips past it. There's a sharp pain in my gut, then a horrible burning. Shaylee runs Fuloch through.

Everything stops.

Pain seeps into the rest of my body and the world begins to blur. Everything's muted. All the information gets burned away before my brain can process it. Shaylee pushes Fuloch off her sword in muffled slow motion. He falls to the ground as a bloody heap. Dominic holds my face in his hands. He's asking if I'm hurt, but I can't form the words. My mouth feels numb. He looks down and his face turns ghostly white.

Curious, I look down too. A dark crimson stain spreads from the center of my shirt.

Rina speaks, but I can't understand her.

The world turns on its side, but I don't remember falling. Everyone's shouting my name, pleading with me, but I don't know why. I look past everyone and meet Fuloch's eye. There's just enough life in them for him to meet mine.

"Now," he gurgles, "you pay."

Twenty-One

TOO FAST.

"Mom, let it go. I looked at the school, and I don't want to go."

"You haven't told me why, though."

The roads are slick.

"It's too expensive. We can't pay for it."

"It wouldn't hurt to at least see what scholarships you might get."

"I promised Dad—"

A dark figure. Too short to be an adult. Too strange to be a child.

"Jocelyn, look out!"

A white flash. Pain. Spinning.

Dark.

...

A voice.

"Dominic, stop. You're using too much magic. You're going to hurt yourself."

"I'm not losing her the way I lost Avery."

The burning starts to fade. It leaves cool waves like I'm being washed ashore.

Something shakes me.

"Jocelyn, you can't leave. You told me you've got a sister, right? She needs you."

Annalise. And Mom. She's awake. I have to go see her. I have to say I'm sorry.

My body needs air.

I shove Rina out of the way and throw myself onto my stomach, gasping for breath and hacking up blood. A heavy hand smacks me on the back, encouraging my body to start up again. It stings, but that means I'm alive.

"Jocelyn, look at us," Dominic begs. "Say something."

He and Rina slowly come into focus, terror etched into their faces. The rest of the group forms a semicircle around me, looking just as horrified.

"What's wrong with me?" I rasp. "I'm freezing, but I was on fire before."

Rina turns to Dominic, hoping for a translation of my babbling.

"Fuloch's dagger was poisoned," Dominic answers. "It's designed to mimic a faerie's reaction to iron. It'll take some time for it to wear off." He slumps back and runs a hand through his hair. "Gods above, Jocelyn, you're going to be the death of me."

"I think I'm okay."

"Jocelyn, don't—"

I scramble to my feet, but the room spins. Shaylee and Iver catch me before I bust my head open on the concrete.

"Lie down before you hurt yourself, or I will tie you down," Dominic barks.

Rina takes my hand and eases me to the ground, cushioning my head with her legs. I drape my left arm over my eyes, hoping the dark will steady me. Breathing deep helps, despite the metallic stench of blood.

After five breaths, I dare to ask, "What happened?"

"Fuloch nearly took you down with him," Dominic answers from the void. "If Rina hadn't mentioned your family, I fear he might have succeeded."

"Where is he now?"

"Brok and Warren are taking care of it. Put him out of your mind."

Easier said than done.

"You brought me back?"

"I closed your wound, but you came back yourself. Though I do hope Essen didn't have any other friends. I think my magic is spent for the next several years."

"I'm sorr—"

"Hush. You don't get to apologize for almost dying."

"I hate to interrupt," Rina cuts in, "but I need answers. Now."

I lift my arm to find her staring down at me, stern and apparently unfazed by any of the insanity she just witnessed.

In a half-dead slur, I tell Rina everything. I tell her about how I swerved to miss a strange creature in the road in a thunderstorm. I tell her how the accident left my mother in a coma, so I went looking for answers and found Mr. Hob instead. Rina listens silently as I explain how he took me to see the queen and how we made our agreement: seven paintings for my mother's life.

As I finish the story, Rina leans back and massages her temples. "This is insane," she mutters. "Absolutely insane."

"You don't believe her?" Dominic asks.

Somehow, Rina laughs. "After the night I just had, how could I not? I got kidnapped by a *faerie.*" She groans. "God, it sounds so embarrassing out loud."

"In your defense," I say, "Fuloch was a redcap. If you got kidnapped by a nymph or a sprite, then you would have to be embarrassed."

"Excuse you," Calista snaps.

Rina jumps like she forgot the others were there. They were so quiet that I almost did too. They're all here, ragged and worn, but in one piece.

"We've cleaned up the best we can," Iver says, chipping a patch of dried blood from his cheek. "Now we need to leave. All that clamor probably drew some human attention."

Dominic gets to his feet, leaning on Shaylee for support. "You're right. Jocelyn, you should be all right to stand. Just go slow...Slow, I said!"

Rina steadies me as I get to my feet. Only then do I realize she's shaking. I wrap one arm around her shoulders and hold her tight.

"I need to get my sword," I say, limping toward the exit. "I dropped it when I fell off the roof."

"No worries. I got it," Shaylee says. "It was just a spare. I'll take care of it."

Sure enough, there's a second sword swinging from Shaylee's belt, streaked to the hilt with drying blood. Weird. I didn't think I'd done that much damage with it.

Dominic cuts through my scrambled thoughts. "Rina, can you get Jocelyn home?"

"Where is home, exactly?" she asks.

"She can direct you. It'll keep her awake. Don't let her fall asleep. And if you could fabricate a believable excuse for your absence, I would be grateful." He hands Rina a small leather purse. Fuloch must have taken it from her. Meeting my eyes, he adds, "Behave. I'll see you at home."

With one arm around my waist, Rina helps me down the stairs, out the door, and into the car. Despite the late October chill, we drive with the windows down. The wind keeps me alert, but does little for the vertigo.

"How are you feeling?" Rina shouts over the wind.

"Like I'm on a carousel from Hell," I reply. My voice resonates on the inside of my skull, making me feel worse. Sleep sounds wonderful. "Didn't Dominic want you to call your roommates?"

Rina slows down a bit and dials a number. Luckily, living on campus means we don't need an alibi for her parents. Her story is simple but believable enough: she's been with me the whole time. We went out to eat, went to watch movie back at my place, and we both fell asleep.

Judging by her roommate's laughter on the other end and the way Rina tells her to shut up, she doesn't believe we just "fell asleep." It makes for an awkward ride home, but that's fine by me. An awkward silence won't try to kill me.

She hangs up as we turn onto my road. Her expression shifts to worry at the sight of the farmhouse. It's an understandable reaction, given the dark windows, broken shutters and peeling paint.

"Please tell me we took a wrong turn." She sighs.

"It's a glamour, a faerie disguise," I explain. "Helps avoid unwanted visitors. Human visitors, anyway."

As we pull up, the illusion dissolves, revealing the neat well-kept house. Dominic stands in the warm glow of the kitchen window, busy at work at the counter.

"See?" I say as Rina parks the car. "You could say it works like a *charm*."

Rina groans and gets out of the car. When she comes around to help me, she mumbles, "You're obviously feeling better."

Once we're inside, Dominic ushers us to the table. In front of us sit three mugs of tea and a spread of fruit and bread.

"Eat," he orders. "Especially you, Jocelyn. It'll help you heal. How are you doing?"

"I'm off the carousel from Hell," I answer, "but I'm still freezing."

Dominic picks an apple from the bowl. "That will pass. How about you, Rina?"

She takes a long sip of tea, her eyes distant. "I don't know.... Still in shock, I guess. It's a lot. Even if Fuloch hadn't...died, it would be a lot."

Dominic nods. "I'm sorry you had to witness that. It wasn't the ending we hoped for, but Jocelyn and I are here for you. And, should you decide you want to forget some or all of it, I can arrange that easily."

Rina shakes her head. "No. I'll deal with it. If Jocelyn can put up with it for four months, I can take it for a little while."

A tired smile creeps onto Dominic's face. "You're perfect for each other."

I'm too tired to argue the details of our relationship. Judging by the way Rina takes another long drink of her tea, so is she. The world goes hazy the more I drink, and for the first time in a while, it feels like everything will turn out all right. Judging by the way Rina slouches in her chair, it's having a similar effect on her.

The three of us sit in silence for a long time, sipping tea and munching on grapes and apple slices. Inside the safety of this house, I don't mind the silence. It provides the first chance to let my mind settle in a long time.

Rina nudges me awake. "We need to get you cleaned up," she says. "Those cuts could get infected."

"They're not that bad," I reply, peeling off my bloodstained jacket. "I'll just wash them extra well and slap some bandages on them."

"You got them in an old rusty building," Rina reminds me.

"I've got some disinfectant in the bathroom."

Rina looks at Dominic. "Is this what being around faeries does to people?"

Dominic lazily raises a hand in defense. "She came to me like that," he argues, "But you both drank enough of the tea to ensure you'll be right as rain. Will you be staying with us for the night, Rina?"

"Given that I don't want to process any of this craziness alone, yeah," Rina answers, getting to her feet. "Sorry, but you're stuck with me."

"No complaints there," I reply. "I'll go find something for you to sleep in."

"*I'll* find her something to sleep in," Dominic argues, getting to his feet. "You go wash up and get to bed."

After his little act at the mill, I have no doubt that he has something more fitting. Too tired to argue, I hobble up the stairs and shut myself in the bathroom. The hot water feels great. Even with the tea, it feels like every muscle and joint are out for revenge. Washing off the streaks of blood and dirt only does so much, though. I still look half-dead and white as the tile. The gash on my arm has already healed to a very long, very obvious scar. I'm too tired to figure out how I'm going to explain it to my family.

Clean, but still cold, I find Rina in the studio, gazing out across the moonlit fields. She glances my way, then looks back out toward the dark shadows of the forest.

"There are more of them out there," she mutters. "Aren't there?"

"You mean faeries? Tons."

Rina cringes at the thought.

"The bad ones can't get us here. Besides, it's over," I reassure her.

She leans back against me. "You're not one of them...are you?"

The idea makes me laugh as I wrap my arms around her. "Nope. I'm human."

Rina wiggles around to face me with skepticism written all over her face. "You sure? Because I'm not about that paranormal-romance life."

"Really, I'm human," I assure her, taking one of her hands in mine. "Faeries run colder than humans. How do I feel to you?"

Rina's mouth scrunches. "Cold, which you've mentioned repeatedly since you woke up."

"Okay, well, faeries don't get this tall."

"Dominic's your height." Rina laughs. It's a relief to see her smile.

"He's two inches shorter. We measured once. Here's one: Faeries can't lie."

Sparks come back to her big brown eyes as she smirks, raising one eyebrow. A curl falls in her face and she huffs at it in vain, refusing to admit defeat by tucking it with her hand.

"I wasn't afraid that I'd lose you," I breathe, tucking back the curl. "Not at all."

Rina blinks a few times. "Okay...you're one for two. What else you got?"

The heat of her body next to mine helps me feel better, feel more like myself. "Now, don't quote me on this, but I hear faeries are pretty lousy kissers."

Rina's eyes go wide, and then she smirks with an eyebrow raised. "You think you're slick, don't you?"

"I don't have to think it," I reply. "I know it."

Rina stands on her toes as she whispers, "Oh, shut up."

With a kiss like this, she doesn't have to tell me twice.

The hot rhythm of her mouth and the flow of her breath pushes the cold away. The slide of her hands, one around my neck and the other through my hair, sends chills through my body that finally make me feel awake. I can't remember the last time I felt this warm. She feels like home, even though I hardly know her.

"Safe to say you're used to the whole liking-girls thing now, huh?" I breathe.

"Only because you're cute, and *not* a faerie," Rina teases. She steals another quick kiss and adds, "I need to take a shower. Save me half the bed, okay?"

I yank my brain out of the gutter and nod as Rina excuses herself.

Five extra blankets later, I hear rushed footsteps and the sudden whoosh of the door. Rina darts across my room and jumps into bed, warm and smelling of soap. My heart rate spikes as she drapes one arm across me. I pray she can't hear it as she lays her head on my chest.

"Did you run here from the bathroom?" I chuckle, trying to relax again.

"Maybe," she mutters, shifting to get comfortable. "Everything looks like a boggle in the dark."

"Don't worry," I whisper back, holding her tight. "It'll all look better in the morning."

Twenty-Two

IT'S QUIET. WARM. Someone strokes my hair, lulling me to sleep, but I don't know who. When I look up, any chance of sleep melts away. It's Mab. Her face contorts into a gloating sneer as she hisses, "This isn't over."

"Jocelyn?"

I jolt awake, and my abdomen spasms in pain, making me double over.

"I'm sorry! Didn't mean to scare you." Rina sits beside me on the bed and touches my shoulder. "Are you okay?"

As my heartbeat slows, I sit up and try not to flinch. "I'm fine," I assure her, rubbing my eyes. "It was just a nightmare." She doesn't look convinced, so I bounce the conversation off of me. "Is something up? Do you need to head back to campus?"

Rina shakes her head. "Can I use your car to go get breakfast?"

"Sure. Want me to come?"

"No, I got it. Any requests?"

"A truckload of bacon would be awesome."

Rina laughs and stands up. She's wearing clean jeans and a sweater she hadn't been wearing yesterday. Dominic's work, I assume.

"I'll see what I can do. You might have to settle for a carload. In the meantime, get some more sleep." She hesitates for a moment, then leans down and kisses me on the forehead.

I could get used to this.

Once she leaves, I try to go back to sleep, by all I do is toss and turn. Every time I close my eyes, I just see Mab's face and hear her voice.

"This isn't over."

That can't be true. What else could she want from me? Instead of driving myself crazy, I get dressed. Surprisingly, my right ankle only feels a bit tender. It's pretty much the only thing that *doesn't* hurt right now. I had no idea putting pants on could be such a painful chore. The stairs are even worse.

Dominic sits at the kitchen table, a mug of tea in his hand and an old weathered book in front of him. He glances up with a tired grin and says, "Look who stayed in the land of the living."

"Thanks to you," I reply, pouring myself a cup of coffee. "How are the others?"

"Fine. We've all seen worse. Mr. Hob didn't open the store today, though."

"He deserves the day off, I think." Coffee in hand, I sit across from Dominic. He manages to read two more pages before I say, "Dominic...Thank you doesn't begin to cover how grateful I am to you."

Dominic shuts his book. "Think nothing of it."

"I can't. You saved my life," I argue. "I wouldn't be sitting here if it wasn't for you. I wouldn't have been able to save Rina if it wasn't for you."

Dominic shrugs. "You would have done the same for me. Besides, you've done more for me than you can imagine. You got me out of the court."

"That's not worth all you've done for me."

"You're wrong." There's a sharp, angry hint to Dominic's voice. "You can't begin to fathom the opportunity you presented me." He takes a long sip of tea, as if he's waiting for his words to sink in. "And besides, look what you've done for Rina. Your mother. Calista. Our friendship aside, I couldn't let you die. The world needs good people like you."

That day on the beach flashes in my mind, and Essen's gasping breaths ring in my ears, bringing back the phantom chill of Fuloch's poison.

I hold my coffee mug in both hands to ward it off. "I want to believe you, but..."

Dominic sits back and drums on the table. "You're talking about Essen, I assume?" He doesn't wait for an answer. "So you killed one person in self-defense—"

"I also put my mother in a coma—"

"Don't interrupt me. I'm at least two hundred years old and I've lost track of how many people I've killed. Some in self-defense, most because my queen told me to, yet you consider me a friend."

I tense as Dominic's eyes bore into my soul, demanding I respond to his words. I can't, though. I don't know how.

Dominic continues, "I won't tell you to forget what happened with that kelpie. I'm not even sure that's possible, but I will tell you to focus on all the good you've done. You braved the depths of Faerie to save your mother. You protected Rina and her friends, though you didn't know them, and you came to Calista's aid yourself.

"And need I say anything about Rina's rescue? You could have backed down when I asked you to form a plan, but you didn't. If you weren't 'good,' I don't think you would have done any of these things."

With each word Dominic says, I shrink further into myself as every defense and weak argument is stripped away.

"You know why I think you don't want to see the good in yourself and move on?" Dominic asks. "Moving forward with the rest of the world presents risks. You could make more mistakes and hurt more people. It's harder to fail again if you're standing still, staring at the ground."

I'm speechless. How am I supposed to argue against any of that?

Dominic continues to drink tea as if all we were discussing is the weather. He gets up to pour himself another cup from the kettle. "It wouldn't be so hard if you let people help you."

Even if he's right, I don't like all this attention focused on me.

"When you brought me back," I remember, "you mentioned someone named Avery."

Dominic goes rigid.

"Who's Avery?"

He looks out the window over the sink and says, "Oh, good. Rina's back with breakfast."

"Hey, that's not fair," I huff. "You can completely break down my psyche, but I can't ask anything about you?"

Dominic glances over his shoulder. "You want me to break down your psyche some more?"

I shut up.

"Didn't think so."

Rina pushes the screen door open with her elbow. A plastic bag of food hangs from each hand. "Hey, you two." Her cheerful expression droops when she looks at me. "Everything okay? Do you need to go lie back down?"

"No, I'm okay," I answer, getting to my feet and rounding the table to help with the bags. "Did the car give you any trouble? How much was breakfast?"

"The car was fine and don't worry about breakfast. It's my treat."

Dominic pops the lid off a Styrofoam tray of pancakes and mutters, "I should have started saving human girls years ago."

I nearly drop the container of eggs in shock. "You're going to eat human food?"

"I was just part of a very dangerous rescue mission," he says defensively, collecting clean plates and silverware. "I've earned it."

"He's got a point," Rina agrees. She hands me a tipped-over container that is slippery with grease from its contents. "Is that enough bacon?"

My stomach growls, and I try to remember the last time I ate. "It's perfect."

Breakfast proves to be pleasant, which feels weird. It's so normal, filled with small talk between Rina and Dominic and delicious syrup-soaked food, that it seems out of place in this house. Dominic's words still play my head, making it hard to really contribute. And there's still my nightmare.

"This isn't over."

"—teen?"

"Huh?"

"I said," Rina repeats, "are you really eighteen?"

Dominic piles food on his plate and stands up. "Well, it's been lovely, but I should go make sure Princess Shaylee sufficiently covered our tracks. Thank you for breakfast, Rina."

She smiles as he scurries off, then turns back to me.

Well, the morning was nice while it lasted.

Running my hands through my hair, I explain, "So, about...me. I'm actually seventeen, the same as you, and I haven't...quite...finished high school yet."

Rina nods, but stays quiet.

"I mean, I plan to finish, but the queen demanded that I live near the court. She wouldn't have made the deal otherwise. I'm sorry I lied."

Rina nods again and takes a sip of juice. "Uh-huh. And that incident at the nightclub? I'm going to take a shot in the dark and say you had something to do with it."

"You have good aim." I sigh.

As we eat, I tell her about bumping into to Calista after Fuloch got kicked out. All the while, Rina alternates from snickering, shaking her head, and smiling.

"You're not mad?" I ask.

"Oh, I *was*," Rina replies. "I was pissed, but you were looking out for us, so...thanks."

"You're awfully chill about all of this," I point out.

Rina goes quiet and lowers her eyes to her plate. "Call me crazy, but I've always wanted to believe that there was more to this world than what we can see. Real scientific, I know." She rolls her eyes and swirls her mug. "One day, we'll find all the answers. I have full faith in that, but I don't know if I want us to. I want some mysteries left in the world. Looks like I found something that'll stay a mystery forever."

"Is that why you keep me around?" I tease.

She shakes her head, then looks down at her mug. "Maybe a little bit at first, but I do really like you."

My heart skips a beat, and my phone rings from across the table.

Rina eyes it and says, "You should probably answer that. It went off all morning."

I groan and pick up my phone. It's Rick. Sure enough, my phone registers seven missed calls from him. I try to ignore the sinking feeling in my gut. It's just a reflex I've developed. That's all. The paintings are done and I'm on my way out of Faerie. Nothing more can go wrong.

"What's up, Rick?" I ask.

On the other side of the line, he snaps, "Finally. Where have you been all morning? And why won't David pick up his phone? Never mind. Have you heard from Anna today? Has she called you? Texted you? Anything?"

My heart sinks.

This isn't over.

"Not today, no," I answer, my mouth drying with every word.

Rina glances at me nervously.

"Did she say anything weird last time you talk to her?" Rick asks. "Anything to make you think something was wrong?"

"No. Nothing." I close my eyes and take a deep breath. "What happened to Anna?"

"I don't know," he exclaims. "She's just gone."

The floor feels like it's falling out from under me.

"I went to wake her up for school and she wasn't in bed," Rick continues. "I thought maybe she left early, but her backpack and bike are still here."

Who would take Annalise?

This isn't over.

Stop. I can't think like that. Not yet.

"I was hoping she called you," Rick continues. "Her phone's gone, but she's not picking up."

"I'm on my way," I say, searching for my keys and wallet.

Rina grabs her purse and waits by the door, arms folded and toes tapping. Dominic stands in the doorway of his room in a similar posture as he waits.

"Okay." Rick says. "Drive careful."

As soon as I hang up, Dominic says, "I'll go to the court and find out if anyone knows anything. Faeries don't snatch children as old as Anna. She's bound to draw attention."

"And I'm coming with you," Rina says. "I can call Anna's phone while you're driving. This isn't the best time to get pulled over."

"No, Rina, you're going back to campus," I argue.

She makes air quotes and says, "Let me guess. 'It's too dangerous'? 'I don't want you to get hurt'? C'mon, Jocelyn. I knocked a redcap over the head with a two-by-four. I can handle a car ride."

"She's right," Dominic affirms. He crosses the kitchen and hands Rina a wrinkled sheet of paper. "This is a list of my contacts here in the Human Realm. If Anna's still over here, they may know something. Rina can call while you drive."

She slips the paper into her pocket. "See? Now let's go find your sister."

I let it go and allow Rina to follow me out to the car. Arguing will just waste time. Truth be told, it probably is for the best that she comes with me. I won't drive like a maniac if she's in the car.

The ride home is filled with one depressing call after another. No one has seen Anna. Most of Dominic's contacts don't even know who she is.

Every time Rina says, "Thank you for your time," and hangs up, I become more convinced of who took her.

A police car sits in the driveway, and an officer talks with Rick on the front steps. My uncle must have been hunting for Anna from the moment he woke up. His hair's a mess and his beard looks scragglier than usual. Both he and the cop look up with grim expressions as we pull up to the curb.

"Could you reach her?" Rick calls.

"No," I answer, jogging up the driveway. "I'm sorry."

Rick looks Rina over. "Who is this?"

I wrap an arm around Rina's shoulders as we step onto the porch. "This is Rina Fischler. Rina, this is my uncle, Rick Marshall."

Rick gives me a quizzical look. "David didn't come?"

"He should be on his way," I lie. Hopefully we can get out of here before my imaginary uncle is supposed to show up.

The police officer chimes in before Rick can ask any more questions. "You're Annalise's sister, right?" he asks, pressing a pen to a clipboard. "I need to take a statement from you."

"Yeah, that's me. What do you need to know?"

"Rick tells me you spoke to her yesterday after your mother woke up from a coma," the officer continues, flipping through a few pages. "First in the hospital room, and then privately. Did she say anything strange?"

As usual, the truth is out of the question. "No. She just wanted to talk about a surprise Halloween costume for a party coming up. It was going to be for our mother, since she woke up from a coma."

The officer jots down my words, believing every one of them. "You moved to Grand Harbor late last summer to live with your uncle, David Lennox, correct? Did you leave behind any bad blood? Anyone who might want to hurt you or your sister? Does David have any unpleasant connections in town?"

"No, I didn't, and he doesn't have any that I know of. Why?"

"Well, we found this in your sister's room." The officer holds up a small plastic bag from the clipboard. Inside sits a wilting branch dotted with onyx-black berries and shriveling purple flowers.

It's deadly nightshade.

Twenty-Three

MY BRAIN STOPS altogether. Somehow, I manage to ask, "What is that?"

"We're still unsure," the officer explains. "But we found it with this. Does it mean anything to you?" He holds up another bag. Inside is a torn square of faded paper with two lines of loopy cursive text. The words threaten to take the ground out from under me.

Because the enchanted way we follow, we bring forth gifts of living things.

Because this night the earth is hallow, we bring to the Ancients this offering.

I can't breathe. It's like there's no air left.

"No," I answer. "Never seen it before."

Another cop hails him inside, and he tips his hat. "Excuse me, folks."

I can't respond. Gravity feels a hundred times stronger and my limbs are numb. Even my vision seems cloudy, as if the magnitude of what's happened is trying to physically manifest itself. I can't think past the words swirling around my head.

Mab took Annalise for the Hallowed Offering.

Rick shakes me, pulling me back reality.

"You know something," he hisses.

My dry mouth makes it hard to speak. "No, I don't."

"You're lying," Rick whispers harshly, squeezing my shoulders. "I can see it on your face."

"My sister has disappeared," I snap back. "I'm allowed to look freaked out."

"I know you, Jocelyn. You're hiding something."

"Why would I hide something at a time like this?"

Rick backs off and scowls. He must not have an answer.

The officer joins us on the porch again. He takes one look at us and asks, "Is everything okay?"

"Yes, officer," I say, backing away. "I'll go look for Anna. I'll call you if I find anything."

Rick lets us go, face still stern. "You had better. And don't do anything crazy."

Stepping off the porch, I call, "I won't," and pull my keys from my pocket.

Rina follows behind and stays quiet as we drive away from the house. I don't want to talk either. I don't want to give words to the horror I've caused.

A few miles down the road, she finally says, "What sort of crazy things are we 'not doing' exactly?"

"Well, you're going back to campus for starters," I answer.

"The hell I am," Rina snaps. Should have seen that coming.

I swing into a random parking lot and stop the car. "I don't think you understand the gravity of what we're dealing with here."

Rina folds her arms and narrows her eyes. "Enlighten me."

"The Queen of Faerie took my sister," I explain. "Which means I have to go back to the Faerie Court. You know, that place where I almost *died* multiple times?"

"You *actually* died not twenty-four hours ago, Jocclyn," Rina reminds me, motioning haphazardly in the direction she assumes the mill is. "Someone needs to go with you."

I groan and massage the back of my neck. "If I don't get Anna in *another* twenty-four hours, the queen is going to use her as a human sacrifice. We don't have time to argue."

Rina pales at the idea. "Then let's go."

"I'm trying to protect you, Rina. Don't you get that?"

"And I'm trying to protect you. You saw me take out Fuloch. I can help."

"This isn't your fight. Enough people have gotten hurt because of me."

"Will you get over this self-deprecating bullshit for five minutes and listen?" Rina shouts. "You don't have to do things on your own."

Her words throw me off.

Rina goes quiet and bites her bottom lip. "All of this eats you up. The accident, Essen, all of it. I get it, but you have to set that guilt aside right now. If you don't want me to help *you*, fine, but let me help save Anna. I owe you that."

I shouldn't let her come. It's too dangerous and I've dragged her deep enough into this mess. There's no telling what could happen, even if everything goes off without a hitch.

But Mab has my sister.

I lock eyes with Rina and hold out my hand. "If I tell you to take Anna and run, you run. You don't wait, and you don't come back for me. Got it?"

Rina looks down at my hand. "You're serious?"

"Dead serious. Promise me, or you're not coming."

Meeting my eyes again, Rina squeezes my hand. "I promise."

I squeeze back, then plant a kiss on the back of her hand. Rina instantly flusters and stutters an incoherent response, playing with her hair as an excuse to focus on something else.

And this is the girl who charges fearlessly against redcaps and boggles.

Rina calls Dominic as we fly down the road and puts him on speakerphone. I tell him what we found at the house, hoping he'll have some idea how it happened in the first place.

"It certainly fits," he says. "Shaylee said that the queen listened to her story, then just dismissed her. Then, a few hours later, she announced that she had chosen the Offering. She plans on presenting her to the court tonight."

"So, Mab didn't buy it. Why?" I ask. "What loose end did we forget?"

Rina folds her arms and raps her fingers. "Shaylee was the girl who came with you two, right?"

"Yeah. She wanted to try being diplomatic first."

Rina wrinkles her nose. "That was pathetic. I don't think she wanted to be diplomatic at all."

"I know she didn't do the best job, but—"

"Listen. What if she never actually wanted a peaceful solution? What if she wanted a fight? If she knew you were on thin ice, she would have tried harder."

"That's preposterous," Dominic scoffs.

"She went all the way down to get Jocelyn's sword, remember?"

"She wanted to cover our tracks."

"She killed Fuloch with it, though, then told Jocelyn she'd take care of it. What exactly did she mean by that?"

Dominic goes quiet on the other end. He would want Rina to be wrong even more than I do, but I have to admit that going down to get my sword before checking on Rina and me is strange. Given how fast those last moments were, I can't say for sure which sword Shaylee used, but Rina's right about one thing: She said she'd take care of mine and it was covered in blood. She's also been strangely adamant about me spending time with Rina.

But those two things can't be related, can they?

Dominic finally speaks again. "Those are some odd coincidences, I'll admit. But Shaylee wouldn't sell Jocelyn out. She's even offered to help with Anna's rescue. She promised to be our distraction while we sneak in, grab her, and get out after the queen presents her tonight."

"Presents her?" I repeat.

"Before the entire realm during the preoffering feast," Dominic explains.

Rina rubs her forehead with an exhausted expression. "How many faeries are we talking about here?"

"Easily in the thousands, though it's impossible to get an accurate number. We're terrible with record keeping. The documents usually get eaten, boiled for potions, or sewn into party dresses."

"Lovely," Rina mumbles.

I try to refocus them. "Dominic, how do we get into the feast?"

"That's easy. We go in through the main gate. Getting out is the real challenge," he says. "We have three options: the kitchen, the tunnels running under the prison cells, and a secret passage behind the mirror in the queen's chamber."

"The kitchen would have too many witnesses," Rina says.

"I agree. The tunnels are our best bet. They require a special charm to walk through successfully, so we don't bother to guard it. Only Mab's closest knights know how to make the charms."

Good thing we have one of Mab's closets knights on our side.

A distant voice comes through the phone speaker. I can't recognize it.

"Jocelyn, I have to go," Dominic says. "We'll talk when you get home."

"'Kay. See you soon."

Rina hangs up the phone.

"You can still back out of this," I say. "I'll understand."

"No way," Rina replies. "I'm not backing out. This Queen Bee-otch has messed with you and your family for the last time. I want to help take her down."

"Now you're *definitely* not coming." I'm not sure whether I should be joking or serious as I say that. Judging by the determination on Rina's face, she wouldn't be deterred either way.

We reach the house and find Dominic and Shaylee in the living room. Shaylee's knees bounce as she sits on the couch and Dominic has practically walked a circular groove into the carpet.

Rina stops short at the sight of Shaylee. Judging by her cold expression and rigid posture, she still thinks Shaylee betrayed me. Whether she's onto something or not, it isn't the time to investigate. We're going to have to trust Dominic for now.

The princess doesn't seem to notice. She greets Rina with equal parts fondness and sympathy. "Hi," she says with a limp wave. "Sorry we keep meeting under crappy circumstances."

"Not your fault," Rina replies coolly.

Shaylee hugs me tight. "I'm so sorry about your sister. We're going to get her back. I promise."

"I know," I reply. "Did Dominic tell you the plan?"

"Yes, and I think it'll work except for one thing: no one can see you. The second someone ties you to this, your whole family is done for."

"So, we dress her as a knight," Dominic suggests. "No one will question her in our armor, and it'll give her an excuse to roam the halls unattended."

"Can we call anyone else for help?" I ask.

"Unfortunately, everyone will be preoccupied," Shaylee says. "But there's a troop of nixies coming that owe me a favor." She turns to Rina without any further explanation. "You're coming too, I assume?"

"Of course," Rina replies with a glare, daring Shaylee to argue otherwise.

Shaylee claps her on the shoulder. "Good. Someone's got to help Jocelyn and keep her from doing something stupid."

I shoot Shaylee a dirty look, but she ignores it.

She turns Rina around and begins shoving her toward the basement. "But for that to work, you're going to have to look like one of us."

"Wait, what are you doing?" Rina asks, digging her heels into the carpet.

"You need to change, obviously," Shaylee answers. "I brought a few things."

Rina scoffs as she looks over Shaylee's rail-thin body. "How am I supposed to fit into your clothes?"

"Magic," Shaylee replies. "Duh."

Having no further arguments, Rina allows herself to be herded down the stairs. She gives me a look, however, that orders me to call the police if she's not back in an hour.

I wait a moment before I speak, wanting to make sure they can't hear us. Even then, I only mutter, "Do you think Rina could be right?"

Dominic sighs. "Truth be told, Jocelyn, I don't know. Faerie royalty has done worse things to get to the crown, but right now, we need her help. We can investigate how this actually came about once it's over."

I play his words back in my head. "Why would getting Mab to come after my family help Shaylee get the crown?"

Dominic blinks several times, then walks toward his room. "You need to change too," he says. "I have a suit of armor you can borrow."

"No, back up," I demand, following him across the living room. "What does any of this have to do with Shaylee becoming queen?"

"I honestly haven't asked enough questions of my own to know. Now, give me a moment to find that armor."

"But—"

He shuts the door. The lock clicks. So much for that conversation. I'm not completely empty-handed, though. Judging by his answer, Dominic is suspicious of Shaylee too, but doesn't have enough information to reach a conclusion. I wonder if any of us ever will.

His answer told me one other thing:

Whatever we're walking into, it's bigger than a rescue mission.

Twenty-Four

I'VE NEVER SEEN the path to the Faerie Court look so alive. Orbs of light line the narrow path, music drifts on the wind, and laughter carries through the envoys that travel toward the court. There's tension underlying all the celebration, though. It's heavy and anxious, waiting for what might happen next. It scrapes at my mind worse than some of the shrill musical instruments. Rina must sense it too, because she's glued to my side as we trail behind the faeries Shaylee sent us with.

They're nixies, freshwater mermaids from lakes and rivers farther north. They ignore me, seeing as I'm supposed to be an escort, and talk amongst themselves in what I think is a variation of German. One of them falls into step beside Rina and switches to English.

"You seem nervous," she says. "Is it your first time witnessing the Hallowed Offering?"

"Yes," Rina answers as she tugs at her dress made of autumn leaves. She grumbled about twigs poking her most of the way here. At least, I think that's what she was complaining about. I was too busy noticing how great her legs look to really listen.

"This is my third time, unfortunately," the nix continues. She gives a bored flip of her perpetually damp hair. Her long turquoise gown is wet too. "I hate watching it, but no one else in my family has the stomach for blood."

"Ditto." Rina sighs.

The nix looks Rina over skeptically. Apparently, faeries don't say *ditto*. Rina goes rigid under her scrutiny.

The nix's gray eyes narrow to slits. "What's your family's name again?"

"Fisher."

"I've never heard of you."

I hold my breath and grip the hilt of my sword.

"We live pretty far north," Rina lies. "Tip of the Upper Peninsula."

"Is that so?" The nix continues to study Rina.

The leader of the nixies calls to her, pulling her away from her silent investigation. The nixie gives Rina one final glace before doing as she's told. The leader's deep-blue eyes meet mine through my helmet, and she nods. I return the gesture.

Both Rina and I exhale in relief.

"That was close," she mutters, clutching her chest. "How much farther?"

The keep looms through the trees, dotted with firefly lights. The trail of faeries pours into the entrance, like a snack to keep the beast happy until the Offering.

"We're here," I whisper.

The longest minute of my life passes as the guard at the gate inspects the nixies' invitation. He hardly spares Rina a glance before handing the paper back to the leader. Eyes down and breath held, we follow them into the faerie keep, hopefully for the last time.

It's never looked so clean. We're greeted with the warm earthy scent of incense rather than the sharp stink of rot and mold. The atmosphere feels festive and the Grand Hall actually looks grand. The torn mildew-infested tablecloths and banners have all been replaced. Sparkling dishware, clean enough to actually eat off of, sits among the succulent spread of food. All the normal guests sport neater versions of their usual attire, though very few look happy about it, and there's not a speck of blood to be seen.

That's where the improvements end.

Mab stands above it all and greets the guests. Despite her festive golden attire, she looks worn out. She doesn't stand as tall as usual and her eyes appear distant. Lyle stands beside her, more focused on her than the guests. His concern is as obvious as Mab's exhaustion. Maybe getting Anna out will be easier than we thought.

I don't have to look far to find my sister. She sits at Mab's feet in a simple white dress with golden leaves woven into her long hair, like a goddess in training. Her legs tuck neatly under her as she sits atop a silky blue cushion as still as a porcelain doll, only moving when the guests lean down to kiss the back of her right hand.

I hold my breath and lower my eyes as we approach the macabre trinity. I'm completely hidden by the armor, but I don't want to risk looking at Mab. Maybe it's paranoia, but I wouldn't be surprised if she recognized me from the tiniest detail.

My hands sweat inside the leather gloves, and my legs shake. I watch as the nixies' leader pays her respects first to Mab, then my sister. All of the nixies, including Rina, give a low curtsy before dissolving into the crowd. The leader hangs back and places a kiss on Anna's hand, then one on her cheek.

That's what it's supposed to look like, anyway.

Anna frowns for the slightest moment. Her eyebrows pull together, and then she's normal again. The queen raises a hand to stop Lyle, who reaches for his sword in response to the nixie's gesture. With a deep bow as an apology, the nixie melts into the crowd with everyone else. Mab and Lyle watch her go, their eyes narrow with suspicion, but finally lose interest as the nixie mingles with the other guests.

"Do you think Anna got the message?" Rina asks as she pretends to inspect a painting on the wall.

"It looks like she did," I reply under my breath.

Like the other guards, I pick a patch of wall and pretend to watch the party. Rina tries to find an excuse to hang by me, but she's running out of things to look at. Just as she finishes studying an embroidered unicorn impaling a man, the leader of the nixies joins us. Rina grins and speaks to her like an old friend.

"Thank you again ever so much for letting me join you," she says, laying on a thick accent that I can't place. If the situation wasn't dire, that voice would be comical. "What a shame the rest of my family couldn't make it."

"A shame indeed," the leader replies. She looks back to Anna. "The queen certainly picked a lovely offering. I heard her sister was recently in service to Her Majesty as a painter. Her works are still hanging here in the keep, supposedly."

"Is that so?" Rina asks, widening her eyes in mock-surprise. "I wonder if they're any good." Then she turns to me. "Dear knight, you've been ever so helpful thus far. Would you happen to know where the paintings are?"

"I do, as a matter of fact," I answer, trying not to snicker.

"Would you be so kind as to show us where they are?"

"You'll have to go alone," the leader says, eyes shifting to me. "I have some urgent business to take care of. It'll tie me up for the rest of the night."

I nod to show I've received the message loud and clear. We're on our own.

Rina gives her "friend" a wave goodbye, and we set out into the corridors. We pass other guests receiving tours of the keep, but most of them are led by servants who pretend to be joyful to preserve the queen's façade. Only one other group is led by a knight, but even they don't pay us any attention. His group of nymphs are too busy giggling and pulling the poor guy down the hall every which way.

The Hall of Vanity is unguarded and empty. The stretch of wall dedicated to my paintings is easy enough to find. Hopefully it'll be easy for Anna to find too.

I begin to pace back and forth as Rina looks at the paintings.

"You're really good," she says, focusing on my first one. In it, Mab lies beside a lake, dozing like a cat, while sprites look on. "Like, *really* good."

I shrug. "I guess."

Rina looks at me like I'm crazy, then back at the painting. "Do you want to turn it into a career?"

"If I could." I mutter. "Unfortunately, it wouldn't pay many bills."

"What else would you want to do?"

I go to speak, but realize I don't have much of an answer. "I'll get back to you on that." I finally say. "I was looking into graphic design programs before this whole mess started. Or maybe web design." The thought makes me laugh. "I don't know if I even remember how to use a computer anymore."

Rina gently elbows me. "You're smart. You'll figure it out."

I'm glad I have a helmet on so Rina can't see me grinning like a dork. "Thanks. Coming from a future astrophysicist, that means a lot."

A sudden *bang* announces the nymphs we saw earlier.

Rina and I dive behind a statue as one giggles. "Where'd our knight go?"

"Shhh, listen," sings the other.

They go silent. All I can hear is my heartbeat in my ears, but the nymphs must hear something down the hall because they shout, "Found you," and rush off again.

Rina and I relax and slide down the base of the statue. We study the alarm on each other's faces and begin to laugh.

"Anna needs to hurry up before I lose any more years off of my life." I chuckle.

"Same," Rina replies. In the panic, we reached for each other's hands. Instead of letting go, Rina squeezes mine and leans against my shoulder.

Well, maybe Anna could take a little more time.

"You're the first girl I've ever dated," she says quietly. "I dated a few guys in the clubs I was in and I really did try to like them." She gives a weak exhale. "There were a few girls I thought might be gay, but I was always too scared to ask. I thought I looked and acted too straight."

"You know there are feminine lesbians, right?" I interject. "My first girlfriend was a cheerleader of all things."

Rina leans back and studies my expression. "You're kidding."

"I swear I'm not. Of course, no one knew we were dating. She didn't want to deal with what people might say. I can't say I blamed her." With a shrug, I conclude, "Anyway, just know that you don't have to prove yourself to anyone. If you like kissing girls, me in particular, you're gay enough. Or bi enough. Or whatever. It's completely up to you."

"You'd still like me if I was bi?"

"Why not?" I lean forward and press my forehead against hers. "I like you however you are."

Rina smirks. "So noble, dear knight."

I cringe. "Please stop calling me that."

"What should I call you then?" Rina snickers.

"Your girlfriend, maybe?"

Rina blinks a few times, then pulls away so that she can lift off my helmet. Her hands linger on my face, hot and soft against the sudden cool air. "You're unbelievable, you know that?"

"Says the girl who followed me into the Faerie Court."

A smirk creeps onto Rina's face as she pulls me closer and whispers, "I have to keep up with your craziness somehow."

Her lips brush mine as I breathe out, "I have to admit, this is a good start."

The door clicks open, and the moment is gone.

I slowly peek around the corner, holding my breath, not sure what to expect.

It's Anna and Warren, one of the elves that helped save Rina. I run to Anna, scooping her up and spinning her around. She squeals, hugs me back, and laughs. The sound makes me squeeze her small body tighter. If I never heard that laugh again, I don't know what I'd do.

"God, Jocelyn, you scared me." She giggles as I put her down. No sooner are her feet on the ground than she wags her finger in my face. "You lying jerk," she huffs. "I *knew* you had something to do with Mom, but faeries too? And you didn't tell me? Lying to Uncle Rick about that art program I can forgive, but lying to me?"

"I promise I'll make it up to you." I laugh. Turning to Warren, I add, "Thanks for bringing her."

He nods and puts his helmet back on. "My pleasure, but you better hurry. Her Majesty will be suspicious soon."

That doesn't sound quite right. "I thought Shaylee was distracting her."

Anna shakes her head. "We can't leave. The queen needs me to be a part of this big ceremony and—"

"That's exactly *why* we need to leave," I retort, dragging Anna toward the opposite end of the hall.

She digs her heels into the floor and yanks away. "Why can't you let me have this?" she whines. "I'm grateful for the deal you made. Really, I am, but why can't you let me have an adventure of my own? I can handle this."

I grit my teeth and take a deep breath. "Anna, this isn't a bedtime story."

"She's right," Rina pipes up. "Anna, you've got to trust your sister on this."

Anna grins from ear to ear. "You're the ice-cream girl, aren't you?"

What little patience I had left evaporates. "Anna, Queen Mab's going to kill you if we don't leave this instant."

The grin melts from Anna's face and she turns pale. "What do you mean? The Faerie Queen wouldn't do that."

Warren snorts.

Anna glances at him, then back to me, eyes wide with desperation. "She invited me. She said she needs me to help—"

"—The Faerie Realm keep their connection to magic?" I finish. "Did she happen to tell you what you needed to do?"

Anna closes her gaping mouth and swallows. "She said I just had to recite a few lines, stand before Faerie, and that she would take care of the rest. She said it wouldn't take long."

I grasp my sister by the shoulders and lean down so that our eyes are level. "You've got to trust *me*, Anna. Not her."

Her eyes narrow to a glare. "I'm sick of being lied to, damn it. Would it kill people to tell me the truth? If the queen had told me, I could have at least put up a fight. That would have been awesome." She takes the wreath from her head and throws it on the ground. "Let's go. I'm too old for this fairy-tale stuff anyway."

Warren, Rina, and I relax, and I pull Anna into another hug.

As I squeeze her tight, I look to Warren. "Will you be okay if we head for the tunnels?"

Warren waves off the concern. "Truth be told, we'll do a lot better with you lot out of the way. Get going." He pats me on the shoulder hard enough to make my knees buckle under his heavy gloved hand. "And take good care of these girls of yours." Rina and Anna both wave as we head in the opposite direction. We don't make it too far before Warren calls to us. "Nearly forgot. Dominic says he'll—"

His words cut to a choked gasp and the wet sound of metal slicing into flesh.

I whirl around and my stomach plummets.

Warren slouches against a statue, face contorted in pain as he grasps at the bloody dagger jutting out from the shoulder of his leather armor. He glares back at his assailant, hissing curses in a language far older than English.

Judging by Lyle's triumphant sneer, the curses aren't doing much good. "Tour's over, Annalise." He snickers. His cold gaze darts to Rina and me. They light up like torches lit with Hell's flames. "But it looks like visiting hours have just started."

Twenty-Five

I DRAW MY sword. Rina tucks Annalise behind her.

"I've met some stupid humans in my time, but you've built your own category, Jocelyn." Lyle cackles.

"Mab has no right to take my sister," I explain coolly. "Our contract was up and I've done nothing wrong."

Lyle's eyebrows perk up. "What do you call killing that redcap?"

"Jocelyn, you killed someone?" Anna whispers.

"You're surprised?" Lyle sneers. "Or has your sister been keeping even more secrets from you?"

"Shut up, Lyle," I growl.

The knight shrugs. "Fine, keep lying to her, but you can't lie about the princess of Faerie."

My mind reels. Shaylee didn't tell Mab the truth?

"Enough," Warren growls. With his free hand, he reaches to his back and yanks out the knife, face contorted in pain and anger. "You'll not touch those children, Lyle."

"Oh?" Lyle chuckles. "And I suppose you think you can stop me?"

Warren lunges at him. Lyle hardly has to lift a finger to defend himself.

I grab Rina and Anna and run.

With the girls in front of me, we sprint toward the exit at the other end of the hall. Queen Mab watches us from above. All her embodiments turn us around, threatening to trap us here forever if we can't find our way out. I spot the exit, but my right ear erupts in pain. A dagger cracks a statue, exactly level with my head, and clatters to the floor.

Lyle.

I face him and brace myself, sword at the ready. Lyle scoffs and wipes the blood from his sword. I try not to think about how it's Warren's.

"Rina, take Anna and run," I mutter.

"Are you crazy?" she snaps. "I can't leave you—"

"You promised. Get out of here."

A hand squeezes my shoulder. "You better be right behind us," Rina says.

"I am, now go."

"Jocelyn," Anna whispers, "I'm sorry."

"Just go."

Lyle looks past me as they slip out the door. His gloating grin spreads wider like their escape is no big deal. I just hope I can keep him busy long enough to prove him wrong.

"We haven't had an Offering try to run in decades," he sneers. "At least your stupidity makes you entertaining."

"Did you kill Warren?" I demand.

"I would have loved to." Lyle sighs. "But unfortunately, Her Majesty will have some questions for him, no doubt. Like what Dominic could possibly have to do with all of this."

Shit. He heard us. But at least he's still talking.

"You're not hurting my sister, Rina, or Dominic."

"You're quite right about that, Jocelyn." One blink and Lyle is in my face, sword raised. "The queen will. I just get to watch."

His sword comes down, and I barely keep my head. Literally.

The strike reverberates up my blade, threatening to knock it from my hand, and I place myself against the door. Lyle's blade is everywhere. Left. Right. Above me. Coming in low. The sound of clashing crystal deafens me. My arms shake and begin to droop. Any chance of me beating a faerie knight is ludicrous. I could never put a scratch on Dominic and he went easy on me. Time to fight dirty.

I rip a tapestry from the wall and fling it in Lyle's face. The knight slices through it like butter, but not without lowering his defenses ever so slightly. It's all I need.

With Lyle's blade raised high in the tapestry, his lower half is wide open. I plunge my sword just below his knee. The blade slices between the leather plates and into his leg. Lyle screams in pain and brings his sword down in blind rage rather than strategic attack.

I roll out of the way and bolt back the way we came.

"Get back here, coward," Lyle shouts, tumbling to the floor. "Get back here and fight me!"

Warren's right where we left him, but he looks like death. Two daggers pin him to the wall through his forearms. He looks up at the sound of my footsteps, his eyelids heavy and his legs buckling.

"Are you mad?" he growls. "Get out of here before Lyle catches up."

"We've got some time," I pant, taking hold of one of the daggers. "And I can't just leave you here. Ready? One, two, three."

Warren grits his teeth and bites back a cry. His model of strength is the only thing that keeps me from throwing up as I pry the other dagger from his arm. I catch him before he crumples to the ground, but he pushes off me.

"Let's go," he hisses, cradling his arms against his chest.

"I need to talk to Shaylee," I hiss, leading Warren toward the exit. "I want to know why the hell she threw me under the bus."

"You don't have time," Warren snapped. "You need to get out."

We reach the door and hesitate. I haven't planned that far.

"Aim for the kitchens," Warren orders. "We'll get the least resistance."

I nod. Holding my breath, I slowly turn the handle. If we move fast—

"Jocelyn, don't!"

The door flies open. A crowd of guards grab at us. I barely touch the hilt of my sword before they slam me into the wall and bind my hands behind my back. The cord bites into my wrists as I push against them and strain to spot Warren. It takes five guards to subdue him.

"Don't hurt my sister!"

I crane my neck and spot Anna held captive. She stands limp in a guard's grasp. They got Rina too. She pulls at her restraints and spouts profanity, glaring murder at everyone.

Lyle limps out the door, blood streaming down his leg. "Sorry about your little rescue operation." He chuckles. "Though I must admit it's admirable. Shall we see what Her Majesty thinks?" He turns to the girls and raises Rina's chin. "I'm particularly interested in what she plans to do with you, stranger."

Rina snarls up at him, "*I'm* planning to bite that hand off if you don't move it." He just laughs at her, so she spits in his face.

Lyle backhands her and snatches her by the front of her dress. "You filthy little—"

"Don't touch her, you bastard," I bellow.

He turns back toward me and wipes Rina's saliva from his face. "I'm sorry. Is this wench important to you? I'll be sure Her Majesty gets extra creative with her."

"Yeah, when it comes to creativity, you don't have *a leg to stand on*, do you, Lyle?" I snicker.

He sucker punches me in the gut, knocking a year's worth of wind out of me. Rina gives me a look as if I'm absolutely insane, and Anna looks on in horror. I can't tell them that I'm okay. It takes all my energy to breathe again, but it was totally worth it.

Lyle does his best to walk on his own as he leads us through the keep. I don't recognize the area. It's certainly not near the Grand Hall, and it doesn't seem to be toward the tunnels. We stop in front of a simple wooden door. Behind it sits an equally simple room with a raised platform and several rows of dusty, decrepit pews. The carpet under our feet wore out long ago and smells of mold and dirt. It reminds me of a chapel that's been out of use for decades, if not centuries. The guards force us to sit in the first pew. We wait in tense silence, only able to ask questions with quick glances and worried looks.

The door bursts open. Mab storms up the aisle, rage practically pouring from her snarling mouth and fire shooting from her vengeful gaze. My heart speeds up with every approaching step. As she towers over us, I swear it's about to explode, but then she strikes me across the face and I forget. My cheek rips open from her rings and stars fill my vision.

"Why don't you ever learn?" she demands, snatching me by the throat. Her nails dig into my neck as she lifts me up onto my toes. I can only gasp in response.

"Your Majesty, let her go," Anna begs.

"Silence, or I'll rip out your tongue, brat," Mab screeches.

"Leave her alone," I wheeze.

Mab lets me go, and I crumple to my knees, gulping down air and trying to see past giant black spots.

"I wanted to, Jocelyn, but you left me no choice," Mab spits. "I warned you *time* and *time* again to leave my subjects alone." She kicks me in the chest with each word. The leather armor only softens the blows a little.

When she pauses, I gasp, "I didn't kill Fuloch. Shaylee's lying."

That earns me another kick.

"Faeries can't lie, you idiot," Mab snarls.

"Pick on someone else for once, bitch," Rina shouts, jumping up from the pew. One of the guards has to pin her back down.

Mab's face shifts to an unreadable cool that terrifies me to my core. She stands up straight and strolls over to Rina. After the longest second of my life, Mab grabs a handful of Rina's hair and yanks her head back.

"You're the girl Jocelyn killed the redcap for, aren't you?" Mab asks, drawing that dagger I've become all too familiar with.

Rina forces a chuckle. "What are you going to do about it? Kidnap me? Slap me around? You don't scare me."

"Such bravado." Mab's mouth curls into a malicious grin. "I should cut it out of your chest."

Mab turns back to me. "You're right, Jocelyn. Annalise is innocent. I shouldn't have dragged her into this. Not when there better ways of punishing you. Anyway, she won't be a willing offering now that she knows the truth." Mab giggles down at Rina. "And I suppose you wouldn't be interested either, hmm?"

"Go to Hell," Rina snarls.

Mab turns Rina's face left and right. "You *are* quite beautiful." The queen's eyes shift to me. "I think I'll keep her for myself. Maybe then you'll learn your place."

"Leave her out of this," I bark.

Mab stands erect, sneering down at Rina. Rina's furious expression slowly goes blank and her body goes limp against the pew like a rag doll. There's no longer anything behind her ebony eyes except Mab's will.

"Stand up, my dear," Mab orders, "and take this knife for me."

Rina obeys, eyes foggy and head lolled.

I fight against the guards. They weigh nothing next to the crushing panic in my chest. "Mab, stop, please. Rina, wake up."

Rina glances my way at the sound of her name, but only for a second. She looks back to Mab, awaiting further orders with the dagger in her hand.

Mab folds her arms and taps her chin. "Since you're mine now, we need to make it obvious, wouldn't you say?" She glances at me with a triumphant grin before giving her final order.

"Carve my mark into your skin. Make sure to cut deep. We'd hate to repeat this process down the road, wouldn't we?"

"Rina, wake up for Christ's sake," I beg, fighting against the guards with everything I have.

"Your Majesty, stop," Anna sobs. "Don't do this."

Rina raises the knife to her bare chest.

Think fast. Think, Jocelyn!

"Mab, let me do it. Take me instead."

"I'm bored of playing with you, Jocelyn."

"What would Titania say?"

The queen winces and glares at me. "Who told you that name?"

"What would *your sister* say?"

Mab's nails dig into her arms. Her eyes lock with mine, stormy and unreadable. Rina holds the dagger centimeters above her skin, like a robot whose program has stopped working.

The room holds its breath.

Mab's eyes clear and snap back to Rina. "I gave you an order."

The dagger presses into her skin.

Anna screams.

"MAKE ME THE OFFERING!"

Mab raises her hand. Rina's eyes flicker back to consciousness. The dagger clatters to the floor. She stares at it in horror and falls to her knees, trembling.

The queen pauses, then glowers down at me with a calculating expression. "What did you say?"

I take a deep breath and repeat myself. "If you let Annalise and Rina go, I'll be your willing sacrifice. I'll be the Hallowed Offering."

Twenty-Six

"TELL THE COURT whatever you want," I beg. "Tell them Anna changed her mind. Tell them I'm so blind with devotion to you that I begged to take my sister's place. I don't care. Just let Annalise and Rina go."

"Jocelyn, no," Annalise cries, still restrained in the pew.

Rina scrambles to her feet. "Jocelyn, don't you dare," she shouts. Two guards intercept her before she can get to me.

My offer hangs in the air like the blade of a guillotine. Mab twists a lock of hair as she weighs it. A wicked grin spreads across her face. The blade comes down.

Mab points to the girls. "Get them out of my court."

One of the guards forces Anna to stand and drags her down the aisle. "No, you can't," she sobs. "Jocelyn, please."

I can't bring myself to face her, so I focus on Mab, even though the delighted light in her eyes makes me want to bolt.

Rina latches onto my arm as she passes, squeezing so tight it hurts. There's a fire built on rage behind her eyes. "Don't let her win, Jocelyn Lennox," she hisses.

"You and Anna are getting out," I remind her. "So, she hasn't."

Rina's grip goes limp and her eyes widen in terror. She and Anna fight every step, refusing to walk, but it doesn't stop them from being dragged out.

"What about Mom?" Anna weeps. "She just woke up. What's it going to do to her if you just disappear?"

Finally, I force myself to look at her. The tears streaming from her big blue eyes nearly break me. I gulp back my fear and disguise it as a laugh. "It'll be okay, Anna."

Terror and pain register on her face just as the door slams shut.

The silence that follows is deafening, like the stillness after a bomb goes off.

Mab doesn't let it stay that way for long. "Jocelyn Mae Lennox, do you give yourself willingly as the Hallowed Offering in exchange for the life of your sister and your lover?"

"I do."

"Do you swear to face death with dignity and courage, so that Faerie may be blessed and flourish for another seven years?"

I swallow hard and force out, "I do."

Mab offers me her hand with a proud grin. "Then we have a deal."

The second my hand touches hers, my chest begins to burn. The searing heat brings me to my knees. The fire feels so deep in my chest that I can't even work up the breath to scream. After what feels like a hundred years, it smolders and I'm left lying on my back as the ceiling swirls above.

One of the guards hoists me to my feet and steadies me as the room spins.

Mab is the one image that stays still. Her nails dig into my cheeks as she holds my face in her hand. "You brought this upon yourself, Jocelyn," she hisses. "I could have left you all alone, but you forced my hand. I can't let a human defy me like this."

"Talk to Shaylee." I cough. "I don't know how, but she's lying."

The queen's eyes narrow. "You accuse my own daughter of lying to me?"

"Why not? You killed your own sister."

Mab winces, digs her nails even deeper, and then thrusts me away.

"Put her somewhere she won't cause any more trouble," she orders. "I'll send Needleworker to get her measurements."

"With pleasure, Your Majesty," sneers the knight holding me up. He hurries me out of the room as Mab stands in front of Warren.

"I heard an interesting story about Dominic," Mab muses. "Care to explain?"

Warren speaks so softly I almost miss his words: "Long live the Queen of Light."

As we march down the corridor, muffled screams cut through the silence.

My legs begin to give out. "I need to stop."

"Keep moving," the knight growls.

Only then do I realize it's Lyle. If it were anyone else, I'd be impressed he's still on his feet, but since it's this asshole, I'd rather give him more grief. If I only have another day to live, I might as well make the most of it.

"You might want to up Mab's medication a bit," I taunt. "I don't think she's going to make it through the day, otherwise."

"Shut up," Lyle spits. "And watch your tongue. How dare you use Her Majesty's name."

"What, she doesn't let you use it? Her closest, most trusted knight?"

"I said shut up, girl."

"Oh, ho, we're putting away the formalities, I see. Sorry you can't do the same with the queen."

Lyle shoves me in the chest right in the still-healing burn and it erupts in waves of pain. I bite back a chain of profanities. I'm not about to give him any satisfaction.

"Hit a nerve, did I?" I scoff, massaging my chest as he glares daggers at me.

"As the Offering, I can't kill you," Lyle growls, "but you don't have to arrive at the altar in one piece. Unless you want to lose that damned tongue, you'll silence it."

He grabs me by the arm and drags me deeper into the keep.

The corridors have completely cleared out, which doesn't make sense. Aren't faeries from all over the realm visiting? It was buzzing with activity before everything went to hell. Now it's deserted. Mab must want to keep them busy until everything's back on schedule. If there's one thing she's told me a thousand times, it's that I can't make her look weak. To be honest, I think she's doing the job fine herself.

By the time we arrive at our destination, my fingers tingle from the lack of circulation, but that's the least of my worries. Empty cells line the walls, illuminated by dim orange torches that dance in the dreary draft. Skeletons of long-forgotten prisoners grin through the crystal bars like warnings for those foolish enough to cross the Faerie Queen.

Fools like me.

With a wave of his hand, Lyle opens one of the cells, throws me in, and slams the door in one quick, fluid motion. "How I wish the Offering ceremony required you to suffer more." He laughs through the bars.

"Yeah, well, we wouldn't want to get any blood on your precious *Mab's* dress, now would we?" I fire back.

A joyful smile spreads across Lyle's face. "No, we wouldn't. I'll just have to settle for watching her slit your throat and bleed you out like a goat."

The thought threatens to make me throw up.

He won that round, but I'm too wired to stop.

"How much time do you think this Offering will give her? A few years, tops? She won't make it to the next one."

"Yes, she will. She's strong enough," Lyle spits.

"No, she's not, and she's a terrible queen. All she does is poison this place."

Lyle socks me in the stomach through the bars. I crumple over.

"Don't you speak of my beloved like that!" he roars.

I look up at him in time to see the shock on his face.

He hides it again and leans close to hiss, "One more insult against Her Majesty, and I mean it, I'll cut out your tongue. Maybe your eyes, too, for good measure." He stands erect and leaves me in the cell to contemplate how much it must suck to be in love with the Queen of Faerie. That explains the pissing contest he's had with me since day one, but if he honestly thought I was trying to compete, he's as crazy as she is.

This doesn't change anything. I still hate him, but I can fume about that later. Right now, I have to think of a way out of this mess. I pace the length of the cell, in part to get my mind going and in part to ward off the chill. It doesn't do much on either account.

Waves of guilt compete for room in my mind. I should have never let Rina come. I should have never gone to that haunted house. I should have protected Anna better. What is she going to tell Mom? If I die, how long will they look for me? How will this affect Mom's recovery? What if her health gets worse?

I stop and lightly slap myself in the face. "Get it together, Jocelyn," I mumble.

If I keep this up, it'll eat me alive. I'll be dead before Mab can lay a finger on me.

And I'll be just like her.

No. That would mean she was right about us. She can't be.

Ugh, focus! What would Dominic say if he were here? Something inspirational about moving forward, no doubt, but it's impossible to move anywhere when you're stuck in a jail cell.

Footsteps echo down the hall, putting me on high alert. The voice that accompanies them makes my blood boil.

"Yeesh," it mutters. "You must have *really* pissed the queen off if she put you down here. Offerings usually get really nice digs."

Two more steps and Shaylee stands in front of me.

The woman who sold me out.

Red tints my vision as I snarl, "You traitor."

Shaylee raises her hands in surrender. "Before you flip out, let me explain."

"You have ten seconds," I growl. "Before I come at you through these bars."

She takes a step back. "I didn't think Mab would take your sister. I figured she would go straight for you and make you the Offering. I miscalculated."

"Are you kidding me?" I bark.

"Look, Jocelyn, this isn't personal. We need to take back the faerie courts and split them up. Mab's a time bomb. When she goes off, she'll plunge the whole realm into chaos. Waiting until December to take her out is too risky, but my mother won't listen to me. Lucky for me, Little Miss Rina showed up. She's the perfect candidate to claim you before the court, giving me time to put our forces in place to overthrow the queen."

My mind races. "Why would Mab *want* you to attack her?"

Shaylee rolls her eyes. "I didn't say Mab. Keep up, Jocelyn."

My anger fizzles out as I piece together the puzzle.

That's why Shaylee kept pushing me to spend time with Rina. She's the final piece of the coup. She needed to like me enough to "claim" me before the court, whatever that means. But that doesn't tell me who Shaylee's mother is. She looks so much like Mab, who else could it be? What had Warren said?

Long live the Queen of Light.

"Queen Titania isn't dead," I conclude. "And she's your real mother. She had you pretend to be Mab's daughter to infiltrate. How does that work?"

"We look a lot alike, don't we?" Shaylee flips her hair, probably for emphasis. "I didn't even have to use a glamour. And it certainly helped that Mab is rumored to have a bastard kid like me running around. Might even have a few. Most faerie monarchs do. It was the perfect alibi."

"I thought faeries couldn't lie," I point out.

Shaylee puts her hands on her hips and leans toward the bars. "I'll let you in a little secret," she whispers. "Being half-human means I can. Lovely little trick, lying. Humans should take more advantage of it."

"You're sick."

Shaylee shakes her head. "Not sick. Just half-faerie."

"That's no excuse," I snap.

Shaylee begins ambling away instead of defending herself. "Well, it's getting late, and I still need to get everyone on board with my plan." She pauses and backtracks. "Oh, and if you could *not* sell me out to the queen, I'd be grateful."

"Are you sure you're not Mab's?" I snap. "You're certainly calloused enough to be hers."

Shaylee shrugs. "I deserve that, but things will work out. Trust me. Besides, in the end, you just might thank me."

"Why the hell would I thank you for this?" I demand.

An elated grin spreads across Shaylee's face and she puffs up like a birthday balloon. If the thought of potential death and bloodshed gets her excited, she's clearly related to Mab, even if she's not her daughter.

"Think about it, Jocelyn," she says, strolling away. "How many humans can say they've been part of a coup for the faerie crown? You'll be a legend." With that, she leaves me alone again.

If I don't think of something soon, that number is going to stay firmly at zero.

Twenty-Seven

FORMALIZING A WAY out of this isn't going well.

If I run, Mab will just come after Anna and Rina. Maybe even Rick and Mom. And an Offering has to be made, or all of Faerie will fade away. That puts Hob, Calista, and countless others in danger too. I don't know how long that would take, though. I should have made Shaylee tell me more about her stupid coup.

Mab said she'd come visit me eventually. What if I just... No. Hell no. No more blood on my hands. The fact that killing her even crossed my mind tells me how desperately I need to get out here. But another Offering is going to have to die in my place no matter what I do.

Shuffling footsteps saves me from pondering anymore. I wind up a few barbs to throw at Shaylee, but they're useless.

"The queen gets loonier every day," whines a scratchy high-pitched voice. "Changing Offerings on a dime. Is she daft? What will people say? Someone is bound to notice that she's going mental. What if they attack before the princess?"

"You should watch your words, Needleworker," says a calmer familiar voice.

"Oh, let her hear me. Then let her find another exquisite seamstress on such short notice."

A pudgy little faerie waves her hand in front of the bars. They swing open and nearly smack me in the face. She strides in, pokes at me, and drops her giant patchwork bag.

"Take this armor off, girl. We have work to do."

"Nice to meet you, too," I snap.

Iver follows close behind and helps me unbuckle the straps. "Forgive her," he says. "She's a bit put out at the moment."

"Hmph. Who isn't?" asks the seamstress, snapping out a stretch of shimmering white fabric. "Who does Princess Shaylee think she is? Dragging innocent mortals into faerie politics? There are plenty of terrible ones she could have put on the chopping block and left there."

Iver ignores her. "Are you all right, Jocelyn?"

"Not really," I answer, slipping off my arm bracers. "I've been down here for hours, and I still don't have a plan to get myself out of here."

"Fret not. There's something in the works. Thanks to Shaylee's insubordination and Warren's capture, Dominic's cover has been blown, so he's retreated to our queen's side. No doubt he'll help get you out of this mess."

"Is Warren okay?" I ask, bracing myself for the answer.

Iver lowers his gaze. "We'd best not talk about it," he mutters. "You'll only blame yourself."

My stomach knots. "He's dead."

Iver stands taller with his chin high. "He knew the risk, just like the rest of us. Shaylee made this much bigger than you, Jocelyn. For that cause, he died with dignity."

"But he—"

"Don't. You'll drive yourself mad. We're going to have a hard enough time getting you out of here without you falling to pieces."

I shake my head. "Everyone can't seriously be considering—"

Needleworker throws a length of the fabric around my shoulders. "Hold still now," she orders. "And we most certainly can. Especially Dominic. He's always had a soft spot for humans."

"Why is that?"

Needleworker and Iver exchange knowing looks.

"That's his tale to tell," Iver answers.

Too bad Calista didn't come with them. She would have told me everything.

"Besides, we have bigger problems," Needleworker says, scowling up at me. "Like your hair. What am I supposed to do with it? It looks like a pile of hay that's been kicked around in the mud."

Throwing shade at faeries is very ill-advised, but when the one spouting insults looks like a ragged pincushion with gnawed-on yarn for hair, it's hard to resist.

I reach deep into my soul and take a calming breath. "Just run a comb through it. If Shaylee's plan fails, I won't be alive long enough for a haircut to be worth it."

Iver and Needleworker pause, taken back by my statement. They're probably right to react that way, but I'm too tired to care.

"The queen's really worn you down, hasn't she?" Needleworker asks, her voice slightly less grating.

"Yeah," I mumble. "She has."

The seamstress works silently, mumbling as she fiddles with the fabric. I let her get on with it, too tired to squirm as she pokes and prods me. I don't even react when she pricks me with pins. Iver watches me with the same concern I've seen on Dominic's face a thousand times.

"There," Needleworker announces. "Now take it off. Careful now. Don't let the pins fall out."

I gingerly pull the fabric over my head and hand it to her. Without the armor, I shiver in the thin white shirt and brown slacks Dominic loaned me. The cold feels deeper than the soil and roots around me, though. It's like Fuloch's poison has settled in again.

Needleworker glances at me from the corner of her eye and slaps her forehead. "Blast it, I nearly forgot." Sticking a few pins between her teeth, she rummages in her bag and pulls out a thick wool shirt and a small knotted handkerchief. "Put that on. It'll keep you warm. And you need to eat. You're too skinny."

I try not to glower at her as I throw on the shirt and untie the handkerchief. Inside sits a vine of grapes and loaf of bread speckled with nuts and grain.

"Sorry it's not more," Needleworker says, going back to work. "With all the guests, there's not much left in the kitchen that you can eat. No point in saving you if you're just going to wind up trapped here."

"It's perfect," I say around a mouthful of bread. "Thank you."

I take a seat beside Iver and watch Needleworker sew at lightning speed. The tunic hangs in the air as if two invisible hands hold it for her. It rises and lowers when she mumbles directions. The calm chatter is soothing after all the shouting in my head.

"At least the girls got out," I mumble.

Iver nods. "That lover of yours certainly has a fire within her."

I choke on a grape. "She's not my lover, Iver," I gasp.

Iver blinks a few times, eyes wide. "Then what are you two?"

"We were working on that."

Needleworker throws the tunic in my face. "Try that on again, but this time without those shirts." She raises an eyebrow at Iver. "Nosy, aren't you, knight?"

"Yes, but this is important," Iver argues.

"Why would my relationship with Rina be important?" I ask, getting to my feet and self-consciously removing my shirts. "Even if she does want to 'claim' me or whatever."

I stop short when I look down at my chest. A cursive "T" glows, irritated and red, against my skin. I hadn't even gotten used to the nightshade mark being gone before putting myself in the exact same spot.

Scratch that. This is way worse.

I feel sick at the idea of Anna having the same mark. She couldn't have, though. She would never have gone along with Mab's plan if she had met the same fate. Mab's made it clear that she takes a special sense of pleasure in torturing me.

"That's why," Iver snarls, jabbing a finger at the burn. "Rina can help us save you from that monster."

"Absolutely not," I snap, throwing the garment over my head. "We need to talk to Shaylee and think of another plan."

"It wouldn't work anyway. They're both women." Needleworker sighs.

"It doesn't matter," Iver corrects. "They just have to be in love—"

"Time out," I exclaim, standing between the two of them. "I've known Rina for three weeks. I like her. Like, *really* like her, but she's definitely not in love with me. What are you going on about?"

"Yep." Needleworker pokes at the fabric. "Won't work."

"It just might. Have a little faith," Iver argues. Finally remembering that I'm in the room, he turns to me. "We can't tell you everything. We're bound to silence, but know that someone who loves you might be the only key to saving you."

If that's the case, I have to agree with Needleworker. Three weeks is way too fast. She can't be in love with me. As much as I like her, I'm *definitely* not in love with her. I can't be, right?

"I'll figure something else out," I say.

"Smart girl," Needleworker affirms. She tugs at my clothes, wanting me to change again. "Love is too fickle to trust at a time like this." She gently folds the tunic and sets it on top of her bag.

"Love is what we need most at a time like this," Iver argues.

Needleworker shoves the handkerchief in her pocket and gnaws on the empty grape vine. "Love is what cost Queen Titania the Seelie Court to begin with."

Iver glares down at her, but doesn't argue. Looking back to me, he says, "If Rina has the audacity to call Her Majesty a 'bitch' to her face, I think she can handle it."

"It's not a matter of what she can handle," I reply. "I'm tired of people getting hurt on my account."

The knight studies me, then follows Needleworker out the door.

"If there's anything else you need," she says. "Just ask."

Maybe if my hands were busier, I could think clearer. The longer I ponder, the more I think that's exactly what I need. "Paint. I want to leave Mab one last portrait."

The seamstress nods. "I'll see what I can do."

Iver lingers as she walks back the way she came. With her out of earshot, he takes ahold of one of the crystal bars and says, "I understand your struggle, Jocelyn. You're proud. You want everyone to rely on you, but you're afraid relying on others will mean you've failed them somehow. To live closed off from others, too cowardly to open up and let them carry you when you need it, forsaking love in the name of your ego—that would be the true failure. Remember that."

"You sound like Dominic." I sigh with a shake of my head. "Are all faerie knights sages of wisdom?"

"No." Iver chuckles. "Just the particularly handsome ones."

Needleworker cackles from down the hall.

Iver glowers at her. "We'll see you soon, Jocelyn. Keep your head up."

"I'll try."

With them gone, I'm stuck planning again. Regardless of how Rina feels about me, I feel about her, or what it means for my ego, I can't put her in harm's way again.

Think. What can I work with? Mab said she thinks we're the same. There has to be something there I can use, even if I refuse to believe her. If only I could convince her that those similarities don't have to spell our demise.

A small scratching sound against the far wall of the cell distracts me. I back away, worried about what faerie vermin could possibly look like. An area crumbles to reveal a tunnel. From it comes a voice I know quite well.

"Gods above. Did Lyle have to pick the farthest cell?"

Dominic crawls out of the hole, coughing and covered in dust.

He's hardly on his feet before I throw my arms around him.

"Dominic, oh my God," I exclaim, "I thought you were with Queen Titania."

He pats me on the back, then dusts himself off. "I was," he answers. "But I couldn't hang around while you were still in the dark."

A crotchety voice comes from within the tunnel. "Is this the right cell? Is she still in one piece?" Mr. Hob emerges second, wheezing and clawing up Dominic's leg to get to his feet.

I kneel to hug the old goblin and try not to let his rotten cabbage odor ruin the moment. "Mr. Hob, what are you doing here?"

He squirms out of my arms and pushes me away. "Rescuing you, obviously. If Her Majesty thinks she's sacrificing my best employee, she's got another thing coming." He looks around. "Where is…" He leans down and calls into the tunnel, "Hurry up, lass."

"I'm coming. This dress isn't exactly tunnel-friendly."

That voice is supposed to be miles away.

Rina pokes her head out and grins.

"Hey there, hero," she says. "Ready to be rescued?"

Twenty-Eight

THE JOY OF seeing Rina and the panic of seeing her *here* make my brain short-circuit. Holding her, soaking up the warmth she radiates, and breathing her in is more important than thinking anyway.

She pulls away and cups my face in her hands. One finger gingerly traces the cut from Mab's ring. "Did she hurt you again?"

"I'm fine," I say. "Are *you* okay?"

"I'm going to have nightmares well into my forties, but I'll make it."

"You promised you wouldn't come back if things went wrong."

Rina drops her hands. "That wasn't *wrong*, Jocelyn. That was batshit insane. We didn't lay ground rules for batshit insane."

I flash Dominic and Mr. Hob a dirty look. "Why didn't you stop her?"

"What, and get more bruises?" Mr. Hob retorts.

"As much as you loathe getting help," Dominic cuts in, "we need her."

Rina rummages through the layers of her dress and pulls out her phone from a pocket. "I did a little research and—"

"You found a solution to this madness with your *smartphone*?"

Rina beams. "Cool, right? Apparently, a previous queen cursed the story. Faeries can't tell it without falling over dead, but there's a human account, which is fair game."

"I will say this for humanity—" Dominic chimes in. "Your methods of storing information are pure marvels."

Rina scrolls down the screen. "So, anyway, there was this girl, Janet, who fell in love with a faerie knight, Tam Lin. He was picked to be the Offering the last time the courts were united, back when they were still in Europe, so she snuck into the ceremony and used this thing called the law of claim to save him."

"That sounds too easy," I say.

"That's because Janet had to go through these trials. Luckily, she passed and they both got to leave."

I pace for a moment, weighing our options. "And while this is going on, Shaylee will put her coup into action, I take it?"

"Exactly," Dominic answers. "The challenges will drain what little magic the queen has left, allowing us to strike."

I'm still not sold. "Where's Anna?"

"At the farmhouse with Calista," Mr. Hob answers. "She refuses to leave without you, and I wasn't about to argue with her."

I look back to Rina. "You're sure you want to do this?"

Rina puts her hands to her hips. "No, I have a gun to my head. Of course I want to do this."

"Maybe we should brainstorm a few other ideas first," I suggest.

Rina rolls her eyes. "We don't have time to brainstorm. The queen wants you dead in less than twelve hours."

"Well, we're going to have to *make* time. There's got to be something that doesn't put you in harm's way. Nobody else needs to get hurt because of me."

Rina groans and makes a strangling motion with her hands, clearly intended for me. "You. Are. Infuriating," she snaps. "Do you hear yourself? You saved my life twice. You endured that psycho-bitch of a queen to save your mother. And yet you..." Rina's voice cracks and she folds her arms, looking away from all of us.

I lay a hand on her shoulder, trying to comfort her, but she jerks away. Dominic and Mr. Hob look on sternly, ignoring my silent pleas for help.

Rina sniffs and takes a deep breath. "You've got to stop this crazy crusade," she says, turning to me. "I can use the law of claim. I know I can. You've done enough. Please...just...stop."

I want to. Really, I do. And I know she can do it, but, even with everything on the line, giving up control is hard. It feels damn near impossible, especially when I've tried to stay in control for so long.

But if I want to live, I'm going to have to learn to let go.

"Okay," I mutter. "You win. Law of claim it is." I pull Rina toward me.

She lets me and lays her forehead on my chest. Tension drains from her body. "Oh, thank God," she exhales. "I thought Dominic was going to have to hex you."

"Don't rule it out yet." Dominic chuckles. He jumps as his right pocket vibrates. One glance at his cell phone makes him scowl. "It's Shaylee."

What little peace I had burns up in rage. "Give her a few choice words for me."

Dominic shoves his phone back in his pocket. "I already did. Believe me." He looks to Mr. Hob and Rina. "Come on, you two. We'll see Jocelyn soon enough."

"Don't lose faith, lass," Mr. Hob says, crouching to crawl into the tunnel. He gives me a final thumbs-up. "We'll see this through."

I return the gesture. "Thanks, Mr. Hob."

Dominic follows suit. "You'll be home with your family before you know it."

"I know," I reply. "Be careful out there."

The knight scoffs, "Unlike you, I'm always careful."

Instead of following Dominic, Rina fiddles with the collar of my shirt. "I can't believe Shaylee sold you out," she grumbles. "She shouldn't be queen of anything."

"Trust me, she could be worse." I sigh.

"That doesn't mean she.... What's this?" She tugs down my collar and gasps at the sight of the burn. "Jesus, Jocelyn. What did she do to you?"

I take Rina's hand in mine, trying to draw her attention away. "Don't worry about it. It doesn't even hurt anymore."

"Don't worry about it?" Rina repeats, voice rising with panic.

"It'll be gone the second this is over."

Rina wiggles out of my grip and looks at the burn again. The warmth of her touch sends chills across my chest. "You're worth saving, you know," she mutters. "You've got yourself pegged all wrong."

"Maybe," I reply. "I'm also incredibly hardheaded, so it'll take some time for that to sink in. I need a learning curve."

She still looks concerned about the burn. There must be something I can do to get her mind off it. I glance at her full lips for a second, then bring them up to meet mine. The heat of her mouth pushes away the chill of the cell and her body pressed against mine feels like a current of electricity. I can hardly remember where we are with the way her hands run through my hair.

She breaks away and quietly asks, "Where's this on the learning curve?"

"It's the origin point," I answer. "Very crucial."

Rina whispers, "You're so full of it," and kisses me again.

A distant creaking sound cuts it short.

I let Rina go and shove her toward the tunnel. "Tell Anna I'll see her soon."

Rina gives an exasperated huff of laughter as she kneels in front of the tunnel.

That isn't what I want to hear.

"What was that for?" I ask, leaning over her.

She reaches up and kisses me on the cheek. "Nothing. Look for the nixies in the crowd. I'll be with them."

"Rina, tell me."

She disappears and the rocks roll back into place. I'm left staring at the seamless wall, heart pounding in my chest. I'm not even sure what for anymore.

"Having a nice conversation with the wall?"

Needleworker stands at the door with a basket of small jars of paint, water, and three paintbrushes. She slides it through the bars and hands it to me.

"It's just too quiet down here," I lie.

Needleworker watches me with skeptical beady eyes as I sort out the paint.

She taps her chin but lets the subject go and hands me a small corked vial. "Sprinkle this on the wall. It'll clean it right up. I'm no artist, but dirt and grime have no place mixing with paint."

I study the white powder inside. "Got it. Thanks."

Needleworker waves away the gratitude and shuffles away. "Don't mention it," she calls, "Just make the best of that paint."

Once she's gone, I pick a smooth patch of wall get to work. I dust it with the powder in the vial, and then put down a layer of white paint. It dries almost instantly. Wonderful. No room for mistakes.

Three faces emerge from the paint. The first is Mab's. I have her features memorized, but painting her looking happy feels alien. Shaylee comes second with flowers in her hair and a matching white dress. I have to resist the urge to paint devil horns on her head. The last woman, Queen Titania, is the most difficult since I've never seen her. I use Mab as a reference and tweak her features, making them softer. She ends up with pale blond hair to contrast against Mab's dark curls, but they have matching bright-green eyes.

"My sister wouldn't be caught dead in white."

The voice startles me, and I drop my brush.

Mab watches me pick it back up. We make eye contact, and she looks like she's expecting me to say something, but I just wash the brush and start painting again. Her nails click against the porcelain mug in her hands. It's a pathetic attempt to mute the deafening silence. She tries speaking instead.

"You're upset."

"I'm not upset," I grumble, eyes still focused on the painting. "'Filled with a murderous rage' is a more apt description."

Mab scoffs. "You could never kill me, Jocelyn."

"Did you need something? Or do you just feel like harassing me one last time?"

"The seamstress said you were painting," she explains, entering the cell. "I wanted to see." She steps close enough to brush against me, making my muscles tense as I wait for her to attack. "Why my family?"

"It's a trinity," I answer, pulling away. "A healthy, peaceful coexistence, each supporting the other—the Seelie, the Unseelie, and the Human. Something you destroyed when you took the throne by force."

Mab winces. "You might not have the resolve to murder me, but you certainly know how to twist a knife," she says, setting down her mug.

"I do what I can," I murmur.

Mab's gaze bore into me as I work on Titania's dress. I have nothing left to say to her. She still apparently has plenty to say, though, because she lays a hand on my shoulder, making me cringe.

"Or maybe you're trying to save me?" she muses.

I jerk away. "Why the hell would I do that?"

She grabs a hold of me again. This time, her nails dig into my skin as she forces me to face her. "Like I said, we're the same," she answers. "Our attempts to save what we love have blown up in our faces and the shrapnel just might kill us."

My stomach plummets. "That's not true," I snap.

"And yet you sit here awaiting your death."

"Let go of me, Your Majesty," I demand.

Mab shakes her head. "You know better than to call me that," she coos, shoving me against the cold damp wall. "And you know there's no way out of this. Just forget for a while." She leans closer, like she has dozens of times before, but my head's still clear. The room is still static and not an inch of my body wants this woman touching me. It must be the Offering. She can't bother wasting magic on something like this.

And I can't bother humoring her.

I shove her away hard enough to make her stumble. "Like you try to forget?" I shout. "I told you that I don't want to."

Mab glares at me. "Give up already," she spits. "There's no turning back for us. All we can do is try to forget so that we don't hurt in the meantime. I'm trying to help you."

"Trying to forget hasn't helped *you*," I fire back. "You're still hurting."

The words catch us both off guard. Mab winces as if I physically attacked her. I recoil too, as if she shocked me. Why should I care if Mab is in pain?

The queen raises her mask again and grinds her teeth. "You're hopeless," she snarls. "Trying to help you was a fool's errand."

"Then why are you still here?"

Mab huffs and snatches up her mug, splashing tea everywhere. "Enjoy your last few hours of life, Jocelyn."

"Will do," I respond.

She storms out of the cell and slams the bars behind her. She's only out of sight a few seconds when something crosses my mind.

"Why did you tell me your name?" I call after her.

A long silence follows. Then, her heels click back toward the cell. She studies me through the bars with that familiar calculation back in her eyes. "I thought being the same gave us a connection." Mab lowers her gaze. "But it seems like I was wrong. The world you see is quite different." As she walks away, she adds, "I thought the world was dark, but now I think I might just be blind."

I hate how those words tear at my heart.

She can't be right. We're nothing alike, and I can't be feeling sympathy for her.

Alone in the cell again, I pick up my brush and continue painting. I try to push Mab's words away, but they weigh on my mind alongside a grim realization:

No magic on earth could ever give sight to those too afraid to open their eyes.

Twenty-Nine

WITH THE PAINTING done, I try to rest. Falling asleep is easy, but actually being asleep doesn't last long enough to be worth anything, thanks to Needleworker.

"Wake up," she barks, banging on the bars. "We have a schedule to keep."

I peel my aching body off the floor. "Is it time already?"

"Unfortunately," she answers. "We need to get you presentable."

My heart sinks at the sight of the two unfamiliar guards beside Needleworker. Once out of the cell, one of them grabs me while the other binds my hands.

Needleworker snatches me by the hem of my shirt and drags me down the hall with the guards following close behind. I try to keep the lid on my panic. Where's Iver? Or Dominic? They didn't get caught, did they?

And where are we? I don't recognize this area. Judging by the rising ceiling and the dripping stalactites, we're farther underground, but it should be getting colder. Instead, the air feels warm and humid.

Needleworker comes to a halt and swats me when I run into her. Turning to the guards, she says, "I can handle her from here, gentlemen."

The two guards shift and look to one another. "But we've been ordered to watch her," one of them says.

"And I've been ordered to get her presentable," Needleworker snaps back. "You'll just get in the way. You want to answer to the queen if she's late?"

They both go pale. "No, ma'am," says the other.

With a huff, Needleworker yanks me around the corner. With a wave of her hand, a stalagmite raises up out of the ground, shielding us from the guards.

"There." She huffs. "I can finally work in peace." She begins to untie my ropes. "What a mess. They're so scared of her they won't even follow her orders."

"I can't say I blame them," I mutter, taking in the chamber around us.

A spring bubbles through the far wall, feeding a deep pool in the center, then trickles into a stream before disappearing under the opposite wall. Beside the pool sits a narrow ledge filled with brightly colored glass bottles and bars of soap. The whole setup would be quite relaxing if I wasn't about to be sacrificed.

"Get washed up," Needleworker orders. "I'll leave the tunic out for you." She makes her way toward another ledge. "And no dawdling. We have—"

"—a schedule to keep, I know."

Needleworker scowls at me before focusing on her patchwork bag. "Cheeky little Offering, aren't you?" she grumbles. She faces the wall as she rummages through her bag, giving me enough privacy to get in the bath.

The hot water melts the soreness from my muscles and relaxes me more than sleeping did. However, it's not relaxing enough to keep my mind off Mab's words for long.

I thought being the same gave us a connection.

She's wrong.

I hold my breath and dip down under the water, as if I can drown the notion.

"Hey, Needleworker," I call as I surface, groping blindly for a towel. "Do you think the queen meant for this to happen?" I find one and wipe off my face.

"What do you mean?" she calls over her shoulder.

"I mean the court being what it is."

The seamstress cackles. "Of course not, girl. No monarch ever would. But I couldn't give a damn about what she intended. Her intentions didn't ruin Faerie. Her actions did."

Fair enough. It was a stupid question. I think of another while I change into the tunic. "Do you think she would ever step down?"

Needleworker examines the blades of a pair of scissors. "I doubt it. She's too proud for that. Besides, stepping down would never atone for everything she's done. Someone would end her the second the crown left her head. For Her Majesty, asking for forgiveness would be asking for death."

Merely existing in Faerie seems akin asking for death, but I won't argue.

"Love her or hate her, and most do hate her, no one can deny the queen has held it together longer than anyone who's ever joined the Faerie Courts, but that's no excuse for the damage she's done." Needleworker faces me, her eyes narrowed in calculation. "But that's not who we're talking about, is it?"

I lower my eyes and fold my arms. "Who else would I be talking about?"

"Who indeed?" Needleworker muses. She snaps her fingers and a hunk of stone morphs into a stool. She gives it a little pat. "Sit."

I plop down in front of her and let her get to work. This haircut has been overdue for a while, so I can't complain. It's too fast for me to even start worrying what a faerie haircut might look like.

"Finally." She sighs, shoving a mirror into my hand. "Your hair was driving me crazy."

I count to three and dare to look at the mirror. It's not bad. The shorter, neater cut makes me look older. Or maybe that's all the lines carved into my face. I wish she had left it a little longer, but Needleworker still has the scissors in her hand, so I think I'll keep that complaint to myself.

"Thanks," I say, handing the mirror back. "I look like a respectable young lesbian again."

"Don't go dying and make my work for nothing," she snaps, taking the towel from my neck.

"I'll do my best."

She shoves me to my feet. "Good, now we need to get you tied back up." Picking the rope up off the floor, she adds, "Sorry I can't do more for you."

"You've done plenty," I reply as we walk toward the exit. "Thank you."

The guards take over and lead me back the way we came. The corridors of the keep are eerily quiet. The emptiness sets me on edge with the realization of just how big this event must be. I can't decide if time needs to speed up or slow down. The sooner this starts, the sooner it'll be over, but how can anyone be ready for something like this?

Needleworker breaks off near the entrance with only a nod as a farewell. If I come back alive, maybe she'll have more to say.

The guards lead me into the night. A winding procession files down the center of a wide dirt road lined with torches. The shifting flames and shadows shroud the guests in mystery. Shifty eyes watch us as we pass. Claws, wings, webbed fingers, and wisps of smoke gesture in our direction. There are more whispered languages than I could ever hope to recognize. Many were probably never spoken among humans.

Looking ahead gives me more hope. Iver stands holding the reins of a milky-white horse. On the other side stands Brok, the other elf from the rescue mission. I do my best to keep my face neutral as the guards hand me off to Iver and exchange a few words of greeting. They untie me so that I can hoist myself up onto the horse and leave my hands free.

"You're supposed to be doing this willingly, after all," Iver whispers.

"Willing or not, I've never ridden a horse in my life," I reply.

Iver pats the beast's neck and mutters back, "Not to worry. It's easy. Just be sure to ride with your legs. Besides, you have bigger things to worry about."

From the depths of the forest comes the drone of a horn. The sound is so low and deep that it rattles my bones and sends my blood racing.

"That, for example, would be a good place to start." Brok comments, taking the horse's reins.

The procession marches through the woods, much to the joy of the onlookers. I dare to glance at the enormous crowd and meet menacing, malicious grins and drunken hoots, as if the ceremony has been going on for hours. Mixed within them are lowered heads and sad eyes. A short stocky faerie dares to fold his hands in prayer and gets slapped aside to make room for those who actually want to watch.

I can't let the crowd distract me. I need to find Rina. All she told me was that she would be with the nixies, but there isn't a familiar face in sight. As the procession winds through the forest, my mind spirals into all sorts of worst-case situations.

A bright glow through the trees distracts me. Judging by the spastic movement and warm colors, it's a roaring fire, threatening to consume the surrounding woods with its angry force.

A distant roar splits through the cheers and music. To my right, a gigantic troll lumbers through the crowd. Its enormous grubby hands stretch toward whatever poor souls it's after. A trail of knights chases after it and its next victims, whoever they are. The conflict spills out into the procession, sending faeries sprawling every which way, and I find out who the troll wants to catch.

It's Mr. Hob and Rina.

The troll lumbers up the road and dives for them. Mr. Hob disappears in the creature's massive fist while Rina tumbles out of the way.

"Rina, over here," I shout.

Our eyes meet. She sprints my direction with the soldiers and troll in tow.

"Ready to improvise?" Iver mutters as he and Brok draw their swords.

"I don't have much of a choice, do I?" I reply, grabbing the reins.

"That's the spirit!"

Iver slaps the horse's rear. It whinnies and bolts into the chaos toward Rina.

Here's hoping my two-minute riding lesson counted for something.

I call Rina's name, and she spots me through the crowd. She reaches for me, and I take hold of her arm, pulling with all my strength while trying to keep my balance. She flies up and lands behind me, arms wrapped tightly around my waist. We duck as the troll swipes our way. It misses as we gallop by.

"This would be awesome if it wasn't dangerous," Rina pants.

"Tell you what," I gasp back, "our first real date can be riding lessons."

She glowers at me over my shoulder.

"What happened to the nixies?" I ask.

"They bailed after our last failed miss—"

The horse shrieks and stumbles, throwing us to the ground. My head hits earth and sends the world spinning as I scramble to my feet, seeing three of everything. The horse lies on its side with an arrow jutting out from its hind leg. It thrashes and whines in agony, desperate to get back up.

Rina and I aren't in much better shape.

Leather-clad hands pin me down and bind my hands. Through the throng of boots, I can see Rina trying to fight back. Blood trickles from her forehead as she tries to push off our captors.

She takes the best breath she can and shouts, "The law of—"

A knight gags her before she can finish. She thrashes around and tries to yell, but it's no use. Without her words, I'm still the Offering. The knights hoist us to our feet to meet a familiar face.

Lyle.

He sneers at us, hands folded and chest out like a proud supervillain. With a shake of his head, he snickers. "You're hopeless, Jocelyn. You can't even die properly."

"Lyle, listen," I pant. "It doesn't have to be this way."

"Of course not," he muses, drawing his sword. "I could kill you and your wench here and now."

Rina lets loose a chain of muffled profanities.

"Talk to Mab. Get her to step down. Divide the courts."

Lyle's eyes narrow to a glare. He raises his blade to my neck. "You don't give me orders. *Especially* concerning the queen."

"If you love her, you'll listen to me."

"Enough," he barks. Slipping his sword back into its sheath, he snaps, "Take them and the traitors to Her Majesty. We'll let her make an example of them."

The knights shove us along and the procession starts again, but the illusion of merriment dissolves. Faeries who were excited about the ceremony now watch with nervous expressions and shifting feet. Some whisper behind their hands while others take giant steps back as if they're ready to run. Iver and Brok join us in our march, both beaten and bloodied. Their faces pale at the sight of Rina struggling against her gag.

"It didn't work." Iver's shoulders slouch. "It was a fool's errand after all."

"Thanks for the vote of confidence," I hiss back.

Iver hangs his head.

The fire grows into a roaring blaze as we come to the end of the trail. It stands atop the faerie mound I pass every time I come to court and towers over the crowd like an ancient god, thirsty for blood. I can hardly look at it directly it's so bright. It silhouettes Mab and Shaylee, like succubi with auras made of hellfire. The rest of the procession fans out around the mound, cowering before their queen. They tremble as if they fear they might be consumed next.

The knights drag us up the mound and force us to kneel before Mab and Shaylee. Behind them stands a stone alter, stained with the blood of past Offerings. A silver goblet sits at one end, sending macabre scenarios racing through my imagination.

Panic rises in my chest. I can't breathe.

"The girl tried to invoke the law of claim, Your Majesty," Lyle whispers with a proud grin, like he single-handedly stopped us.

Mab's face contorts to a snarl of rage. "I should never have let you leave this place," she hisses at me. "I should have turned your eyes to stone and locked you up."

Rina shouts at her, regardless of the gag that muffles her words.

Mab grabs her by the jaw. "Someone should cut out that tongue of yours."

"Harm her and you lose your willing Offering," I snarl.

Mab pauses, then releases Rina. "Fair enough. Making her watch you die will be more satisfying anyway." Looking to the knights holding Rina, she snaps, "Get her out of the way so I can get this over with."

Rina kicks and screams, nailing a few good blows on Mab's knights, but they overpower her and drag her off to the side. They force her head up so that she has no choice but to watch Mab yank me to my feet. My view of the crowd swirls and blurs as terror threatens to win. If Mab wasn't holding me up, I wouldn't be able to stay on my feet. Every fiber of my being trembles and my mouth went dry long ago, despite the fact that I want to hurl what little is left in my stomach.

Beside me, Mab shouts, "Today, we renew our bond with the Other World and breathe life into the Faerie Realm."

The crowd cheers, confident that the unrest has passed.

"Do you, peoples of Faerie, believe this sacrifice to be suitable?"

A somber, sincere "We do believe" rises from the masses.

Shaylee steps forward and places a long dagger, bejeweled with rubies, in Mab's hand. "Do you, Mab Draiota Dofeith, willingly give yourself as queen to bind the Other World and Faerie together for another seven years?"

Facing her people, Mab proudly proclaims, "I give myself willingly." Then, she stands before me. The fire set to consume me dances in her eyes. "And do you, Jocelyn Mae Lennox, willingly give yourself to replenish the magic that makes Faerie thrive?"

I manage to choke out, "I give myself willingly."

Mab turns back to the throng. "Let our pact, conceived by our words, be birthed by blood."

A knight takes me tightly by the shoulders and leads me to the altar. He forces me down, chest against the hot stone and eyes facing the wooden bowl below. It's exactly level with my neck.

Despite the fire, I'm freezing cold.

Mab whispers, "Because the enchanted will we follow, we bring forth gifts of living things."

I crane my neck to meet Mab's eyes. Her eyes glow in the blazing fire.

"It's not too late," I mutter, voice trembling. "You can stop this. You can save both of us."

Mab snatches me by my hair and yanks my head back. The cool of the blade bites my neck, then pulls back again.

"Because this night the earth is hallowed…"

I squeeze my eyes shut. "Please don't do this."

"We bring to the Ancients this—"

A sharp clang rings out.

"*I invoke the law of claim!*"

The world falls silent.

There's no pain, no agony, so I slowly open my eyes.

The knife lays in the grass beside a smaller dagger. The sight of it turns me into a trembling puddle against the altar. Thank God I'm already lying down.

Mab stares over her shoulder, then stands up straight and statue-still. "Who dares invoke the law?" she barks.

I twist to see Dominic, out of breath and standing at the edge of the hilltop with a girl at his side, looking just as winded. Her tattered white gown and the flowers in her wild blonde hair make her look more like a feral angel than either faerie or human. I know her blue eyes, though. I know that narrow nose and that thin serious mouth. I meet them every time I look in the mirror.

It's Annalise.

Thirty

MAB BLOCKS ANNA'S path to me as she comes forward.

"What makes you think you have a right to claim Jocelyn?" she scoffs.

"She's my sister," Annalise fires back. She lowers her gaze to me and smiles. "The law doesn't specify what kind of love I have to feel."

How does she know about the law? I crane my neck to meet Rina's eyes, hoping for a silent answer, but she's too focused on Annalise.

Mab's shoulders shake as she begins to laugh. "You're a fool if you think love is enough." She snickers. Looking to me, she snaps, "Untie her. Let her up."

A knight yanks me to my feet. Annalise throws herself into my arms and holds me tight. I don't think I could stand otherwise.

"That was too close," she mutters, voice shaking. "Too damn close. I'm so sorry, Jocelyn. Dominic had to come get me. The knights wouldn't let me get close enough to the faerie mound to—"

"Anna, you need to leave. Now," I demand. "I can't let you do this."

She squeezes me tighter. "You're not Dad, Jocelyn."

I don't know what shocks me into silence, her anger or her words.

She looks up at me with tears in her eyes. "I know he told you to look out for me and Mom, but you were *thirteen*. I know how much you miss him, but this is insane. I miss him too, but don't you think Dad would want us to look out for *each other*?"

I pull away and hold her shoulders. "Anna, you don't understand. Mab's—"

The queen's booming voice cuts me off. "Peoples of Faerie," she announces, "our Offering has been claimed. Will you bear witness to the challenge placed before this girl?"

The crowd shifts, eyeing their neighbors as if they wonder who might be the unlucky replacement. Hesitantly, they say in unison, "We do agree."

Mab turns back to us and glowers down at Annalise. With her steely gaze unyielding, she says, "Do you accept whatever challenges I lay before you?"

Anna narrows her eyes to a frosty glare. "Bring it."

Judging by the smug look on Mab's face, my sister should be more worried.

Mab leans forward and says quietly, "Brave words for one so young." She turns to me. "I think I'll bring you along, Jocelyn."

I can't imagine it's just to spectate, but I nod in agreement.

With a snap of Mab's fingers, the faerie mound disappears.

I blink to find a strangely human setting.

Red curtains tower above me on either side. Thick black wires beneath my feet lead to a shadowy room filled with timpani drums, music stands, and wound-up ropes. The only illumination comes from the stage on my right. Under the blinding lights stands the Northland High School choir, dressed in simple black dresses and tuxedoes, backs straight and folders held tall in front of them. Their conductor lifts her arms and the performers stand a little taller. The elderly woman at the piano waits for a glance from her, then begins the tranquil introduction to *Silent Night*.

All attention shifts toward my corner of the stage, where Annalise stands alone in front of a packed auditorium. Her face turns pale green as she looks down at her abrupt wardrobe change and over toward the conductor and pianist. Both women give her curious looks and the pianist begins the intro over again, waiting for Anna to sing.

Instead, my sister drops her folder and bolts behind the curtains.

She needs me.

I run forward to meet her, only to run face-first into nothing, resulting in a wicked headache. "Son of a bitch! Hold on, Anna." I back up to get a running start.

"Careful," warns a voice. "Break that barrier and she automatically loses."

I come to a halt and look to find Mab standing off to the side. Like me, her clothing hasn't changed, but her expression is smug and amused.

"What is this?" I demand.

"I decided that your sister's challenges should be her three greatest fears. We don't have time to go the usual route," Mab explains. I imagine that means she doesn't have the energy to do much more than this. The queen folds her arms and keeps talking. "If she gives up or if you step in, shattering the illusion and showing her that none of this is real, she loses."

"You're sick," I snarl.

Mab shrugs. "True, but you both agreed to this."

Fighting with the queen won't do either of us any good. Looks like all I can do now is send Anna good vibes. On the other side of the barrier, she wraps her arms around her waist and leans forward as if she might throw up.

"I can't do this," she cries, shaking her head. "I can't do this."

Desperate to do something, I lean against the barrier. "Yes, you can, Annalise," I whisper. "If you can face these last four months alone and infiltrate the Faerie Court, you can do this. Please, Anna. You have to." I hold my breath and watch helplessly as my sister tries to catch hers.

She closes her eyes and takes several deep breaths. "C'mon, Anna. Get it together," she murmurs. "It's only one song. Get out there." She opens her eyes, and the fire is back. Arms at her side, and face determined, Anna turns on her heels and marches back onstage. With a nod to both the conductor and the pianist, she stands in front of the microphone and squares her shoulders.

She takes a deep breath and begins to sing in the purest voice I've ever heard.

"Silent night, holy night..."

Come to think of it, I don't think I've ever heard Anna sing by herself. I listen in awe, wondering where my sister got such a gift and proud that she brought herself to use it when it really counted. Once the rest of the choir joins in, I turn back to Mab to gloat.

"Is that seriously all you got?" I taunt.

Mab smiles at me as if Anna's triumph doesn't faze her at all. She raises her right hand, ready to snap her fingers again. "You wish."

The concert hall melts into a lakeside view. Mab and I stand on the bank and look up at the overcast sky. The chilly breeze makes me shiver and wish for more clothes, but it's worse for Anna. She stands at the edge of a dock, trembling in a black one-piece bathing suit as she looks around to get her bearings. Laughter from the other side of the lake draws both our attention.

Across the water, doubles of my mother and I sit at a picnic table, laying out a spread of food, despite the bad weather. The sight makes me squirm, even though I know it's just a fancy glamour designed to trick Annalise. A car door slams, drawing my eyes past me and my mother. What I see nearly makes my legs give out. It's Dad.

He strolls toward the picnic table with a two-liter of cola and a bright smile on his face. As he sets it down, he kisses Mom's hair and ruffles mine. Fake-me pretends to be embarrassed and wiggles out from under his hand. Once he sits down next to Mom, he looks out across the lake at Anna.

"Come on, sweetheart," he calls. "It's time to eat."

"Daddy?" Anna calls, voice cracking. "Is that really you?"

"Who else would it be?" he yells back. "You're not thinking about swimming, are you? It's too cold. Besides, you hate the water."

My sister nods, turns, and speed walks toward shore.

My stomach plummets.

"Anna, no," I shout. "You gotta swim."

She comes to a stop on her own, one foot hovering above the sand. Her eyebrows pull together for a moment as she thinks it over. With a groan, she turns back to the lake.

With a deep breath, Anna takes off running toward the water and skids to a stop.

"One more time," she says to herself. "One more time. I can do this."

Again, she sprints forward, only to stop short of falling in.

"Third time's a charm." She sighs, walking back toward land.

"Anna, you're killing me," I grumble, beginning to pace.

Mab titters from the sidelines.

From the other side, fake-me shouts, "Hurry up, sis, I'm hungry."

"Screw you, Jocelyn," Anna yells back. I get the feeling that's intended for *me* me.

Annalise shifts from foot to foot, shakes out her arms, races toward the water with a crazed battle cry, and plummets into the lake. Her head breaks the surface seconds later with a scream.

"*Shit* that's cold," she yells, beginning to swim.

I grin and punch the air in triumph. "Way to go, baby sister."

"Don't celebrate just yet," Mab taunts. "She has to make it all the way across."

Of course she does.

Luckily, it turns out that the barrier only surrounds the lake. I can follow Annalise as long as I stay on the bank. I walk alongside her as she makes her way across the lake, listening to her complain about the cold the entire time.

She stops abruptly a third of the way.

My sister treads water and twirls around frantically. "Is something there?" she calls through chattering teeth. "What touched my leg?"

Oh, no.

She jolts again, searching the water for the culprit. I freeze and pray she keeps going.

Anna shrieks and flails about. "Please, no," she pleads. "Please, don't be real."

"Just keep going," I beg under my breath. "C'mon, Annalise. Keep going."

Dad comes to the edge of the lake. "Honey, go back," he calls. "It's too cold to swim all the way across."

Anna's head swivels between the distant bank and the dock. It's hard to tell if her face is pale from fear or cold. I hold my breath and wait to see what she'll do. Something must have touched her again, because she jumps, but it propels her toward the imitation family.

"Way to go, Anna," I cheer, following along. I run ahead to the edge of the barrier and shout encouragement that I know she can't hear. The idea that she just might beat Mab at her own game is too encouraging for me to stay quiet.

Annalise reaches the shallows and stumbles to her feet. Her face contorts into a sob as she runs into our father's arms. He holds them open, ready to catch his tired, terrified, freezing baby girl, but dissolves the second Anna touches him. The shock on her face breaks my heart. I don't want to break through to help her. I just want to cradle her as she holds her head in her hands and mourns the loss of our father a second time.

"She's stronger than I thought," Mab says coolly, appearing beside me. "She came along with me so easily to be the Offering. I never imagined she'd have the gall to resist taking the easier paths."

"It's a Lennox thing. We're full of surprises," I scoff. "Want to quit now? Save yourself the embarrassment?"

"Oh, no, Jocelyn," Mab replies. "Weren't you the one worried about what the court might think if I went back on my word?" She raises her hand to snap her fingers. "Besides, I'm particularly excited for this next one."

The scenery shifts again.

Soot black clouds rumble overhead and icy rain slants as it falls, thanks to angry, roaring gales. A small chapel sits atop a gently sloping hill, looking ominous against the dark skies. Tombstones and plaques dot the surrounding field with drowning bouquets that let the dead know they're not forgotten. I know I'll certainly never forget this place, because this is where Dad's buried.

I don't have to look far for his tombstone, but two sit beside it that I've never seen before. Anna stands before all three. The names on the new stones leave me colder than the rain.

Susan Marie Lennox

Jocelyn Mae Lennox

My sister brings her hands to her mouth in terror.

"Anna, they're not real," I choke. "You have to see past this. They're not real."

"Careful, Jocelyn," Mab taunts. "Wouldn't want to—"

"Shut up," I bark and point to the tormenting scene in front of us. "This is demented. What if someone shoved your grave in Shaylee's face?"

The queen's expression grows somber. "My daughter would act in a way befitting a queen of Faerie," she snaps. "Besides," she adds bitterly, "even if she were allowed to cry, I know she wouldn't."

"Don't you think that's wrong?" I demand. "Do you really think saving your realm has been worth the fact that your own daughter won't mourn you? Has seizing all this control been worth every relationship that's ever mattered to you?"

Mab winces.

Behind us, Anna sobs and doubles over with grief, "Don't leave me like this. I can't do this on my own."

My fury boils over, and I punch the barrier. It stays firmly in place.

My sister drops to her knees, crumpled in the rain. "I'm not you, Jocelyn. I can't live alone. I'm not strong enough." She really thinks I was being strong all this time?

I hit the barrier again, this time leaving my fist there. "Yes, you are, Annalise," I mutter. "Get up. You have to."

Instead, she leans toward the ground as if she's ready to lie down.

"Annalise Grace Lennox, don't you dare," I order.

"I can't do this without you guys," she cries. "Please, don't leave me."

"I'm here, Anna. I won't ever abandon you again, but you have to stand up."

There's nothing I can do. It's all up to her now.

So, I wait for what feels like an eternity.

Finally, Annalise lifts her face to the gravestones. "I can't...just lie here, can I?" She slowly sits up straight again. "That's not what any of you would want, is it?"

A near-hysterical laugh escapes my lips. "Damn right, we wouldn't. Get up."

Anna looks at each of the stones in turn. "If Dad could fight for as long as he did, and Mom could raise us on her own, and Jocelyn could face the Faerie Queen, I can do this."

"Yes, you can, baby sister."

Anna takes in a deep breath and lets it out again. "Guess I should start with going to change these wet clothes, huh? Jocelyn will probably haunt me if I let myself get sick like this."

"I probably would, yeah."

Anna pushes herself back onto her feet and steps away from the graves.

As she turns to face our direction, the world shatters.

I crumple to the grass of the faerie mound and struggle to breathe past the white-hot burning in my chest. All I can see is the roaring fire and the shadows it casts.

Rina's voice breaks through as she tries to pull me up. "Jocelyn, stay with us. You're almost there."

I glance up to see Anna looking around in a daze as if she's forgotten where she is. When she finds me, she shakes it off and shouts at Mab, "I beat the challenges. Let her go."

The fire in my chest fades to dying embers. I glance down and see that the Offering mark is gone, replaced by smooth red skin. "She did," I croak, holding onto both Rina and Anna as I get up. "It's over."

Judging by the crazed look on Mab's face, that's not true. Lyle rushes to her side, but she shoves him away.

"No," she growls, striding toward us. "No, no, no!"

I pull Anna behind me alongside Rina, but Mab hardly seems to notice them anymore.

"We're not alike after all," she spits at me. "You're weak. You let your sister fight this battle for you instead of protecting her and dying with dignity."

"You're the one who's weak," Annalise fires back. "From what I've seen of Faerie, you're destroying this world. All for the sake of your ego."

"She's right," Rina agrees. "Admit it. Jocelyn's got us. That makes her stronger than you. We're *all* stronger than you."

"You nasty little brats," Mab snarls at her. "I should—"

"Should what? What can you do, really?" A proud smirk comes to Anna's face. "Since the Offering hasn't been paid, I don't think you'll be doing much for a while."

Only then do I realize that the air feels thicker and smells sweet with the rot of autumn. The colors are duller. Even the inferno behind Mab burns dimmer.

Anna's right. The magic is *literally* gone.

Mab turns on Lyle and draws his sword.

"Your Majesty, don't," he begs.

"I will save this realm from anything and everything that threatens it," Mab screams.

I shove Anna and Rina back, only to be knocked out of the way too.

I scramble to my feet to see who it could be, expecting one of the knights.

It's Shaylee. She stands with her blade parried against Mab's and her eyes cold as steel. "You're done abusing these children," she hisses. "And you're done abusing that crown."

Mab stagers back. "You dare turn against your own mother?" she barks.

A female voice in the crowd calls out, "Well, she learned from the best."

The crowd parts, giving a tall cloaked figure room to walk up the faerie mound. Similar figures emerge, their black cloaks hiding their identities until they shed them in unison. The cloaks falls away to reveal armor the color of fresh spring leaves, the color of the Seelie Court. The figures and the rest of the audience watch as their leader ascends the mound, hood still raised and surrounded by Seelie knights. As they pass, the scent of roses hits me so hard that my head spins.

Mab's expression shifts to absolute horror. Lowering her sword, she staggers back. "It can't be," she whimpers. "You can't have crawled out of my skin." With a desperate cry, she charges the stranger.

The figure's hood falls as she blocks the blow.

The woman before Mab has identical features, minus the distortion of horror. They share the same high cheekbones, full curved mouth, and heart-shaped face, but the stranger's eyes are the lightest blue I've ever seen. Her hair falls down her back in a thick net of strawberry blonde braids.

"Dominic killed you," Mab screeches. "I made him."

Titania, Queen of the Seelie Court, snickers. "You should pick your subordinates more carefully, sister." Her gaze shifts to Shaylee, and she grins. "Adopting my daughter, for starters, was not the wisest decision."

Shaylee sneers at Mab.

The queen frantically swings her sword, screaming the same words over and over again. "You're dead. Get back under my skin. You're dead."

Her sister knocks the sword from her hand.

"It looks like your crown has grown too heavy, sister," Titania taunts. "Let me take it for you."

Thirty-One

MAB'S EXPRESSION TURNS to disgust. "I should have killed you myself."

"No, sister," Titania says coldly. "You should never have taken my court."

"It will never be your court again," Mab snarls. "You'll lead us to ruin."

"Stagnation is ruin," Titania spits. "Which you've proven beautifully."

Mab tightens her grip on her sword. "You talk too much for a dead woman."

She swings her blade. Titania blocks. The clash of their sword sends the world into chaos. Knights both green and black spring to protect their queens. The rest break into hysteria. Some disappear, others take to the sky, or burrow underground. The rest run. I'm taking a page from their book.

I grab Rina and Anna and sprint down the mound, tripping over my feet as the ground gives way underneath. We dodge Seelie and Unseelie knights alike, ducking under clashing swords and jumping over fallen bodies. The common faeries have worse luck. Small ones get trampled underfoot. Some make the mistake of fighting and pay with their lives. Others end up as living shields for the opposite sides.

A Seelie knight runs a pixie clean through to take down his Unseelie enemy. The bodies collapse in unison while the knight runs off to find another opponent. The sight threatens to make me sick. I thought Titania wanted to take back her court to save her people, not to treat them like cattle.

An Unseelie knight falls across our path, her eyes dull and glassy with death. I snatch the sword out of her limp hand and shove it in Rina's. I pull a dagger from her belt and give it to Anna, keeping another knight's holstered sword for myself.

I push the girls under a cart abandoned in the struggle and dive behind them. In the midst of the spreading frenzy, I have no way to orient myself back toward the farmhouse. The faerie mound is still in clear sight with the fire blazing high enough to touch the branches of the trees above. We didn't get as far as I thought.

"Holding up okay?" I ask, taking deep breaths between words.

"Physically? Yes. Mentally, not so much," Rina answers. "Watching faeries slaughter each other and whatnot."

"Annalise?"

"I'll need years of therapy, but I can still move."

"Good enough. We need to mo—"A strong hand yanks me out from under the cart. I twist to attack whoever it is with the best battle cry I can muster.

The Unseelie knight tilts his head to dodge. "Is that how you greet a friend?" he snaps, lifting off his helmet. It's Iver.

I don't think I've been happier to see him. "Where have you been?"

"Escaping," he answers, yanking me to my feet. Together, we shepherd the girls into a nearby path. "Our capture wasn't part of the plan."

"Neither was the nixies bailing," Rina grumbles. "At least Anna pulled it off."

Annalise beams up at us with pride.

"I'm grateful, but why does Annalise know about any of this?" I demand.

Rina bites her bottom lip. "She was meant to claim you all along. None of us were sure it would work with me, so we had Calista bring her from the farmhouse. You wouldn't have followed the plan if you knew, so I had to lie."

Right on cue, Calista peeks out from a nearby house made into a hill. "There you are. What took you so long? C'mon, we need to get out of here."

"Take Rina and Annalise," I say, shoving them toward the door. A nearby crash convinces me and Iver to follow them in. Judging by the cramped space, the house was designed for faeries smaller than us.

"I'm going back. I have a score to settle with Mab," I say.

Iver rolls his eyes. "The whole Seelie Court has a score to settle with her."

"I might be able to end this sooner. Fewer people have to die. Just let me help." I turn to Calista. "Get my sister and Rina out of here."

"Don't tell her what to do with us," Rina snaps.

"You can't go back out there," Annalise seconds.

"It's not just you two," I explain, putting a hand on each of their shoulders. "It's a bloodbath out there, and the farmhouse will be safe. Snag as many people as you can with Calista and get out of here."

Rina scowls. "You're giving us this mission to get rid of us."

"Well, yeah, but it's a good mission."

Tension hangs in the air between the three of us as the fighting continues outside. Finally, Anna whimpers and flings her arms around my waist. Rina joins her and squeezes us both tightly.

Placing a hand on Anna's head, Rina raises her eyes to me. "I'll take care of her. Go do what you need to do." Cupping my face, she kisses me and whispers, "You better come back. You still owe me a date."

Despite the insanity of the situation, I laugh. "I guess I have no choice, then." Letting them both go, I bend down to meet Anna's eyes. "You're incredible, Annalise. Be brave just a little longer, okay?"

She nods and dries her eyes. "You better come home safe."

The window shatters. Iver and I shove the girls behind us. A Seelie solider hangs through the broken glass. I take his sword and shove it into Calista's hand while Iver mutters a prayer under his breath. Once finished, he meets my eyes and we head for the door.

With one hand on the nob, he looks at me and asks, "Ready?"

"Let's just get this over with," I mutter.

He nods and opens the door. I follow him into the fray.

Those still standing are mostly knights from the two sides. Not many notice us as we sprint down the narrow road. Those that do don't last long against Iver. He only disarms those in green armor, but knights who wear the black of the Unseelie Court are cut down never to rise again. He's almost as dangerous as Dominic.

I focus on the faerie mound instead. More green knights stand than black. They keep each other busy as the sisters continue to hack at one another. Even Shaylee is kept away from their duel thanks to Lyle. By the way she's slowing down, it looks like it's getting to her. If she can just hold on until I can get to Mab…

"Watch my back," Iver mutters as we ascend the hill. "I can get you to the sisters, but you'll be on your own to get to Mab."

I brace myself as an Unseelie blade meets Iver's. He pushes through, hardly pausing long enough to cut the knights down. I begin to count down how many stand between us and the sisters. Five, four, three, two—

A familiar face catches my eye.

Dominic slashes an Unseelie knight across the chest.

Lyle darts toward his unprotected flank.

"Dominic, look out!"

I knock Lyle's blade off its aim. It cuts a deep graze into my shoulder, but I'm too relieved to care. He came too close to running Dominic through.

"I should have killed you the day you darkened our court," Lyle snarls. He swings a blow too fast for me to block. Dominic slides between us and parries the attack. "I won't let either of you hurt her," Lyle barks. "To Hell with you both."

"I'm trying to save Mab, not hurt her," I shout.

Both knights falter in their attacks and stare at me.

Lyle recovers first and attacks while Dominic's defenses are down. Luckily, it doesn't work. His and Dominic's swords grind together in an impasse. "Do you take me for a fool, girl?"

"No, I take you for an absolute tool, but that's not the point," I snap. "Mab thinks we're the same. Maybe I can get her to surrender."

"To let Titania win would mean the downfall of this realm."

"Isn't Mab more important to you?"

Lyle flinches, spelling his own defeat. Dominic whirls his sword, knocking Lyle's from his hand. The champion raises his hands in surrender as Dominic raises his sword to his throat.

Lyle looks to me and asks, "Can you really save her?"

A battle cry cuts me off before I can answer.

Shaylee leaps from the throng of knights, the right side of her face dripping in blood. Lyle draws a dagger to keep her at bay and Dominic holds her back as she yells something about making sure one's opponent is really dead.

I sprint for the two sisters. They're easy to spot, locked in battle in front of the blazing ancient inferno. It roars and rages at the battle, not caring who wins so long as it's fed. By the look of it, that won't be long now.

Mab looks nothing like the queen I knew. Her gown hangs in shreds while blood streaks her face and arms and her hair hangs in a tangled wild mess. Titania, on the other hand, looks flawless. I don't think Mab has put a single scratch on her. With her grace, precision, and the ice in her eyes, she's every bit the nightmare Mab imagined her to be. She pushes her sister back until Mab's hem singes in the fire. If Titania doesn't kill her, the fire will. Mab looks from the flames to her sister, then raises her sword for one final try, but her arc is too high.

Titania has a clear shot.

She jabs her sword forward.

It bounces off mine.

The world freezes. Even the fire seems to slow.

Titania wipes the shock off her face and holds her sword at the ready. "Move, girl," she hisses. "This is not your concern."

"Your sister made it my concern," I reply, bracing myself for a possible impact. "I have a score to settle."

Titania lowers her sword and gives me a wry smile. "Is that so? I heard the contract you made and becoming the Offering were both your ideas."

"That's not what I mean." Turning to Mab, I explain, "I can't believe I'm saying this, but you were right about us. We're similar. You gave me the chance to see what we needed to do to save ourselves, and I'll be damned if I leave here owing you anything."

Mab blinks.

"Give up the crown. Let your sister take the weight and split up the courts. Anna and Rina were right. They're what makes me strong. Them and Dominic and Iver and Hob and everyone else, too. Things can't go back to the way they were, but this doesn't have to crush you. Just let Titania help you."

Mab simply stares at me. She looks more like a lost wild child than a queen.

"Did she rob you of your wits completely?" Titania snickers. "You can't honestly think I'm going to let her walk away—"

"If she steps down, will you at least spare her?" I ask. "Put her on trial. Lock her up. You don't want to kill your own sister, do you?"

"Jocelyn—"

"*Do you?*"

"What say you, sister?" Titania's icy gaze darts over my shoulder and melts. "This is your last chance."

I freeze as Mab's arms wrap around my waist. There's nothing suggestive in her touch, nothing playful in the way she rests her head on my shoulder, nothing manipulative in the way she gently pries one hand from my sword and places her amulet in it.

"Do with my trespasses what you want, sister," Mab hisses, "But you *will* be Faerie's undoing. The fact that I could not stop you is a weight greater than my pride."

She releases me. "I will protect this realm the only way I have left."

"Mab, no!"

The fire blazes hot with its new fuel.

The flames consume Mab's dress and hair before a hand covers my eyes. My remaining strength drains from my body. The distant screams make it worse. They must belong to Lyle.

"Get her out of here, Dominic," Shaylee hisses as she drags me away, prying the amulet from my hand. "Now."

Her hand comes away, and Dominic gently leads me down the mound by my uninjured arm, but I yank out of his grip. He doesn't fight me. I watch Shaylee rejoin her mother.

Lifting the amulet so that the remaining knights can see it, Shaylee snaps it in half, separating the trees. Knights in both green and black armor cheer wildly while a few try their best to slink off before the renewed fire can illuminate the lingering shadows.

The flames glow bright green and dance as if elated with the sacrifice. Titania takes the silver goblet from the stone alter and dips it into the fire. The cup comes back overflowing with flames. They don't seem to hurt Titania as she holds it, nor when she drinks them. Shaylee takes the goblet from her and does the same, equally unharmed.

Together, they lift their hands to the fire. It bows to their command and rises as they beckon it out of its hearth. The flames flow through the air like waves of long grass, dancing above the court. Those who took shelter now emerge and lift their hands to touch the wisps of magic-incarnate.

The flames fade back to red and yellow. The lingering wisps rise and change hues, making the sky look like a glowing sunrise.

Titania hangs the emerald tree around her neck and looks out over those who remain. "From this day forth, the Realm of Faerie shall be split and governed separately, coexisting in peace, as intended by the queens of old." She picks up her sister's crown. Mab must have cast it aside before throwing herself into the fire. Shaylee kneels before her, head bowed in respect for her true mother and queen.

"From this day forward, I, Titania Draiota Dofeith, shall be your Seelie Queen." She gently sets the crown on Shaylee's head. "My daughter, Shaylee Draiota Dofeith, who has proven herself to be one of us, the unseen people, shall be your queen of the Unseelie Court."

Quite a few of the Unseelie faeries cheer for their new leader alongside those now under Titania's rule.

Titania gestures to the fire. "Anyone who objects may follow my sister."

No one says a word.

As Shaylee rises to her feet, Titania kneels like the rest of us. "Now bow," she orders, "before the Queen of the Unseelie Court."

A wave sweeps through the crowd as Seelie, Unseelie, and solitary folk kneel before their monarchs. Above, the flames dissipate from the air, leaving only the stars to light the remaining night.

Words escape my mouth before I can think better of it. "What happens now?"

"Now," Dominic mutters, raising his gaze to his true queen, "we move forward."

Thirty-Two

NO ONE AGREES to let me go home until I've had some proper medical attention. Of course, "proper medical attention" around here includes a lot of herbs, tea, and enchantments, but it all mellows me out too much for me to complain.

When Calista brings Anna and Rina back, I forget the fact that they should be miles away. I don't ever want to let them go.

Rina wiggles just far enough away to look up at me. "What happened? Where's Mab?"

I shake my head. Rina accepts that as enough.

"I think we accidentally gave you a few new roommates," Annalise says. "A bunch of the faeries wouldn't leave the farmhouse when we heard it was over."

"They can have the place," I reply. "I'm moving out."

Calista pouts. "You mean you don't want us as neighbors anymore?"

"No offense, but I'd rather live next to a den of cobras."

"That's fair, to tell the truth."

A knock comes at the door. It opens to reveal the two queens with a small ensemble of knights, including Dominic. Titania doesn't look like she broke a sweat during the fight, but Shaylee is even more patched up than I am. A long strip of bandages wraps around her head to cover her right eye, no thanks to Lyle. Dominic looks relatively unscathed, thankfully.

Calista drops to her knees and lowers her gaze. When Rina, Anna, and I begin to do the same, Titania raises her hand to stop us.

"That won't be necessary, you three," she says.

I still take a small bow. "Thank you, Your Majesty."

She nods in return and shoos Calista away. The nymph waves at us and slips out the door. With her gone, the queen asks, "How are you feeling?" When none of us answer, Titania's expression droops. "I'm so sorry for what happened tonight. We had no business dragging you into our mess, but *someone* got crafty when I wasn't looking." She glares at Shaylee, who pretends to study a painting on the wall. "And I'm sorry for everything my wretched sister put you through. Especially in the end. She didn't deserve such compassion from you."

My stomach churns, and I hold Anna's hand a little tighter. "But we—"

"Like so many things my sister said, she was only partially correct about your similarities," Titania explains. "The choices you made planted in you the same sense of burden, but how you nurtured it is what defines you. You learned to humble yourself. In the end, you learned to share your load and trust those you love. She hid behind her pride and refused to even entertain such threatening ideas. You became a hero, in a way. She became poison."

"With all due respect, Majesty, I'm no hero," I mutter.

Dominic scoffs, Shaylee rolls her good eye, and Rina lightly jabs me in the arm.

A soft smile comes to Titania's face. "Whatever you are, I wish to reward you for the kindness you showed her. What do you desire with all your heart, Jocelyn Lennox? If it is in my power to give it, you shall have it."

I only have to think for a second. "I want your protection, Your Majesty," I say, meeting her eyes. "That goes for my entire family and Rina's. Unless we know them personally, no one from your realm is allowed near us."

The queen raises an eyebrow. "That's one I haven't heard before."

"Let's just say I've learned about more than humility. Not everyone is going to be happy with us, and I'm done playing games with your subjects."

Titania nods. "So be it then. You and yours are under the protection of the faerie crown. Anything else?"

I look to Rina and Annalise. Rina shakes her head, but Anna looks up at me with wide, begging eyes.

"We'll take one faerie-tailored dress, a sword, and..." I look to Rina again.

"I'm good," she says, "I've had my fill of magic."

"So have I, but I'm not going to let you walk away empty-handed." I look back to Titania. "This has seriously cut into Rina's study time, so if there is a way to help out when grades come due, we'd both be incredibly grateful."

"Jocelyn—"

"I'm sure you'll do fine without it," I assure her. "It's just insurance."

She shakes her head. "Absolutely not...but if you're insistent, it might be cool to see what the night sky looks like to faeries. Some star charts or books, maybe?"

Titania nods again and pats me on the head, earning herself a few negative strikes in my book. "Modest mortals, aren't you?" she chuckles. "Get some rest. We'll send you home in the safety of morning."

As she takes her leave, Shaylee and Dominic hang back.

"We would like to speak with them alone, Your Majesty," Dominic explains in response to the queen's quizzical looks. "Since we won't be able to see them off."

Titania continues toward the door. "Just don't be too long."

One of her knights pulls the door shut behind her. As soon as it clicks shut, Dominic pulls me into a strong hug, crushing my injured arm.

"Dominic, stop! Ow, ow, ow!"

He lets me go with a laugh, his hands still gently resting on my shoulders. "I'm sorry." He studies me with a bit more intensity than I would like. "You did well." He lets me go and takes both Rina's and Annalise's hands. "And you two ladies were incredible."

"Says the double agent," Rina replies with a grin. "Well played, I must say."

Dominic sighs. "I need to have a chat with Calista. If she tells one more person that's what I am—"

"Let her. It's a cool story," Shaylee says, slapping him on the back. She opens her arms for a hug, but only receives glares. Annalise folds her arms, looking far from impressed. I gently push Rina's hands down as she cracks her knuckles. Even Dominic looks cross with her.

Letting her arms fall, Shaylee sighs. "I'm sorry I used you like that."

"You sure as hell better be," I snap.

Shaylee perks up instantaneously. "But hey, what did I tell you? We had it under control."

"If that was 'under control,' I would hate to see chaos," Rina grumbles.

"Me too, to tell you the truth," Shaylee says, scratching the back of her head. "I promise to make it up to you one day."

A heavy silence follows her words. There probably will never be a "one day."

Dominic doesn't let it last for long. "We really should prepare to depart. Shaylee and I will be leaving for the Unseelie Court in a few hours. The sooner we start cleaning up that mess, the better."

I believe him, but the fact that I'll never see him again doesn't feel real. There aren't proper words in the English language to explain how grateful I am to Dominic. I wouldn't have made it through these past months without him.

"If you ever need anything in the Human Realm, don't hesitate to ask," I say. "I owe you my life."

"Don't take this the wrong way, Jocelyn—" Dominic sighs, clapping me on the shoulder. "—but it would probably be best if I never saw you again."

"You're probably right about that," I agree with a smile.

"I'll cash in that favor for him," Shaylee says.

"No, you won't," he snaps, shooing her toward the door. "Come on, Queen Shaylee. They need to rest." He pauses for a moment. "There's something I forgot."

Before I can ask what it is, he throws a punch my way. I block it with almost no effort. I guess he can't send me off without one final test. When we realize Rina and Anna have caught their breath, we begin to laugh.

"Well done." Dominic chuckles, letting his fist drop, and herding Shaylee toward the door. "I have nothing more to teach you. Keep on your toes and, all of you"—he points to each of us—"take good care of each other."

"We will," I say. "Bye, Dominic."

"Farewell, Jocelyn."

The two shut the door behind them, leaving the three of us.

I don't move until Rina pulls me toward the bed and tugs back the covers. Annalise has already burrowed under the blankets.

"I can sleep on the couch."

"Give it a rest, Jocelyn," Anna yawns. "We all faced death together. I think we can stand squeezing in the same bed for a few hours."

She has a point, and I'm too burned out to argue, so I lie between them with Anna clinging to my arm and Rina curled up beside me. While peace still feels far away, I can feel a shift in the very Earth around us, as if the whole world is on the road toward it together.

The second my mind stops, I'm awake again.

Late morning sun streams through a window and a chilly autumn breeze blows through the curtains. The mingling smells of dust and oil paint disorients and calms me with its familiarity. It takes me a solid thirty seconds to realize I'm back in the farmhouse.

Rina too. She dozes with her head on my chest and one arm resting across my stomach. When I reach out for Annalise, I only find a scrap of paper with the words, *Don't panic. I'm downstairs,* scribbled on it.

Rina stirs, stretches, and sits up, looking dazed. "How'd we get back here?" she murmurs, rubbing her eyes. Before I can answer, she stands and stretches. "Right. Magic. Duh."

I chuckle and prop myself up to watch her as she tries to wake up. Her beautiful eyes stay sleepy as she looks around the room. Her gorgeous hair is still wild and filled with leaves. After a moment of just blinking, she begins twisting a curl between her fingers nervously.

"I'm sorry I couldn't claim you," she blurts, eyes still downcast.

"Don't be," I replied, throwing off the covers. "It was too much to ask of anyone."

"But I put your sister in danger after everything you did to protect her and your mother even though I was *so* sure that—"

I get to my feet, bringing Rina's face up to mine as I stand. She melts against me, wrapping her arms around my waist and standing on her toes to kiss me harder.

When she pulls away for air, I mutter, "You did more than you needed to and you were incredible. Don't take any of this on yourself."

Her gaze darts across my face, looking for answers. "What do we do now?" she mutters. "This was just supposed to be casual, but..."

"It still can be if you want," I answer, raising a hand to my chest. "Cross my heart."

Rina takes my hand before I can finish the X and stands on her toes again. "Let it go, Jocelyn."

With her body warm against mine, I can feel some unseen part of myself begin to stitch back together. Her breath fills my lungs fuller than any perfume at the Faerie Court ever could. She shivers as my lips brush her neck and grips my T-shirt tight against my back. The fingers of her free hand trace where the burns on my chest used to be. The very memory of the pain they once caused begins to melt away.

Bringing my face back to hers, she whispers, "Jocelyn, I—"

The door opens. Of course the door opens.

"Jocelyn Lennox, what have you—Oh, shit. Sorry."

Anna slams it shut again, but the damage is done. Rina jumps away, panting and straightening her disheveled dress. "I, um...I should change out of this."

I try to catch my breath. "Okay."

She scurries out of the room, careful not to meet Anna's eyes as she leaves.

My sister leans on the doorframe, arms folded and expression still flabbergasted. "Well, that was more excitement than I wanted this morning."

"Sorry, Anna," I say, hunting for clean clothes in an attempt to avoid her eyes.

My sister shrugs. "It's okay. I should have knocked. Besides, after last night, you two are the least of my trauma."

Her words make me pause. "Listen, Anna, I'm sorry if I ever made you feel like I abandoned you. With Dad gone and Mom in the hospital, I should have been more sensitive to that, even if Mab did order me to stay close."

She shakes her head and meanders into the room. "Everything you did you did for us. Don't sweat it." A smile spreads across her face. "Besides, maybe I should thank you. With my three greatest fears conquered, what's to stop me from taking over the world?"

"Absolutely nothing," I reply.

Her smile wilts. "Still...that last one..."

I pull Anna against me and hold her as tight as I can. "I'm not going anywhere, Annalise. Not like that."

She buries her face in my chest and draws a shaky breath. "I swore I wouldn't cry anymore," she whimpered.

"Cry all you want," I reply, kissing her temple. "You earned it."

"Damn right I did." She laughs. "And that faerie dress better be the most beautiful in the whole Faerie Realm. That sword better be made of the finest materials, too."

"Only the best for my hero." I chuckle.

Annalise pulls herself together by the time Rina rejoins us. By the time I get cleaned up, the make-out incident must already be ancient history, because they keep sharing knowing looks that worry me.

It's noon by the time we leave the farmhouse. Even with signs that faeries have already moved in—random objects out of place, trails of leaves and acorns, and the odd anonymous giggle—it feels empty. Hopefully the new tenants don't steal too much stuff before I can come back for it.

The girls let me make one more stop before heading out. They sit in the car and work together on their cover stories as I ignore the CLOSED sign and enter the Novel Spell.

Mr. Hob greets me at the door, cross and ornery as ever. "You have some nerve, showing up late," he says, tapping his cane impatiently. "Even if you *did* help separate the courts."

"Cut me some slack. I almost died last night. Repeatedly."

"And I got trampled by a troll," Hob reminds me. "Sorry if that stunts my sympathy." Waddling off toward the counter, he adds, "Something tells me you're not here to clock in."

"Yeah, about working..." I take a long, last look around the store. "I'm really sorry, Mr. Hob, but I'm going to have to quit." He snaps his cane at me, and I dodge out of the way. "This can be my two weeks' notice, if that helps. I can commute from home for a while."

"Don't bother. I'll be fine," Mr. Hob replies. "And believe it or not, that's not me being spiteful. You have a lot to sort out. A lot to process." His eyes soften a bit. "Just know you did all you could. You can't always save everyone."

I know exactly what he's talking about, but I can't bring myself to reply one way or another.

"If you decided to come back to Grand Harbor to be closer to that girlfriend of yours, the Novel Spell will be waiting for you." The goblin lowers his eyes and taps his cane against the cement. "But I'll miss you in the meantime, Jocelyn. You're the best human employee I've ever had."

"That means a lot, sir," I say, extending my hand. "Thank you."

Mr. Hob takes it and nearly crushes it in his stony grip. "Take care, Jocelyn."

"You too. And cut Walter some slack. He's a good guy."

My boss waddles away, muttering "I'll think about it" under his breath. When he reaches the door of his office, he looks back at me and barks, "If you're not going to work or buy anything, scurry home."

"Yes, sir."

As I turn to leave, I swear I see the old goblin smile.

I find Iver in the Time Between, wiping out glasses like nothing happened. He chats up a young Asian woman who sits at the bar, slumped over and nursing something on the rocks. Judging by her unfocused eyes, she's drunk.

I give her a small wave but focus on Iver. "Do you know how to rest? Like, ever?"

"I have a business to run, regardless of who runs Faerie," he replies with a shrug. "Besides, it's peaceful in here when it's empty and I don't have to worry about humans starting brawls."

I laugh and lean on the bar counter. "Can I at least get a celebratory drink?"

"Absolutely not," Iver replies, gently nudging me off the counter. "Come back for your twenty-first birthday, then we'll talk."

I nod and head for the door. If Iver's busy, I don't want to bother him too much. "I'll hold you to that. See you around."

"See you, Jocelyn." Iver turns back to the girl and places his hands on his hips. "Now, as I was saying, this is just sad. You're too good of a customer for me to let you sulk your life away. What about a job?"

A job at the Time Between for a human? That sounds like a story I need to hear.

WHILE DRIVING TOWARD town, I listen to Anna's alibi and hold tightly to Rina's hand. No matter how good our story is, this is going to be rocky. But I'm okay with it. It's nothing we can't tackle together.

The air from the open window makes us all shiver, but no one asks to close them. The November chill is a reminder that we've made it to another day. The cold wind fills my chest and I realize something:

Finally, I can breathe.

About the Author

Tay grew up reading too many fairy tales and watching too many movies, which is probably why she writes fantasy now. When she's not at her day job or writing, she can be found taking spontaneous drives to new places and drinking way too much coffee. "Portraits of a Faerie Queen" is her first book.

Facebook: www.facebook.com/taylaroi

Twitter: @TayLaRoi

Blog: www.taylaroi.wordpress.com

Coming Soon from Tay LaRoi

Smile Like You Mean It
Into The Mystic Anthology

INGRID'S PHONE HATED Sendai. Between the narrow roads, foot paths that taxi drivers thought were roads, and businesses stacked on businesses, the poor GPS hardly knew which way was up. Thankfully, Ingrid spoke a fair amount of Japanese and plenty of people were out for Halloween.

Too bad no one knew where Blue Star Night Club was. After asking two witches, three cats, and one vampire, Ingrid felt more lost than ever. With a defeated sigh, she took off her top hat and dialed her friend. A cacophony of blasting music and drunken cheers nearly blew her eardrum before she heard his voice.

"Where are you?" Thomas shouted over the racket. "You said you'd be here by eleven."

"I'm lost," Ingrid grumbled. "I'm standing outside the Family Mart near Clis Road. The one by the bank."

Thomas chuckled on the other end. "You *really* suck with directions, huh?"

"Just get me to the club."

"Okay, okay. Get back on Clis Road and take a left. Go through the light and take the first right. Then take a left. The club's three buildings down."

"Thanks. See you soon."

Ingrid went back the way she came, embarrassed by the fact that she had lived in Sendai for a year and still had trouble getting around. But she got to strut around in a cape for a while. That was cool. Judging by the occasional double take from men and women alike, a lot of people agreed. The glances and whispers made her stand a little taller and puff out her chest. Her bright red hair usually drew gawks of wonder, but this felt different. It felt like being cool for once.

Too bad it went to her head and caused her to miss her turn.

With a frustrated groan, Ingrid weighed her options. She could go back, but there was a diagonal alley to her right that no doubt led to the same road. Convinced that would work well enough, she set off again, determined not to be distracted, especially considering how dim her route turned out to be. Ingrid had never seen a road this dark within Sendai's city limits. Not until the early hours of the morning, at least.

Weird or not, it was only a few steps until she'd be back in the light.

"Excuse me."

Ingrid nearly jumped out of her skin as a pale hand snatched her wrist. Before she could scream, she realized the fright had been for nothing.

Ingrid's captor let go and lowered the hood of a long black fur-like coat to reveal a feminine face hidden by a white surgical mask. Ingrid saw thousands of women like her on her commute to work, especially now that flu season had set in.

Judging by the way the woman's eyes widened at the sight of Ingrid, she had made a mistake. "I'm sorry," she muttered in a soft timid voice. "Please excuse me."

Ingrid smiled down at the woman and tried to look untroubled. "It's okay, but you should be careful. This doesn't look like a safe place to hang out."

A glint came to the woman's eye. "You speak Japanese?"

Ingrid shrugged. "Well enough."

The woman's eyes crinkled, giving Ingrid the only sign of her smile. "I have a question for you, then. Am I pretty?"

Ingrid's stomach dropped at the question. Why did she have to tell her that she spoke Japanese? There was no right way to answer this question. Her ex-girlfriends had proven that.

"I'd say you're pretty," Ingrid answered hesitantly. "I think everyone's pretty in their own way."

The woman's eyes lit up with glee. For some reason, that just made Ingrid more uneasy. The woman reached up to pull down her mask, and Ingrid's blood turned to ice. She knew she had to stop the woman, but she couldn't say why. When the woman revealed her face, Ingrid got her answer, and it shook her to her very core.

The woman's smile ran from ear to ear.

Literally.

Identical ragged scars ran from the corner of the woman's mouth up to the far sides of her cheekbones as if her face had been split in two. It didn't look as though the ghastly wound had healed properly either, given the way her mouth spread past the corners of her lips when she spoke. Forget speaking. She shouldn't even be alive.

"How about now?" the woman asked, slipping a pair of long scissors from her coat pocket. "Am I pretty?"

Ingrid couldn't gather the breath to speak. It was frozen in her chest along with the rest of her muscles. The only thing that still worked were her eyes. They darted down to the scissors and calculated the likelihood of the woman using them. Something told Ingrid it would depend on her answer.

The woman's smile spread wider. "Well?"

Ingrid forced herself to inhale. "You have beautiful eyes."

The woman's grin faltered, and her eyebrows pulled together. "What?"

"I said you have beautiful eyes. And you hair's really pretty. It has a nice wave to it. You have a cute nose too—"

"Stop dodging the question," the woman barked as her eyes narrowed into a sharp glare. "What about my mouth?"

Ingrid eyed the gnarly gashes again, trying to stop her stomach from churning at the sight. "What happened to you? Doesn't it hurt?"

The woman blinked and lowered the scissors. For a spine-chilling moment, she studied Ingrid's face and then opened her mouth to speak.

A sudden shout cut her off. "Ingrid, is that you?"

Ingrid's heart jumped into her throat at the sight of her friend, Sam, coming toward her and the monster.

"Sam, no," she ordered. "Go back."

Sam approached her with a newfound sense of urgency. "What? Why? Are you okay?"

Ingrid held her hands out to stop him. "Sam, don't! She'll hurt us both."

Sam came to a halt with his face pale with worry. His green eyes darted over Ingrid's shoulder as his hand reached cautiously for his cellphone. "Who will?"

Ingrid turned to find nothing more than an empty alleyway. There wasn't even the sound of departing footsteps. With Sam close behind, Ingrid jogged back to Clis Road, afraid for the woman's next victim. The black fur-trimmed coat was nowhere in sight in either direction, nor down the narrow road across from them.

"She couldn't have just disappeared," Ingrid exclaimed, making her way down the street. After a panicked moment, she turned around and went the other way.

Sam caught her by the shoulders before she could go any further. "Slow down, Ingrid. Breathe. What exactly did you see?"

Ingrid removed her top hat and ran her hands over her hair, trying to calm herself and process what had happened. "A woman grabbed me on my way to the club," she explained between deep breaths. "Long hair, big eyes, black coat. She was wearing a mask and asked if I thought she was pretty; then she took off the mask and…" Ingrid's chest knotted at the memory of the woman's disfigured face "She had these giant cuts across her cheeks, Sam. They were horrible, like someone split her face wide open."

Sam let out a deep sigh that ended in a chuckle. "God, Ingrid. Don't scare me like that."

"Don't scare *you* like that?" Ingrid snapped, voice shrill with panic. "Some psycho is out here with a messed-up face chasing people with scissors!"

"It's just a lady in a Kuchisake-Onna costume messing with people."

"The what now?"

"Kuchisake-Onna, the split-mouthed woman. It's a Japanese urban legend. She asks you if she's pretty, and if you say no, she kills you. If you say yes, she cuts your face to look like hers." Sam studied the panic he most likely saw on Ingrid's face. "You've seriously never heard that story?"

Ingrid retraced her memory. Sakura, her childhood best friend, never mentioned such a tale. Nor had any of her Japanese teachers growing up. All of her independent studies had focused on the country's society, history, and occasionally religion. She had never bothered with ghost stories.

"So what if she's in a costume, Sam? She's still dangerous," Ingrid concluded. "We need to at least tell the police what I saw."

Sam sighed and looked around. "You're probably right. I actually passed a police car when Thomas sent me to look for you. We'll tell them and then head to the club. Deal?"

Ingrid followed Sam back the way they came. "You're seriously not freaked out?"

"She was five hundred feet away from the most crowded street in Sendai on Halloween," Sam replied. "If she wanted to hurt someone, she wouldn't do it here."

That didn't stop Ingrid from eyeing the crowds as they made their way to the nightclub.

A cop car sat on the corner of the opposite road, just like Sam had said. They listened to Ingrid in earnest, but something in their smiles told her that they didn't believe her. Nonetheless, they took down the woman's description and assured her they would put out a message for people to be on the alert.

With that taken care of and Ingrid's nerves slightly more at ease, she finally let Sam drag her down the street and up three flights of stairs to the club.

"What are you supposed to be, anyway?" Sam asked over the music pounding from above.

Ingrid held out her cape. "I'm Tuxedo Mask from *Sailor Moon*, remember?"

"Oh, I remember," Sam replied, rolling his eyes, "I also remember telling you to just be Sailor Moon."

"And have guys hitting on me all night? No, thanks," Ingrid scoffed.

"You like free booze, don't you?"

"Yeah, but it's not actually free. I have to pay attention to them and I'm not in the mood. I'd rather just pay for my drinks and dance with you guys." Ingrid looked over Sam's T-Shirt featuring a cartoon slice of bread, and the toast earrings dangling from his ears. "What are you supposed to be?"

Sam pointed to his hair, which was a deeper red than Ingrid's, and his bread-related clothing with a sneaky grin. "I'm a ginger-bread man."

Ingrid groaned, paid the man at the door, and wove through the dancing crowd in search of Thomas, with Sam close behind. As she did, she couldn't help but glance over her shoulder, waiting for the strange woman to suddenly appear.

A sudden slap on her back startled her out of her worry.

"There you two are. I was starting to worry you *both* got lost," Thomas chuckled, handing Ingrid a drink. "Where have you been?"

Ingrid took in her friend's tall muscular frame sparkling under the flashing lights. The sequins of his merman pants glimmered as he bobbed to the music, as did the cheap plastic trident in his free hand. From their first training session together a year before, Ingrid knew Thomas had a taste for the theatrical and eccentric.

"Ingrid got held up by a Kuchisake-Onna," Sam chimed in.

Thomas craned his neck to survey the crowd. "There was a few here earlier, I think."

"How do both of you know what that is?" Ingrid demanded, taking a sip of her drink.

"My girlfriend told me about it," Sam explained. "She's big into horror flicks."

"Some students told me," Thomas added. "They had to write about their ideal Halloween costume last week."

"So, if I told you I thought the woman was actually dangerous, you wouldn't believe me?" Ingrid sighed.

"I would believe that whoever you saw shouldn't be messing with people like that," Thomas answered. "But it's over and you're safe, so enjoy yourself."

Given that the woman had disappeared, the police were aware, and she'd most likely be in the club until morning, Ingrid decided to try to take her friends' advice. Even if she left and searched Sendai for the rest of the weekend, Ingrid knew she'd never find her. The city was too big and the woman probably didn't want to be found.

So, Ingrid finished her drink, ordered another, and tried to focus on her friends instead of strange women in alleyways. It proved to be easier than she expected when the alcohol kicked in. Once the boys started to get tipsy, the party really got started and ran until the sun began to rise.

Also Available from NineStar Press

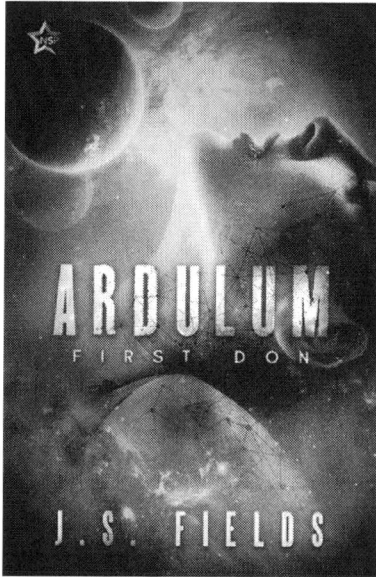

ARDULUM
FIRST DON

J. S. FIELDS

ADDICT

MATT DOYLE

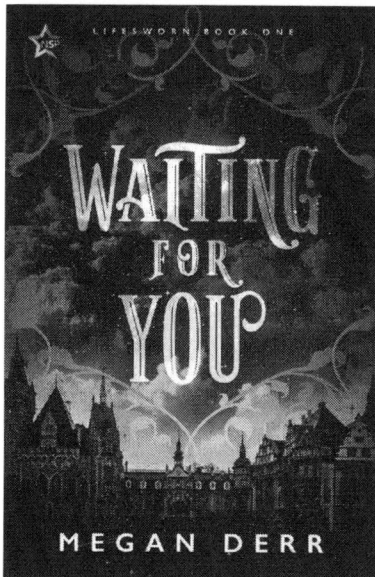

WAITING FOR YOU

MEGAN DERR

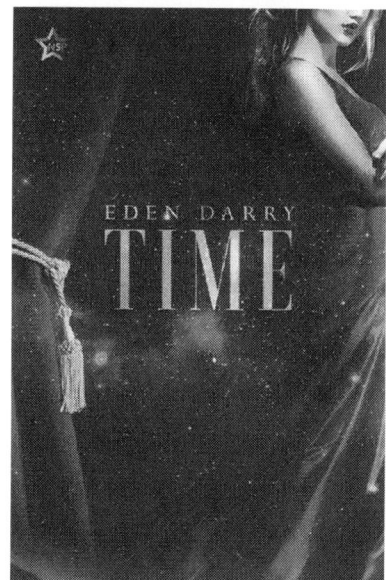

EDEN DARRY
TIME

www.ninestarpress.com

Printed in Great Britain
by Amazon